Ωmega Force: Soldiers of Fortune

Prologue:

It had been nearly fourteen Earth-months since the incidents at The Vault and a sparsely populated planet, Kaldsh-4. The unintended consequences of those actions had kept the six members of Omega Force on the run, struggling to stay one step ahead of the powerful enemies they had unwittingly crossed. Through it all, the six beings, each of a different species, had remained dedicated and loyal to both the team and their new mandate. This heartened Captain Jason Burke greatly; of the six, only three could be considered trained soldiers, himself included. When the heat had been turned up on them he had feared that the group cohesion would begin to deteriorate.

Although he would never admit it to the others, Jason was somewhat pleased with the turn of events; trying to operate while evading professional kill-teams had been an irreplaceable training opportunity for them. Not only that, but the further they fled up one of the Milky Way's spiral arms, the further away from Earth they went. He considered protecting the secret of his homeworld's existence and its location one of his primary functions.

The *Phoenix*, the Jepsen Aero DL7 heavy gunship that Jason captained, had also not escaped without needing drastic changes. They had been forced to completely replace the ship's com nodes and transponders, at great cost, in order to eliminate one of the methods their enemies had been using to track them. While they were at it, Jason had the ship's engineer, Twingo, overhaul the interior to more comfortably accommodate them on long flights as well as replace the ship's flight controls as he had never been able to fully grasp the twin-stalk system that Jepsen had originally equipped the ship with. Instead, Twingo had changed it over to a modified stick-and-rudder system that would be familiar to any human aircraft pilot.

The last step in shedding off their past lives had been to have Kage, Omega Force's resident code slicer, hack into as many public record databases as he could find and delete any and all records of their existence. They all assumed new, clean identities afterwards and hoped it would throw the dogs off their scent, so to speak. These steps had been moderately successful, but one issue that still remained was that they were easily identifiable based on their appearance. Jason was the only human for hundreds of lightyears in any direction and, although his appearance wasn't that exotic when compared to other species, his mannerisms still stood out.

There was also Lucky, a sentient synthetic being that was built specifically for combat. Synths of any variety were rare already, and a battlesynth even more so. Wherever they went, the large combat unit caused quite a stir. The other warrior in their retinue was Crusher, an alien straight out of any human child's nightmare. At nearly seven feet tall, Crusher was heavily muscled and all teeth, claws, and unbridled ferocity. He was Galvetic, a species that only existed on one planet and employed a rigid caste system within their society. Crusher was of that world's warrior class and was the result of millennia of careful, systematic selective breeding programs. While he was normally exquisitely courteous, Jason had witnessed the monster come unhinged in hand-to-hand combat situations, and it was absolutely terrifying. Thankfully, Crusher's loyalty to both his Captain and Omega Force was unflappable.

Besides Twingo and Kage, Omega Force had one other non-combatant; Dr. Jorvren Ma'Fredich, or "Doc." Doc was their elder statesman as well as their medic, he was easily the most traveled and most highly educated of the lot. He also had a certain finesse when dealing with clients and a knack for ferreting out whether or not the job was legitimately one they should take.

Omega Force operated under one guiding principle; to help others that didn't have the power to help themselves. This often entailed aiding people who lived under corrupt or uncaring governments and, more often than not, necessitated the judicious application of force. It was a hard life, but also hugely rewarding.

Chapter 1

High in the upper atmosphere of Corran, a world under political quarantine, white hot plasma streamers heralded the arrival of an enormous intersystem cargo freighter that was beginning its attempt at making landfall. The ship was never designed for this, and there was no guarantee it was even going to work. During the subduing of Corran all the orbital platforms with tethers capable of ferrying cargo to and from the surface had been destroyed, so in order to get critical supplies planetside during the subsequent negotiations radical steps had to be taken. One of these steps was to try and land massive cargo ships laden with medical supplies, food, and infrastructure equipment.

Now past the point of no return, the ship was engulfed in superheated gasses as it slammed into the planet's mesosphere, its thrusters and gravimetric drives howling in protest as they worked to slow the ship's descent. The sensors from tracking stations on the ground were blinded as the thermal signature of the ship climbed several thousand degrees and the ablative thermal shielding began to slough off in the slipstream... and this was exactly what the six beings aboard the comparatively tiny Jepsen Aero DL7 gunship were counting on.

The *Phoenix* was tucked up between the aft drive pods of the plummeting freighter, fighting to maintain position in the violent turbulence created by the atmosphere breaking around the irregularly shaped hull of the larger ship. The pilot of the gunship, Captain Jason Burke, struggled mightily at the controls without the aid of the ship's grav-drive to keep it under control. In fact, all the grav generators were powered down (including deck plating) to minimize their chances of being detected by one of the picket ships in orbit.

"Stop fighting her!" Kage shouted from the copilot seat. "Just keep your control inputs smooth and let the computer worry about keeping the interval between us and the freighter."

"Do you want to do this?" Jason ground out between clenched teeth.

"Not even a little bit," the smaller alien answered glibly.

"Then shut the hell up and let me do it," Jason replied, sweat beading up on his forehead from both the temperature of the ship's bridge and the stress of the situation. While his piloting had improved exponentially over the last year, trying to dead-stick the gunship down through the atmosphere while hiding up under a freighter that was nearly a kilometer long was taxing him. With the exception of Twingo, who was in the engineering bay, the rest of his crew were on the bridge and displaying varying degrees of the terror they felt as they watched through the forward canopy. Most of them wisely kept silent, afraid to distract their captain during the atmospheric entry as they bounced around in their restraints.

"It looks like it's starting to shed the thermal blanket," Kage said. The freighter had a woefully underpowered drive for what it was being asked to do so, in order to protect the ship during re-entry, the contractor had applied an auxiliary heat shield that was designed to burn away as it descended through the atmosphere. The ship's de-orbit burn had it coming in over the Western Sea on a direct approach to Corran City Starport, so most of the larger chucks that were blasted off in the slipstream would fall harmlessly into the water.

"I see that," Jason acknowledged. "Get ready for the rough part." Crusher moaned mournfully at this, the hulking alien was not all that fond of flying to begin with. Running the ship through a violent storm of superheated gas while trying to manually maintain precise spacing with another ship, without the grav-plating of the deck active, was making him miserable. He sat at one of the bridge stations, maintaining a death-grip on the console in front of him. *I guess Twingo will be repairing that later.* Jason kept a sharp eye on the thick pieces of shielding that were peeling away from the freighter's hull; he wanted to try to blend in with them, but also would prefer not to fly headlong into one.

"Now!"

Jason shoved the stick forward and the *Phoenix* pitched over sharply, falling away from the freighter. He fought to maintain control as the gunship bucked like a wild animal in the turbulent wake vortex left by the larger vessel's passing. He ignored the curses and yelps from his crew and the litany of warnings from the computer as he concentrated on the largest piece of shielding he could find and chased it down into the atmosphere. His neural implant painted the target with a reticle that floated in his field of view thanks to this ocular implants. The ship had decelerated dramatically and was now in freefall as it pursued the large sheet of thermal shielding, the idea was to appear as just another piece of spent thermal blanket falling to the sea.

The target decelerated much more quickly than the *Phoenix*, however, and ended up passing below and behind them before Jason could react. Suffering from target-fixation, he kept pushing the nose over as he followed its path and failed to realize that he was approaching the ship's stall speed while not under power. The warning from the computer came too late as the left wing slowed enough to stop providing lift and the big gunship rolled over onto her back and began an inverted, spinning fall towards the surface.

Other than Crusher, the crew was too startled to cry out as they were thrown against their restraints. "Activate the deck-plating!" Jason called to Kage. A split second later the pull of gravity reversed and they were slammed back into their seats as the artificial gravity

8

was restored. The effect was wildly disorienting, but at least Jason wasn't trying to control the ship while hanging upside-down in his harness. He reached over and flipped the four main engine controls to *ENGAGE/RUN* and watched as the switches went from a steady red to a flashing amber, indicating that the main engines were going into their startup sequence.

The first twinges of true panic began to creep up on him as the ship fell out of control through the atmosphere and the engines seemed to be taking an especially long time to come online. The plan had been to fly in cold and use the *Phoenix's* lifting-body to glide far enough down into the atmosphere that the engines' heat signature wouldn't show up on anybody's scan when they finally engaged them. The tumble they were in had ruined that plan; if the main engines didn't light off in time, he wouldn't be able to power out of the stall and the mission would be cut short by virtue of them plunging to their deaths into the Western Sea.

Rumbling signs of life from the aft section of the ship gave Jason a sliver of hope that the engines would come up in time as they descended through forty-five thousand feet. It would still be close though. The flight control surfaces were useless, so he fired the auxiliary reactive thrusters to try and get the nose pointed down to restore the airflow over the wings, allowing them to get some bite into the atmosphere and provide some stability.

The unorthodox maneuver worked and the gunship grudgingly righted herself and pointed her nose down, allowing them to pick up some airspeed. The *Phoenix* wasn't a glider, however, and they were still losing ten feet of altitude for every foot they flew forward, the nose pitched too far down due to the steep rake of the wings. He was about to offer up a silent prayer when all the engine indicators greened up at once and a healthy *BOOM!* resonated throughout the entire ship; the mains had come online and were providing thrust. Jason shoved the throttle forward and the *Phoenix* surged, picking up airspeed and allowing the wings to start generating sufficient lift to keep them in the air. They leveled out a little less than one-thousand feet above the sea and settled into stable, controlled flight.

Finally trusting himself to speak, Jason turned to Kage, "Start feeding me navigational waypoints and get ready to bring the grav emitters back online once we're clear of Corran City's sensor net."

"Yes, sir," Kage said, still shaken up by the close call.

The *Phoenix* streaked over the Western Sea low enough to whip up a foamy, turbulent wake in the water. They were paralleling the coast in a northerly direction, keeping just far enough off shore to avoid line of sight detection. Compared to the previous few harrowing hours under the freighter, flying at near-supersonic speeds at only a couple of hundred feet was child's play. The timing of their entry looked like it was going to work out in their favor; the sun was now on the horizon and it would likely be dark when they reached their destination. Jason told the computer to maintain a constant velocity and released the throttle, now only concentrating on keeping them on course, flying towards the waypoints on his display that Kage had identified.

"He almost kill us again?" Twingo asked, walking onto the bridge. He then stopped, frowning at the crumpled console surface in front of Crusher, who actually managed to look apologetic.

"It wasn't that bad this time," Doc said. "We were almost all the way to the ground before we gave up all hope."

"When the grav emitters are charged, set the field for minimum null," Jason said to Kage, refusing to take the bait. "What are you doing up here, Twingo?"

"I can monitor engineering from up here," the short, blue-skinned alien said in a hurt voice. "I'm always stuck down there and everybody else is up here."

"We're not exactly having a party," Jason said. "But since you're here go ahead and start going through all these warnings the ship spit out during our entry, I can't tell which are real and which ones she's just being overly dramatic about."

"On it," Twingo said, giving Jason an odd look. The crew had begun to notice Jason sometimes referring to the ship as if it were a person more and more. For six males that were still young for their respective species, they gossiped like old women. Doc surmised that

Jason was feeling frustrated since he was cut off from human female companionship for over a year, but he admitted to the others that he didn't know what was normal for human mating cycles. Twingo couldn't help himself as his mouth started to move before his brain could stop it, "You know, Captain... some of the females we've run into out here aren't that different looking from you. I'd imagine all the hardware is compatible..." He trailed off at the look Jason gave him,

"Twingo," he said slowly, "what in the fuck are you talking about?"

"We're clear of the sensor net's range," Kage said, saving Twingo from having to give an awkward answer. "Emitters set to minimum null." The minimum null setting would zero out the gravitational pull of the planet in relation to the ship. It allowed them to stay aloft without needing repulsors and reduced the engine output needed to push them along, but since the gravimetric drive wasn't actually propelling the ship they were still hidden from most sensors.

"Very good," Jason said. "Ok everyone, tighten it up. We're still in the middle of an op." He looked pointedly at Twingo at that last part. He then realized that he hadn't heard from Lucky since they had begun atmospheric entry. When he looked over his left shoulder the stoic synth was in his usual spot, to the left and behind his captain. "Lucky, how the hell did you stay planted during all that?"

"I have mag-locks built into my feet, Captain," he said, raising one foot as if to show Jason. "It makes EVA operations much easier." As a synthetic, a race of constructed, sentient beings, Lucky didn't need to go through the rigmarole of suiting up for extravehicular activities, or EVA He could just walk out the hatch as if he were taking a stroll down the street.

"Yeah, and you also weigh a ton," Twingo said irritably. "You keep warping the deck wherever you drop anchor when we're maneuvering without artificial gravity. I don't know why you can't just sit in a damn chair."

"I do not weigh anywhere near a..."

"ENOUGH!" Jason barked over the brewing argument. It was harmless banter, but it was a dangerous distraction. "You *do* still remember that we're in the middle of a dangerous mission, right? Get serious, and get to work. I don't want to hear another word that isn't related to our target until we're meshing out of this system."

"Sorry, Captain," the pair said in unison.

It's like babysitting a bunch of damn children sometimes.

The crew sat in silence as the *Phoenix* pushed north while the terminator crossed over them and the sky darkened. Jason swung the ship west as soon as they crossed their last waypoint and bled off some more airspeed, wanting to keep the noise signature to a minimum as they headed back towards land. He also tweaked the engine configuration, closing the exhaust nozzles down to about twenty percent and putting them into a low-power mode. They would have to pass quite closely to someone to be spotted from the ground while flying thusly.

They approached the coast right on target, their goal was a river mouth that led inland from the Western Sea. This particular river not only was close to their target, but it was too small to be used for any real commerce, just the occasional fisherman. The *Phoenix* ghosted up the river at only three-hundred kilometers per hour, her engines almost idling, Jason wanted to eliminate the high-pitched whistle of air moving over the hull that occurred at high subsonic speeds. Supersonic was obviously out of the question; it was important they get in and out without being detected on this job. Fortunately, the night had decided to cooperate and, as the air cooled, a dense blanket of fog had settled over the landscape.

"Turn off in twenty seconds, fly to the indicators," Kage said.

"Copy," Jason replied. "Ground team, go suit up and prep the party bus." Crusher and Lucky immediately left the bridge to get ready for the next phase of the operation. After another few seconds Jason banked gently north and climbed up and over the hills that lined the small, muddy river. While his eyes had been improved to see in an expanded spectrum thanks to the nanotech implants that were in him, for now he was piping the ship's sensor feed directly into his visual cortex via his neural implant. The effect was astonishing, if a little disorienting; he was able to look down *through* the hull of the ship and view the landscape as if he were riding in his seat out in the open. Due to the heavy fog, he had chosen long-wave infrared with a false-color overlay so he could penetrate the misty blanket and view the ground as they rushed over it. This was quite necessary as he was flying with their active sensors offline; no radar, lidar, or tachyon bursts to navigate with lest they be detected. He pushed on over the heavily wooded hills, continuing his northerly course as the *Phoenix's* vertical stabilizers occasionally broke through the low-lying clouds like dual shark fins.

"I'm going to set her down in that clearing we spotted from orbit; the basin that was twelve klicks from the house," Jason announced as he slowed even further and let the ship coast in on the momentum it already had.

"Copy that," Kage said. "Doc, better ping our contact and let them know tonight is the night and we're already inbound."

"Right you are," Doc answered, turning towards the console he was sitting at and entering the commands to activate the ship's com array. The crew fell silent once again as the seconds counted down and the tension ticked up. Without warning, Jason cycled the landing gear and brought the nose up, flaring the ship to slow it without needing to apply any retro-thrust. He allowed the *Phoenix* to settle into a steady hover on her grav emitters over a large, depressed field that he could see through his enhanced sight, but was otherwise completely obscured by the fog and night. He began to incrementally scale back the power being fed to the grav emitters and let the ship slowly sink through the fog until only the tips of the vertical stabilizers were showing as it touched down.

"Launch the twins," Jason said as he placed the engines in *STANDBY* and leveled out the landing gear. "I need eyes on target before I risk rolling in there." At his command, two panels slid back on the forward part of the hull on either side of the backbone and, with two loud *pops,* a pair of sleek, autonomous probes launched themselves into the air and zipped off quietly into the night. They were semi-intelligent, but not self-aware. They would hold pattern over the target and provide the team with real-time visual intel as they approached. Once the "twins" were gone, a deathly silence descended over the small valley. "Kage, you have the hot seat. Doc, Twingo; stay up here and monitor things. Also, shut the grav drive down completely. I don't think we were detected coming in, but better safe than sorry."

"You can count on it, Captain," Twingo said. Kage moved around and hopped into the vacated pilot seat as Jason left the bridge to join the rest of the ground team in the ship's armory. He quickly descended the stairs from the upper command deck and broke into a jog through the galley/common area. Walking down another short flight of stairs and through the engineering bay he found Crusher and Lucky in the armory nearly ready to depart. Actually, Crusher was still mulling over which assortment of weapons he wanted to take while Lucky, whose weapons were integrated into his very body, stood watching and giving helpful suggestions.

"Just make sure you grab a stunner as well, Crusher," Jason said by way of greeting as he made his way over to his own bench and started stripping off his gray, utilitarian uniform that Omega Force had adopted as their standard attire while shipboard.

"You know, it would be easier if..."

"No killing. Remember last time? We need to get in and out without being identified, that means not leaving any unnecessary evidence. Like dead bodies," Jason said firmly. Crusher grumbled, but grabbed a stun rifle nonetheless. The fierce alien was sometimes a bit unpredictable once a fight started, but there was nobody else Jason would ever want watching his back.

He looked over at Lucky and noted that the battlesynth had adjusted the coloration of his armor plating to a foliage camouflage pattern. Jason was sure it was just so he could feel like he was also a part of the preparations. Although he was an incredibly powerful soldier from the moment he was brought online, in a lot of ways he was quite childlike. Jason marveled as he watched the synth's emotional growth as he found a home with Omega Force and the group of people who looked at him as a part of the family and not just a piece of ordinance. "You ready, big guy?" Jason asked.

"Of course, Captain," Lucky replied. "In and out, piece of cake." Jason chuckled at that. In their time together it seemed the crew had been adopting a lot of Earth's idioms, probably from the Hollywood movies Jason watched in the common area during long slip-space flights.

"Ok then... you two are going to be backup for this one. Lucky, I'm dropping you off one klick out. Crusher, you'll wait in the vehicle in case I can't bluff my way in," he said as he pulled on the black uniform of a Corran Internal Security officer.

"We know the plan, Captain," Crusher rumbled. Then muttered, "We've only been over it twenty times."

The trio exited the armory through the heavy blast doors that separated the room from the main cargo bay. Sitting in the hold, strapped to the deck with no less than two dozen straps, was a black, wheeled ground vehicle with Corran Internal Security emblazoned on the side along with that agency's crest. Jason, now looking the part of

18

a CIS agent, climbed into the driver's seat while the other two unstrapped the vehicle before climbing in themselves.

Once everyone was inside, they all sat in silence for a long moment, looking at each other. Jason sighed, got back out of the van, and walked over to the control panel to lower the ramp and open the cargo bay to the night. As he climbed back in he could tell from the stunted silence that they had been laughing at him. He refused to acknowledge them as he engaged the vehicle's drive and eased down the ramp and into the grassy clearing.

They had picked this landing zone for a few critical reasons: it offered excellent concealment for the *Phoenix*, it was close (but not too close) to their target, and it had a path that led to the main road that was traversable by their ground vehicle. The high moisture content in the air meant a heavy dew that evening and the vehicle's wheels slipped and struggled for traction in the grass, but they were soon easing up to the edge of the road without Jason having had to make his friends get out to push.

After sitting on the side of the road for nearly ten minutes, listening to the insects of the night sing away, Doc contacted them via Lucky's com node and gave them the go ahead to begin the op; their contact had pinged back confirming they were ready. Once they were on the road and up to speed, Jason flipped on the marker lights and tried to drive as if he belonged there. He forced the tension out of his bunched shoulders as he realized they were still fifteen minutes away from their objective at their current speed.

The trio rode in a relaxed, alert silence as the "van", as Jason insisted on calling it, rolled down the road on its ultra-quiet electric

19

drive system. He slowed to a little under thirty KPH when they were one kilometer, or "klick," away from their target and signaled to Lucky. The synth wordlessly slid open the side door and launched himself from the moving vehicle, rolling once and coming up in a full run before plunging into the forest and disappearing completely into the dense undergrowth. Crusher looked at him with one raised eyebrow.

"I know I could have stopped... but you have to admit, that was pretty fucking cool," Jason said. Crusher just grunted. There was an unspoken competitiveness between the two warriors and Lucky's leap from a moving vehicle meant that Jason could look forward to something similarly spectacular from his other crewmate in the near future.

As they rolled up to their target, a well appointed two-story residence with a gated driveway, they could see another vehicle, almost identical to their own, parked in front of the house. There was another non-descript vehicle parked in the shadows further down the street. Before Jason could enter the code he'd been given the gate began to roll aside to allow them entry and a real CIS agent exited the vehicle parked by the house.

Rolling up slowly, Jason put his uniform hat on and motioned Crusher to stay down in the back. Exiting the vehicle, he was struck at how similar to humans the Corranian were, and it gave him a sudden twinge of homesickness. The relaxed manner in which the agent approached Jason let him know that his cover was still intact and the Corranian thought he was simply the relief shift. "Not a great night to pull swing shift," the agent said, gesturing to the weather. "How are things, Agent..."

"Burke," Jason supplied.

"Burke? An odd name. Where are you from?"

"The highlands of the Eastern Continent," Jason said smoothly. The agent before him froze, however, and stiffened visibly. Jason realized his mistake too late, even though the translator implanted in his head (and likely in the agent's as well) would allow them to understand each other, his mouth movements made it apparent he wasn't speaking Corran or Jenovian Standard, the accepted cross-system language in that part of the galaxy.

To his credit, the agent didn't hesitate at all and swung out with his right fist directly at Jason's head. The Corranians were on par with humans in physical strength, but Jason had been enhanced both biomechanically and genetically over the last year and he was more than a match for the native. He jerked his head back and the punch swung wide, missing him entirely. He moved in swiftly and crashed his elbow viciously into the Corranian's temple, dropping him into a heap. He barely registered that the vehicle on the road was approaching rapidly; that was what Crusher was there for. Instead, he drew his sidearm, set to incapacitate, and looked for the second agent he knew would have been with the one that was laying at his feet.

He saw the far door of the vehicle standing open and knew the agent had fled. One of the twins was overhead jamming com transmissions, but if he was able to get off the property or find a hard line and call for help, things would get very bad, very quickly. He moved swiftly around the side of the house, following the path he knew his quarry must have taken. Viewing the yard and the surrounding woods in infrared, Jason couldn't see any trace of the agent. *Shit.* He was about to turn the corner and move along the rear of the house when he heard a sharp cry and the sound of a body hitting the ground. Breaking into a run he came around in time to see Lucky standing over an unconscious CIS agent near the rear security wall.

"He was trying to come over the wall," the synth explained. "I stunned him, but he fell off before I could grab him. He may be injured," he finished apologetically.

"No worries. Injured isn't dead and we knew there would be some collateral damage. Grab him and let's get around to the front and help Crusher." Jason turned and ran back to the front of the house, the synth easily keeping pace while carrying the injured agent. When they came within view of the front gate they saw their comrade needed no backup; Crusher was leaning casually against their fake CIS van while looking at four neatly lined up agents in full "battle rattle." While the two at the house were your average, uniformed cops, the four in the driveway looked to be the CIS equivalent to SWAT on Earth.

"Nicely done, boys. I'm going up to the house to make contact. You two range out and check the property one more time, meet back here in ten," Jason said, straightening out his uniform jacket.

"Let's be quick about it," Crusher rumbled. "I can't say for sure, but I think one of these guys may have gotten a message out before I could hit him."

"That doesn't give us a lot of time," Jason agreed. "Let's get to it."

He approached the house warily. Although the people here were expecting him, he didn't want any misunderstandings with a trigger-happy servant. Knocking twice on the door, pausing, and then twice more, he was relieved when it was opened immediately. If he didn't know better, Jason would swear the person standing in front of him was a human male in his late fifties. Incredible.

"Yes?"

"Senator Hallis Vongaard?" Jason asked.

"Of course. What do you want?" Senator Vongaard snapped irritably.

"Prime Minister Colleston sends his regards, sir." The words had no sooner left Jason's mouth when a look of overwhelming relief crossed the senator's face. He opened the door wide and invited the human into his home.

"Thank the Creators! I had gotten the signal that tonight was the extraction, but I didn't know what to expect. Who would you be, son?"

"I'm Captain Burke of Omega Force, we're here to get you and your family out as soon as possible. We received intel that negotiations have broken down and dissidents are to be rounded up soon, and I doubt it's for a picnic." He looked around, taking in his surroundings as he spoke. "Please get your family and get them outside, we'll be leaving in a few minutes." Without waiting for a response, he went back outside to take up a watch of the front gate while Crusher and Lucky patrolled the rest of the property.

It was nearly fifteen minutes later when Senator Vongaard led out his family: three females, one of whom appeared to be a teenager in a surly mood, judging by the hostile glare she gave Jason. "Captain Burke, I apologize for the delay. You know how it is with daughters... sometimes they don't fully understand the dangers."

"Thankfully, I don't," Jason said. He hit the transmit button on his com unit to recall his friends and began herding the civilians into the van. "If you would all please pile in and get seated, we'll be on our way momentarily." Things seemed to be going relatively smoothly, so he was hardly surprised when his com unit chirped an incoming signal even as Crusher and Lucky ran up to him from opposite ends of the property. "Go," he said.

"*Captain*," Kage began, "*you've got to get out of there. CIS is scrambling a fast-response team to your position. Their agents failed to check in so they're assuming the worst, they have orders to kill everyone on site who isn't an agent.*" Jason was genuinely shocked at that last bit. *These guys don't fuck around with their internal politics.*

"We're on our way. Get the ship ready to fly, I want to be in the air less than thirty seconds after we arrive," Jason terminated the signal before Kage could reply. He poked his head into the van, "New development; CIS has dispatched a kill-team to this location to take out everyone on the property that isn't an agent, I assume this means you as well. This may get a bit bumpy." He could see the Senator and his wife blanche at the news while the oldest daughter rolled her eyes and sucked in a breath to express her skepticism. She was cowed into silence, however, as Crusher and Lucky climbed into the van. The interior of the vehicle seemed to shrink considerable as they bunched up into seats that were too small for them. Jason grinned tightly and hopped into the driver's seat, wanting to be well away from the house by the time the fast-response team arrived.

Wasting no time, he pulled the van out onto the street and stomped down the throttle, but with the additional four people and their sparse luggage, the acceleration was tepid. They had made it nearly three kilometers before Jason began to relax, but it would be short-lived; he could see in the rear-view monitor that another vehicle was approaching at high speed. He had no doubt who was in it, and he also knew he had no hope of outrunning them in the overloaded, wallowing van. "We've got company, boys," he said to Lucky and Crusher. "Do your thing."

Grinning a feral smile that promised violence, Crusher slid open one of the side doors and leaned out with a wicked looking plasma rifle. Lucky slid open the roof panel and stood up, energizing his integrated weapons as he did. Crusher got the first shots off; three impressively placed blasts that impacted the windscreen and the left, front wheel. The wheel exploded and the vehicle yawed violently before rolling onto its side and sliding to a stop in a cascade of sparks.

Crusher smiled at Lucky as he slid the door closed, "You need to be quicker on the draw to beat me, my friend."

"So it would appear," Lucky said as he sat back down. Jason could see his armament was still powered up and appreciated his prudence, no telling what awaited them now that the op had gone to hell. Nearly missing the turnoff, he slammed on the brakes, failing to warn his passengers first, and pulled the van off onto an unmarked path that led into the dark, misty forest. He could see the apprehension on the faces of his passengers as the van bounced over the uneven terrain at a semi-safe speed.

As Jason rolled the vehicle up to the *Phoenix's* lowered cargo ramp he could see the engines were glowing a muted red, ready to be engaged at the touch of a button. Her grav-emitters, which ran the length of the trailing edges of the wings, were still dark, however. As he shut the van off he could hear and feel the pulsating hum of the engines. "We need to hurry, folks. Grab your bags and please make your way up the ramp as quickly as you can. Lucky, get up to the bridge and tell Twingo to start prepping for an emergency start of the slip-drive."

"At once, Captain," Lucky said, bounding up the ramp and into the ship. Jason looked back and could see that the family of the Senator was extremely distressed after the exchange of fire on the roadway. Crusher, being surprisingly gentle, was herding them out of the van and up the ramp.

"Take them up to the bridge and strap them in, Crusher. This is likely to get bumpy. Again," Jason said. Crusher simply nodded and led the four Corranians into the gunship's interior. Jason quickly went about wiring up the van with a series of thermite charges that would reduce the vehicle to a lump of molten slag. He set the remote and walked up the ramp himself.

Chapter 2

Senior Agent Caalum of the CIS sat in the passenger seat of the ground vehicle pensively. He was in charge of a two-vehicle convoy that was meant to back up the initial assault team that had been dispatched to the home of the traitor, Senator Vongaard. While he was surprised that the call to apprehend the Senator came at the late hour it did, he was thankful he was on duty at the time. The surveillance team had called in suspicious activity before they had lost contact, then the assault team also went silent, so he decided to move on the house himself.

When he arrived on-scene, he had found his surveillance team stunned and one injured quite badly by a blow to the head. The muddy tire tracks leading to the property from the west, and leaving as well, left little doubt as to which way the guilty party had fled. A quick check had verified what he had feared; the Vongaard family was missing.

"Slow down... what's that?" Caalum asked the agent driving the vehicle. Ahead of them, illuminated by the vehicle's running lights, was an unrecognizable heap in the road.

"Looks like our missing assault team, sir," the driver said quietly, eyes scanning all around his field of view. When they pulled closer Caalum could clearly make out the van, sitting on its side and showing no signs of activity.

"Stop here. Squad two, move forward and look it over." At Agent Caalum's command, the troops in the trailing vehicle disembarked and moved forward slowly, weapons ready, to investigate the wreckage. It didn't take long to get an answer.

"Sir, it's assault team Alpha. It looks like they've got some injuries and are trapped inside, but no fatalities. They're telling me they were in pursuit of another CIS surveillance vehicle that had been fleeing the scene." The report came in over the com as squad two began to help the injured in the disabled vehicle.

"Why didn't they call this in?" Caalum snapped irritably. A fake CIS vehicle? This was starting to reek of a professional job, which usually came with professional soldiers. He would have to proceed much more cautiously.

"They said the vehicle's com repeater was knocked out and the hand-held units didn't have the range to reach dispatch."

Agent Caalum signaled his driver forward, leaving the second vehicle behind. The tracks from their quarry had faded away, so they were just proceeding along in the hopes they could intercept the vehicle. There were no side streets off of this stretch of road, but Caalum didn't want his vehicle to end up like that of Team Alpha's, so he ordered it slow and steady so they didn't rush headlong into a trap.

It was another couple of kilometers when he ordered a stop again. Something had caught his eye, but he couldn't readily identify it. The team sat in silence for a few more seconds before he ordered everyone out of the vehicle, "Spread out and search both sides of the road. Something doesn't look right, keep an eye out for anything that may have been discarded or anything else that looks out of the ordinary."

After a few minutes of searching, Caalum found what he was looking for: tracks that clearly led off of the road and into the woods. The overgrown path had been trampled down recently by something large passing through and led steeply down into a low-lying set of fields that were completely obscured by fog. He knew this must have been where they went, but he hesitated.

"Are we continuing pursuit, sir?" Caalum looked over to the young agent that had asked the question. He didn't want to appear to be a coward in front of his subordinates, but he really didn't want to walk down that path into whatever may be lying in wait either. At least not with only a four man fire-team. Before he could open his mouth to speak, the quiet of the night was shattered by a deep, violent rumbling that he could feel in his chest and seemed to shake the very ground.

"Look!"

He directed his gaze to where one of his men was pointing and froze; rising slowly out of the fog was a ship, a warship by the looks of it. The mist slid off its hull, clinging to the wings and fuselage as it rose up on its repulsors. It must have been sitting in the valley, hidden in the fog. Senior Agent Caalum was convinced this was the end for him, there was no way he and his men could withstand an assault from such a craft. But he'd be damned if he went out without a fight. "Listen up! Form up in a skirmish line, single file! Fire at will!" To their credit, his men let out an enthusiastic war cry and engaged the hovering ship with their small infantry-style weapons.

*   *   *   *   *

"We're being engaged by small arms fire, Captain," Kage said as Jason was getting his bearings and setting up his nav waypoints.

"What the fuck?" he asked, looking up as energy bolts splashed harmlessly against the ablative coating of the hull. He had to admire their courage, however misguided. "Put the shields up and jam their com transmissions. We're out of here," he said as he grabbed the throttle. He had absolutely no intention of firing on a group of law enforcement officers who only thought they were doing their jobs. However, he wasn't above scaring the living hell out of them. Smiling, he slammed the throttle forward, eliciting an explosive roar from the main engines. The *Phoenix* eagerly lunged ahead towards the street and the still-firing CIS agents. Jason dipped the nose towards them and brought the gunship roaring over their heads before climbing away into the night. Fortunately, the mains were still in low-output mode with the exhaust nozzles choked down, so the ringing in their ears would fade in a few hours. Instead of never.

The *Phoenix* ghosted over the trees, her captain intent on making it back to the river and out to the Western Sea. The original plan was to try and sneak up and under the next scheduled freighter that would be trying to make orbit and ride out with it, but that plan had been dependent on them not being detected. Now things were in a state of flux. *Eh... I didn't think that plan would actually work anyway.*

"Recall the twins, they can't do anymore out there and I don't want to leave them behind if we have to shoot our way out of here," he said quietly to Kage. He was trying to exude confidence for the sake of his passengers, but inside he had grave misgivings about their chances on making it out of the system. The picket ships were powerful, plentiful, and itching for a chance like this. *We may have bitten off more than we can chew on this one...*

"The twins are inbound," Kage said. "Slip-reactor is prepped and the emitters are ready for emergency charge. Our range might be limited depending on how quickly you try to engage the slip-drive."

"Understood." Jason weighed his options carefully, trying to push ahead with their original exfiltration plan would require them to fly dangerously close to Corran City and its extensive sensor network. It would also mean flying in blind since their own sensors would pinpoint their location instantly. Trying to simply fly up out of the atmosphere on a random vector also would end badly; the planet was still heavily contested and low orbit positively seethed with powerful military vessels. Jason believed one of the tenants of being a good leader was knowing when he didn't have the answer, so he asked, "I don't like our planned exfil. Options?"

"I've been working on that, Captain," Doc spoke up from one of the sensor stations. He had been monitoring the passive sensors and intercepting com traffic. "Corran's EM field is particularly strong and, like most planets, destabilizes near the poles. We could fly up through the charged particle influx and it may mask us long enough to get clear and mesh out of the system." Jason looked at him skeptically, he was certain there would be a picket ship sitting in polar orbit just waiting for them.

"I concur, Captain," Twingo's voice came over the intercom. As per Omega Force's standard operating procedure during a mission, everyone was on an open com channel. "It's not perfect, but it's better than trying to hang around Corran City until a ship heads back up to orbit. For all we know the spaceport is on lockdown after we were reported."

"Plot me a course that avoids major population centers," Jason said, not dithering between options while the clock was ticking down. "We're going to have to climb up out of the ground clutter; we can't fly terrain-following all the way to the pole. Keep monitoring com traffic and let me know if we've been detected."

"Of course," Kage said, his four nimble hands flying over his controls. Jason pulled the nose up and began to swing around onto a northerly course. He was in a gentle climb that would take them up to the beginnings of Corran's stratosphere, allowing them to push up to supersonic speeds without leaving such a large sonic footprint as they crossed over the continent. Thankfully, the northern regions were sparsely populated; Corran's axis tilt ensured the winters there were especially brutal. "The twins are on final approach, lowering the shields to let them in," Kage told Jason without looking up from his console. The two intelligent probes zipped in close to the *Phoenix* and then eased down onto their respective landing hooks. Once they were pulled back inside and the hatches were closed Kage reactivated the dorsal shielding. Like the engines, the shield emitters were operating in a low-power mode to keep the chances of detection to a minimum without leaving them completely vulnerable.

"We're climbing up through flight level zero-three-zero, everyone stay sharp," Jason said. Zero-three-zero represented their altitude, in this case thirty-thousand feet. As an American expatriate, Jason frequently shifted between metric and English units of measure naturally, but for his crew (especially Twingo), who were relying on

34

their translations being accurate, this idiosyncrasy drove them almost insane. Kage looked over at him in annoyance, but said nothing. The ship was now flying at the altitude most commercial flights would be found at, but due to her size and configuration, Jason didn't hold out much hope of the *Phoenix* fooling even the most inattentive sensor operator. They were still quite a distance from the pole when their luck ran out.

"Contact! Two destroyer class ships transferring to a lower orbit and moving to shadow us. We can assume they'll be launching fighters when they're within range." Doc's voice was calm and measured, but the Vongaard family looked fearfully between him and Jason.

"So much for sneaking out of here," Jason said tightly, flipping the engine mode to full output. "Let's hit it!" As soon as his engine indicators greened up he slammed the throttle against the stops. The *Phoenix* roared as her main engines came to full power and millions of pounds of thrust blasted them through the Corranian atmosphere. He intended to see just how good the picket ships really were. The DL7 was designed especially for this scenario: outrun much larger and more powerful ships within a planet's atmosphere or low orbit. He glanced down at his indicators to make sure there were no issues with cooling to the engines or hull temperature on the leading edges, all were well within norms, so he kept the hammer down and let the *Phoenix* race to hypersonic velocities as she tore a hole through the clear northern sky. Despite the imminent danger, the chance to let his powerful ship off her leash sent an electric thrill up Jason's spine.

"Weapons and shields coming up," Kage said without being prompted.

"Reactor output is coming up to one-hundred percent, grav-emitters are in emergency charge mode; we'll have limited slip-drive in two minutes," Twingo said over the intercom.

"Very good," Jason said. "Senator Vongaard, would you and your family please activate your seat restraints, the ride might not stay so smooth." He watched the civilians scramble to get the seat harnesses activated and took some small pleasure in the abject terror on the face of the oldest daughter. *Not quite so sullen now, are you?*

"The heat signatures on the destroyers are spiking. They're pushing their engines hard to try and keep up," Doc said from the sensor station. "We also have a cruiser descending into the upper atmosphere over the pole. I think they realize what we're trying to do."

"Can we slip between them and stay out of weapons range of both formations? There's no point in trying to sneak up the polar axis at this point," Jason said as he pulled the power back on the engines to maintain their current speed.

"If we can get to orbit within the next forty-five seconds we'll clear both groups before they can maneuver back up out of their current orbits. There are ships still patrolling in high-synchronous orbit, though, and they're moving to cover us as well."

"Shit. Hold on!" Jason pulled the stick smoothly back and stood the *Phoenix* on her tail. The ship clawed up out of the atmosphere in a vertical climb that would put them right in the middle of the waiting hornets' nest above in mere seconds. "Kage, plot a jump directly away from Corran, seven light seconds."

"Plotting... It's going to be close, Captain. We've just barely got enough charge in the emitters to pull it off. If they use an interdiction field we're screwed," Kage said as he set up their short slip-space hop.

"I'll chance it," Jason said as the sky blackened around them. He saw a green pop-up indicator on his main display letting him know that the jump was programmed and ready, all he had to do was engage the drive. He waited a few more seconds as the *Phoenix* shot up between the two groups of ships that had descended to pin them down and aimed for the smaller gap in the ships that were waiting above them. The instant they were at the extreme outer range for most interdiction field generators, Jason smacked the "engage" button that was blinking on his right. There was a high-pitched whine, the canopy darkened, and then a split second later they were sitting in open space. "Report!"

"Jump successful," Kage said. "We're seven light seconds away from Corran."

"Go dark," Jason said. "Shut down all potential emission sources. Plot me a course into the interior asteroid belt, five second burn on the main engines. Twingo: after the engine burn I'm killing the mains, I need the slip-drive to full power as fast as you can manage it."

"You got it, Captain," Twingo's disembodied voice came across the bridge. "It'll be a bit; that short hop almost discharged the emitter coils completely."

"Understood, just do your best," Jason answered. He swung the ship onto the indicated course that Kage had provided and nudged the engines up to fifty percent power for five seconds before chopping the throttle and then shutting the engines down altogether. He was hoping the heat bloom from the short burn wouldn't be detected. Now they were just an inert piece of space junk floating towards the closer of the two asteroid belts in the Corran System. With any luck, the ships involved in the blockade would think their slip-space jump was completely out of the system and not come ranging out looking for them. It was a gamble, but once in open space the advantage would have shifted to the larger warships as the smaller *Phoenix* would have been hard pressed to keep their big guns at bay.

"Captain?" The shaky voice had emanated from the forward part of the bridge.

"Yes, Senator?"

"Would it be possible for me to take my family and sit down someplace comfortable? They've been through a lot and it seems everything up here is well in hand," Senator Vongaard asked respectfully, seeming overwhelmed by the events of the previous few hours.

"Of course. Doc?"

"Sir, if you'd please follow me I'll show you and your family to our galley and lounge area. It isn't much, but you can get something to drink and sit in a comfortable chair," Doc said as he rose from his seat, indicating towards the bridge exit with a flourish. The four Corranians filed out and Doc turned to follow, giving Jason a sideways smile as he did. Jason smiled as well; it was a rush to cheat certain death yet again. *The crew is really coming together.*

He got up out of the pilot's seat and made his way over to the sensor station Doc had only recently vacated to scan the surrounding space. While the passive sensors weren't great, it was better than nothing at all.

"I'm going to get something to eat," Crusher announced and stood to leave the bridge.

"Put your toys away first," Jason said, referring to the weaponry still hanging from various locations on the hulking warrior. Crusher gave him an unfriendly glare before clomping off the bridge towards the armory.

"You love pushing his buttons," Kage said, shaking his head with a smile.

"It's good for him," Jason replied. "With other people on board he'll eat in the armory anyway. He's still a little self-conscious about that." Crusher's diet tended to be rather bland; a simple lean protein and some sort of fiber or leafy green vegetable, often the same thing every day for weeks on end. But the shape of his blunted muzzle, coupled with his oversized teeth, made for some interesting noises and the occasional food projectile. He had grown comfortable around the rest of Omega Force, but when others were on board he either ate in his room or in the armory. While it was mildly amusing to see such a ferocious person be shy about something as mundane as eating, it also reminded him that the big guy was actually fairly sensitive under that terrifying exterior. "So... what do we think?"

"About the mission?" Kage asked.

"Yep."

"It went pretty well once we were on the ground. We seem to have gotten away clean. Well... so far at least," the smaller alien said. "Lucky?"

"It could have gone better, in my opinion," the battlesynth said, still standing by the bridge entrance.

"Care to elaborate?" Jason asked.

"It was unnecessarily complicated. The ruse with the CIS vehicle and you dressing as an agent... we could have simply snuck through the forest, infiltrated through the back wall, and been out before the Senator was noticed missing," Lucky said. The longer he spent around his friends, the more comfortable he was offering an opinion the others may not like. It was something that Jason encouraged at every opportunity.

"Fair enough..." Jason began.

"We didn't know the back would be unguarded," Kage interrupted. The van had been his idea so he felt compelled to defend it. "Our intel stated there were regular patrols of the property and surrounding area."

"True," Lucky conceded, "but as Captain Burke is fond of saying: 'No plan survives first contact.' We should have sent the twins to scout the area first and then adjusted our strategy accordingly. The confrontation with the CIS agents at the house led to our detection and pursuit."

"I'd say you're both right," Jason said. In truth, he was happy neither had brought up the fact he had almost crashed the ship again during atmospheric entry. "But I think ultimately Lucky is the most correct, we need to stop getting so locked into one plan or idea that we fail to see a better way when it presents itself. We'll go through a full debrief later. Once we're in slip-space we're going to have a few days to go over the missteps. Kage, you've got the bridge, I'm going to go stow my gear and grab a quick bite. I'll come back up in a few to relieve you so you can do the same."

"Thanks, Captain," Kage answered. "I'll be here." Jason turned to walk off the bridge, patting Lucky fondly on the shoulder on his way out.

As he suspected, Crusher was in the armory with an empty tray from the galley when he entered. The big warrior was sitting on one of the benches fiddling with a small plasma sidearm. "Nice job out there tonight," Jason said as he walked in through the door.

"Thank you, Captain. It wasn't all that difficult," he said modestly.

"Not for you, maybe. I don't have your training or background," Jason said as he made his weapons safe and began putting them away on their appropriate racks.

"You sell yourself short. You were a good soldier when I met you, and you've gotten quite a bit better over the last year. Your body is almost strong enough that we can begin some serious hand-to-hand combat training, if you're interested," Crusher said. In truth, the prospect made Jason more than a little nervous. He was nowhere near a match for the warrior's strength and ability despite his recent upgrades.

"I appreciate the offer," he said neutrally. "I may take you up on that during the longer slip-space flights." He stood up and headed towards the door, "You about done in here?"

"I don't think the Senator's family is comfortable around me. I'll probably stay here for a while longer."

"Suit yourself. But this is your home; you're free to go where you want and any passengers we take on will need to adjust to that. Or not. That's their business, but don't feel that you have to skulk around the ship on their account." Jason walked out of the armory without another word. He almost stopped to talk to Twingo in the engineering bay, but the steady stream of profanity coming from the general vicinity of the slip-reactor dissuaded him. Instead, he made his way to the galley to grab a sandwich to go and relieve Kage so the code slicer could get something to eat and unwind a bit.

He was lounging in the pilot's seat when Senator Vongaard entered the bridge, pausing slightly as Lucky turned to him. While the gesture looked harmless, Jason knew the synth was scanning the Senator for weapons. Both he and Crusher took internal security very seriously, and when they were carrying passengers they were doubly cautious. "Captain Burke, now that the...excitement... is somewhat concluded, I would like to again offer you my thanks. I must confess, I'm shocked that my own people would send a hit squad to eliminate me and my family," Vongaard said sadly as he sat slowly in one of the sensor station seats.

"Don't mention it, Senator. After all, we're being well paid for this," Jason said.

"Forgive me, but you don't strike me as your average, run of the mill mercenaries."

"Oh?"

"No. For one, our mutual friend wouldn't have hired you. For another, you spared every CIS agent you encountered during the rescue when it would have been in your best interests to simply kill them," Vongaard concluded. "Your team operates more like a military unit than a random group of guns for hire." Jason took the statement as the compliment it was intended.

"No, Senator," he said, "we don't kill indiscriminately. The agents were misguided, but not evil. However, if we had arrived a bit later and they had already been attempting to carry out their orders... things would have gone differently. Orders or no, every man is responsible for his own actions and the consequences or rewards they may bring."

"Quite right," Vongaard conceded. "So... the make-up of Omega Force seems to be quite unique. You look like a Corranian, but I know that you're not. Not only that, you have a Galvetic warrior, which is extremely rare, and a real battlesynth, an even more rare species. How is it such an eclectic group formed and travels together like you do?"

"Lucky, care to explain it to the Senator?" Jason asked his friend.

"It is not all that difficult, Senator Vongaard. We did not so much 'form' as we rescued each other, each from their own form of captivity. Captain Burke pulled us out of lives that held torture and certain death, and now we wish to continue that work for all who need it," Lucky said softly. The synth was rarely so introspective, but Jason couldn't fault his logic. Before Vongaard could answer, the rest of his family entered the bridge, led by Doc.

"Ah! Come here my dears, let me introduce you properly to the Captain," Vongaard said expansively. His little brood huddled around him and looked at Jason while keeping a wary eye on Lucky. "Captain, may I introduce my beautiful wife, Saffreena. My eldest daughter, Calleeá. And lastly my youngest angel, Seleste." The women of the Vongaard family smiled shyly at Jason, seeming to have dropped some of their early indignation for being rushed from their home in the middle of the night.

"Ladies," Jason said with a nod of his head, "welcome aboard the *Phoenix*. She's not the most luxurious thing in the sky, but she'll keep you safe until we reach our destination. We're currently drifting unpowered towards your inner asteroid belt to avoid detection from the blockade ships in orbit over your planet. So far, it's working. As soon as the slip-drive is fully online, we'll mesh out of the Corran System and be on our way. Doc will see to your comfort. I'm sure you all must be tired after your ordeal." Doc looked up and gave Jason an unfriendly look as he was volunteered for chaperone duty again.

"Of course, Captain," Vongaard said smoothly. "We'll leave you to your task." With a half bow he led his family off the bridge, trailed by Doc. The youngest daughter, Seleste, smiled shyly at Lucky and offered a little wave. The big synth winked one of his eyes at her, eliciting a delighted giggle before she was through the hatchway. Jason smiled to himself and shook his head.

As Kage was walking back onto the bridge, Twingo's voice broke over the intercom, "Jason, the slip-drive is now fully active. Emitter coils are charged and the reactor is capable of sustained output. I'll be in the galley if you need me."

"Thanks, bud. I appreciate it," Jason said.

"My ass is on this tub too..." Twingo's voice trailed off as he continued to mumble out of range of the audio pick-up in engineering. Jason rolled his eyes before turning to Kage.

"So the million credit question is: do we continue to try and drift through the asteroid belt or do we just mesh out of here and be done with it?" he asked. Kage took a moment to weigh both options before speaking.

"Waiting to get into the belt would shield our slip signature somewhat, but if we just jump now we may still be undetected. And we can always do a series of dummy jumps to throw anyone off like we usually do."

"We're flying completely blind out here with the active sensors shut down, there could be a cruiser bearing down on us and we'd never know it until it was too late," Jason said. "We're out of here. Plot out first jump and then get me three dummy jumps before we come onto our final course." A "dummy jump" was a short slip-space jump followed by another, and usually another, in order to throw any potential pursuers off their trail. The energy released in initiating a slip-space field saturated surrounding space to the point that a tracking ship's sensors would be hard pressed to ferret them out. On the last dummy jump Jason liked to send out the damage control bots to

48

inspect the exterior of the ship for any active trackers that may have been placed on the hull.

Thirty minutes later, the *Phoenix* was tearing through slip-space towards their destination (and payment) to drop off the Vongaard family. It would be a four-day flight at the speed Jason had chosen, quick enough that their passengers wouldn't become restless but not so fast that they burned an excessive amount of fuel and ate away at their profit for the job. He sat on the bridge in his seat for another hour to monitor the ship's systems during the beginning of the long flight and to unwind a bit in the relative quiet the command deck offered. Kage, as was usual, seemed completely absorbed by his own displays. In truth, he was hooked into the computer via his own unique neural implants and was probably only vaguely aware of his surroundings. As a Veran, Kage had the ability to partition off sections of his over-sized brain and dedicate those to parallel functions. The "sectioning" of his brain made him an especially effective code slicer.

Jason leaned back further into his seat and watched the indicated velocity on his display creep up towards their final cruising speed. It was all abstract to him; they were moving at nearly a thousand times the speed of light in relation to objects in normal space, but within the cocoon of slip-space energy, the ship was motionless. He was getting a firmer grasp on the principles involved, but much of the technology on his ship may as well have been magic to him. He figured he had as long as he needed to get himself up to speed; he had no plans on settling down anytime soon.

Standing and stretching, he nodded to Kage (who either didn't see him or chose to ignore him) and walked off the bridge. As he expected, Lucky turned and followed him out. "I'm heading to bed,

Lucky," he told the synth. "Keep an eye on everything and wake me up if anything goes sideways on us."

"Of course, Captain," Lucky replied as he posted up against one of the forward bulkheads. The vantage point would allow him to monitor the only entrance to the bridge as well as the only passageway that led to his Captain's quarters. Never requiring rest, he would remain at his post for as long as necessary and control access to either of these areas. Although the Senator and his family seemed harmless and the job had seemed legit, past experience told them things weren't always what they "seemed" to be.

Jason stripped off the CIS uniform and tossed it carelessly into the corner of his room. The cleaning bot that handled his quarters would find it and feed it back into the fabricators. He walked into the attached restroom, or "head," and turned on the shower. A set of misting water jets that did a remarkable job of cleaning him off. He stepped over to the sink and stared at himself in the mirror. Sometimes, when the light was just right, he could see the glint of the nanotech implants in his eyes; a series of auxiliary retinas he could access to see in an expanded spectrum. He knew that these interfaced with his neural implants, basically a series of powerful computers that were tied directly into his nervous system that allowed him to access information over data networks, send instructions to the ship, and understand all of the alien languages being spoken around him.

As his eyes moved down to his torso, he couldn't help but reflect on the other changes he'd made to himself. He had paid to have

50

his skeleton modified to increase its strength by having the large bones clad in a type of bio-compatible carbon fiber that had been threaded in over the course of days. He had also let Doc, a geneticist by trade, tweak his genetic make-up to work in conjunction with the available nanotech to increase his physical strength by an order of magnitude. If the isolation hadn't caused him to begin to lose touch with his humanity, each new tweak and twist to his body certainly did. "Bah," he said aloud and turned away from the mirror, entering the shower stall.

He wasn't sure why he was feeling so moody about being separated from his own world. Perhaps it was because the Corranians looked so very human, perhaps it was something else. During his last visit home, during which he had given all his worldly possessions to an old love, he had also left a discreet payload in orbit that he had not bothered trying to access as of yet. It was a small, stealthy com drone that was capable of intercepting all Earthly broadcasts, and even access the internet, and send them via slip-space transceiver directly to the ship. So, as he dried himself off, he ordered the computer to activate the com array and download the contents the small probe had stored up so far, mostly television and radio broadcasts.

After donning a pair of loose basketball shorts and a t-shirt, he grabbed a beer and flopped onto the bed. A quick look through the data package contents from the probe brought a smile to his face. "Computer, dim lights and play Top Gear, UK version. Newest episode first," he said.

"Acknowledged." As the first notes of "Jessica" by the Allman Brothers announced the beginning of his favorite show, Jason leaned back and suddenly didn't feel so far from home anymore.

Chapter 3

The remainder of the flight proved to be uneventful; the Senator's family were perfect passengers, neither making a fuss nor getting in the way of the crew as they went about the daily operations of flying the ship through slip-space. Not surprisingly, Doc and Senator Vongaard had become quite friendly and were often seen in conversation together in the common area. Saffreena, Hallis Vongaard's wife, spend much of the time reading off a tablet computer (Kage took it upon himself to hack into it to make sure there was nothing on there that shouldn't be) and didn't interact with the others very often except for mealtimes. The oldest daughter, Calleeá, was quiet and sullen, often emerging from their quarters in crew berthing with red, puffy eyes. During the long, boring flight it had begun to sink in for the young woman that she would never be able to return to her life or her friends. For a teenage girl of any species, this was devastating.

Seleste, the youngest daughter, surprised them all by instantly bonding, and wanting to spend time constantly with, the two most fearsome members of Omega Force: Crusher and Lucky. For their part, the pair of soldiers were exquisitely gentle and kind with the young girl, answering her questions and even submitting to playing games with her at the galley table. It was a startling visual at first, but Jason and Kage soon got used to it. At the threatening look from Crusher, both wisely chose to forgo the obvious jokes that came to mind.

"It is quite the visual contrast, is it not?" Senator Vongaard asked Jason when they were on the bridge one evening. "I think the night we had to escape Corran frightened her more than she's letting on, and those two represent a sense of security. Who could possibly hurt you with them standing watch?" He shook his head with a smile, obviously amused.

"For Crusher, the fact that she's not terrified of his appearance is a bit unique. I think he's enjoying being around someone so innocent and who doesn't run the other way screaming when he walks into a room," Jason said, equally amused.

Some days after their dramatic escape from Corran, the crew all sat on the bridge, as did Senator Vongaard, as they neared within hours of their destination. As was their usual procedure, the ship was cleaned up, weapons were inspected, and everyone was at their station and alert while they waited for the slip-drive to disengage and pop them back into real space.

"Eshquaria System transition in ten minutes," the computer announced. Everyone on the bridge involuntarily sat up straighter in their seat and looked forward despite the canopy still being blacked out for slip-space flight. Jason tensed up in the pilot seat as the seconds ticked down, even though they were hired to do this job by someone from Eshquaria, and Doc swore it checked out, this would be the first time they would meet their employer, or even set foot on the planet.

The system was controlled by a sovereign government, a type of representative democracy, but it still maintained official commerce relations with the ConFed government without submitting to the overarching authority of the ConFed Council. The Confederated Systems were more a wide-ranging alliance than a true governmental body, each system still handled internal affairs as they saw fit in order to simplify the logistics involved due to interstellar distances. It reminded Jason of the United Nations from Earth, but with more teeth. Maybe NATO would be more accurate, but the ConFed was heavily involved in regulating commerce and social issues as well as defense. It seemed to work okay for what it was, but he was so new to the subtleties of galactic politics that he usually only understood the broad strokes from the newscasts, and even then Doc had to paraphrase them for his benefit. From his perspective, it looked like the ConFed skimmed an enormous amount of wealth off the top and used it to build an incredibly powerful fleet that answered only to them. Ostensibly this was to provide for the common defense, but Jason had his doubts.

The *Phoenix* shuddered slightly as the slip-drive disengaged and the universe, who abhors things not being in their natural order, popped them out into real space with a flash of dissipating slip energy. A quick glance at the status display confirmed that they had meshed in-system precisely on target and were drifting down the primary star's gravity well towards Eshquaria, the main planet in a system made up of three habitable worlds, five habitable moons, and a handful of large industrial and commercial orbiting platforms.

Jason engaged the ship's autopilot once he confirmed their position, leaving the manual flight controls in their stowed positions. Eshquaria's traffic controllers were notoriously insistent on accurate approaches to their planet since the space traffic was normally quite heavy. He didn't feel they'd appreciate him practicing on the new flight control system in their clogged shipping lanes, so he sat back and simply monitored their progress instead. "Twingo," he called out, "are we running with clean codes?"

"Of course we are. I've got us covered, Captain," Twingo said casually from one of the bridge stations. They'd spent an incredible amount of money to refit the *Phoenix* with a set of switchable transponders, complete with all new registry codes from various worlds around the galaxy. After some of their more memorable missions, they had been pursued heavily by law enforcement agencies from half a dozen different planets. They'd had to adopt the old smugglers' trick of rotating transponders in order to stay a step ahead. There was one transponder which they kept "clean" that identified the *Phoenix* as a light courier freighter.

The DL7 slipped easily into their designated approach lane which would put them on an orbital insertion vector that bypassed most of the holding and transfer orbits. This would queue them up for a quick atmospheric entry. Jason was happy about the clout their employer seemed to have on the surface; while he didn't mind cooling his heels above a planet, the longer they were airborne the more likely it was that someone would get a good visual of the *Phoenix* and realize she wasn't just some light freighter and raise an alarm.

Luck stayed on their side and they passed unseen, and largely ignored, through the Eshquarian traffic and began their descent. Like their approach, entry was rigidly controlled and they were ordered into a tight, spiraling descent through the atmosphere that was almost directly over their intended landing zone: a small, commercial spaceport near the coast of the southern continent. This maneuver would be impossible without a gravimetric drive to control their speed and angle of attack, but even with it, there was still considerable friction heating over the hull. They continued down in the lazy, eighty-mile wide spiral as the thickening atmosphere began to buffet the gunship slightly.

With the ship's computer actually doing his job, Jason was free to enjoy the view of the planet as they descended. Eshquaria was very much like the other Earth-type planets he had visited since he started working in space. It had brilliant blue oceans and rolling green landmasses, just like his home. The more of them he saw, the more he realized Earth wasn't really all *that* unique. Instead of being upset at that, he found it oddly comforting that humans fit snugly into a "norm", albeit many, many years behind technologically.

"Heads up, Captain. We're approaching the handoff," Kage said.

"I've got it," he said testily. The handoff was when the autopilot would kick off since it wouldn't be receiving instructions from ground control on their final approach.

"Really? It looked like you were daydreaming."

"That's what humans look like when we're anticipating something," Jason replied. Both Doc and Twingo gave him a look that clearly showed how much they disbelieved that statement. Jason ignored them as the flight controls extended up from the console and the floor in preparation of the transition to manual flight.

The computer passed control of the gunship over to him and the nav system began feeding him fly-to indicators on his display, leading him to the spaceport's main landing area. The final approach was easy since the landing pad was a semi-private section of the facility that catered to private shuttles and the occasional slip-capable yacht. The *Phoenix* most definitely looked out of place as Jason cycled the landing gear down and settled her onto the tarmac. No sooner had they touched down when a coded message came through the coms, text only, directing them to the hanger complex ahead and to the right. Jason kept the grav-drive active in order to keep most of the ship's weight off the landing gear and began to taxi towards the indicated building, an enormous, non-descript metal hanger that looked like all the others around it.

Peering into the hanger, Jason could make out a half-dozen vehicles lining the wall and twice as many armed men milling about. He knew his cargo (er... passengers) were of high value, so he didn't look too much into it as he nudged the *Phoenix* over the threshold and all the way inside. A man on a mezzanine directly in front of him marshaled them forward and then crossed his arms, indicating that they come to a stop. Jason leveled the ship out on the landing gear, shut down the drives, and began putting the various systems in standby or killing them altogether. The others stood and began filing out of the bridge with the Vongaard family to gather their belongings and finish securing the ship.

"No, it's ok... really. I'll finish up here," he said to himself since everyone else had left. He went to two other stations and made sure things were in their proper setting before walking off the bridge and heading towards the cargo bay. He was discreetly armed with a small sidearm tucked into a rear waistband, but he stopped by the armory to deposit the weapon before meeting the others by the rear ramp. Besides, with Lucky beside him, the small weapon wouldn't amount to much anyways.

"We all ready?" He asked as he approached the group. There were nervous nods from the Vongaard family and a studied indifference from his crew. He walked over to the control panel and opened the interior pressure doors of the cargo bay and then hit the control to lower the rear ramp. As it hummed down towards the ground, Jason could see the handful of men in black uniforms waiting at the bottom. Although well-armed, there was a casual air about them that said they didn't expect any trouble.

He walked down the ramp confidently with Lucky and Crusher flanking him one step behind. The effect it had on the men at the bottom of the ramp was amusing, and intentional; nobody in their right mind would think they had the upper hand when a Galvetic warrior and a full-fledged battlesynth were coming towards them. "Gentlemen," he said cordially. "I'm Captain Burke. I believe we're expected."

"Of course, Captain," one of the men said, identifying himself as in-command. "Would you be so kind as to consent to a hand scan? That goes for the rest of your crew and the passengers as well."

"I don't see why not," Jason said, relieved he had left the small sidearm in the ship. He had expected this; nobody paid the kind of money they were getting for this simple job without being prudent. "Can we do this here, at the bottom of the ramp?"

"Yes, sir. And thank you for cooperating without a fuss," the commander said with some relief in his voice. He had mistaken Omega Force for simple mercenaries and his experience told him that they were usually an uncooperative lot if for no other reason than the chance to be uncooperative. Two other men in black uniforms came forward with scanners and cleared the six members of the crew (although Lucky's readings caused some discussion) and the four Vongaards. Once that was finished, the commander of the group called an "all-clear" into his com unit and stepped back. Jason looked around, confused, until a small group of well dressed individuals came around from under the *Phoenix's* left wing and into view. Senator Vongaard broke into a large smile immediately.

"Prime Minister Colleston! This is truly a pleasure; I had no idea you'd be meeting us yourself," he said, approaching the Prime Minister with his hand outstretched for a very human-looking handshake.

"When I heard you were inbound I had to come down and see for myself," Colleston said. "The reports from Corran were that the ship you fled on was destroyed. But, since they never produced even a molecule of wreckage, we all held out hope you'd made it." The Prime Minister looked over to take in the rest of the Senator's family and the crew of the *Phoenix*. Vongaard saw the look and rushed to make introductions:

"Mister Prime Minister, you already know my family..."

"...Hello, ladies..."

"... and let me introduce you to the members of Omega Force. Without them we certainly wouldn't have made it off Corran, not alive anyway. This is Captain Burke, Chief Engineer Twingo, Doctor Ma'Fredich, Kage, Lucky, and Crusher," Vongaard said, rounding out the introductions.

"Lucky?" Colleston asked in genuine confusion as he eyed the synth up and down.

"Not my official designation, of course. It is the name my friends have given me," Lucky said quietly.

"How interesting," Colleston said. "Anyway, I can't thank you enough for the job you've done. My advisor was right when he insisted on hiring you. You understand we couldn't have sent in Eshquarian military units, even special forces, to affect a rescue; the political fallout if they failed would have been considerable. But I was told you guys were at least as good... and here you all are," the Prime Minister beamed, arms held wide, "safe and sound.

"Now, if you'll all excuse me, I'll leave you in the capable hands of my Chief of Staff, Mr. Kross." With a final, curt nod the Prime Minister of Eshquaria turned and made his way back to one of the waiting vehicles with most of the security force in tow. Mr. Kross, a distinguished looking man with longer silver-violet hair and an impeccable suit, walked directly up to Jason.

"Captain Jason Burke," he said in a clipped, formal tone. "I'd also like to extend my congratulations on a job well done. You came recommended to us very highly, and, I must say, you didn't disappoint. The Senator's safety has greater implications than just a saved life, but we can talk about that later. If you and your crew would be so kind as to grab what you need, I'd like you to be my guest in the Capital at the

Prime Minister's compound. You'll meet the man who hired you there so he can arrange payment." Jason would have rather been backing the *Phoenix* out of the hanger and preparing to lift off, but leaving without payment wasn't an option.

"It appears we're at your disposal, Mr. Kross. We'll be just a moment," he said. He turned and saw the crew was already heading back up the ramp to grab their things. In truth, a little time planetside and off the ship wouldn't hurt; they'd been at it pretty hard the last few months. Lucky, who didn't need to get anything, stood at the bottom of the ramp in a manner that made it obvious he was guarding the entrance to the ship.

Jason grabbed his "go-bag" out of his quarters that had his toiletries, an assortment of "civilian" clothing, and a few other interesting little items that he knew would make it through a security scan, and then went up to the bridge to give things a once over to ensure they were properly shutdown or in standby. Some other systems, like internal and perimeter security, were still on full alert. He set external security so that someone would actually need to be touching the hull before they were stunned, but if an unauthorized person tried to force their way on board, it was unlikely they would survive. Harsh measures, but the *Phoenix* was their life out there. They couldn't take the risk that someone would want to damage or steal her.

"Computer," he said as he walked back down the cargo ramp to meet up with his crew, "lock up and initiate defensive protocol Burke-Bravo."

"Confirmed," the computer said. When Jason's boots hit the hanger floor, the internal pressure doors slid shut and the ramp raised and locked. The marker lights on the tips of the wings and vertical stabilizers remained on, but muted, as fair warning to any would-be vandals that the ship wasn't sitting helpless.

"After you, Mr. Kross," Jason said as he hefted his bag. The Vongaard family had already left in one of the other vehicles while they had been on board gathering their things, so the crew divided themselves between the remaining two vehicles and rolled out of the door near the nose of the ship and made their way down the service road that paralleled the taxiway. Jason remained quiet and stared out the window. *I hope I'm not walking us into something we can't walk out of.*

The trip to the compound that housed an assortment of government officials and foreign diplomats was about an hour and a half in the ground vehicle. Jason didn't like being so far away from his ship, but he knew if they didn't collect on this job, things would begin to get very tight for them; operating the DL7 gunship was horrifically expensive and the cost of trying to disappear after some of their more exciting jobs was daunting. But, despite the rough patch, Omega Force had remained true to its core beliefs: they never brought harm on someone who didn't deserve it and they had remained loyal to each other throughout. Jason was proud to serve with all of them and he hoped they would be able to continue to make a real difference.

The compound was actually a campus of tall, graceful buildings that was surrounded by a high decorative wall that looked quite substantial. Their vehicle rolled through a security gate unopposed and pulled up to one of the taller towers on the grounds. "Your accommodations will be in this building, Captain," Mr. Kross was saying. "I think you'll find them slightly more comfortable than a deep-space combat vessel. At least I hope so, if not we'll have to talk to the interior decorators." Jason knew the man was making meaningless small-talk so he didn't bother answering. The Chief of Staff smoothly moved on, talking to Doc instead as they all piled out of the passenger vehicles. "There will be a reception for Senator Vongaard this evening that you're all invited to attend. The dress will be dinner formal. Someone will come to collect you in order to take you to the event and the man who contracted you will meet you there." Jason sighed audibly; jumping through hoops to get paid after a job was completed was not something he usually entertained.

"Of course, Mr. Kross," Doc said smoothly. "We'll be sure to have ourselves ready." Once Kross had departed, the crew followed one of the security troops into the building and up to their suite. As promised, it was fairly luxurious with seven separate bedrooms arranged around a large common/entertainment area. It seemed to encompass at least half the floor they were on.

Jason walked into one of the bedrooms, dropped his bag on the floor, and flopped backwards onto the enormous bed with a huge sigh of contentment. *I may need to see about replacing the mattress on my own bed. I didn't know what I was missing.* While he could have instantly fallen asleep on the ultra-comfortable bed, an argument in the common area seemed to be gaining momentum in both volume and number of participants. Reluctantly, he got up and walked out to see just what everyone was so worked up about.

"I didn't sign on for this sort of thing, hobnobbing with politicians and sycophants isn't my game," Kage was saying.

"It wouldn't kill you to stay disconnected from a computer terminal once in awhile," Doc said. "A little culture wouldn't hurt either. That goes for you too, Crusher."

"Fuck that," Crusher rumbled, repeating one of his Captain's favorite phrases. "I'm not going." The big warrior had already found the bar and was splayed out on a couch with a bottle of something green in his massive hand.

"Captain..." Doc said helplessly, relieved when he saw Jason walk out.

"Ok," Jason began, holding up his hand for silence. "Who actually wants to go to this?" Only Doc raised his hand, who then turned and openly glared at his crewmates who did not raise theirs. "Fine. Doc and I are really the only ones who *need* to be there. If the rest of you want to sit here and get drunk while we go and get the money from the job, so be it." The smiles he saw in return told Jason he hadn't quite gotten the hang of guilt tripping them into anything yet.

"So you are insistent that you will not be going, Crusher?" Lucky asked.

"You heard me."

"Captain," the synth said, "I will be accompanying you and Doc this evening."

"Really?" Doc asked, surprised. "You don't especially like crowds, Lucky."

"This is true. But I will not let Captain Burke go anywhere without proper protection, no offense intended," Lucky said.

"None taken," Doc laughed. "Anything he can't handle himself is going to be out of my league."

"I appreciate that, big guy," Jason said sincerely. While he didn't think he was in any danger, he wouldn't insult his friend by turning down the offer. Lucky was still somewhat uncomfortable around groups of people in social settings after his abduction by Bondrass' slave traders, so the gesture was viewed by the Captain as a profound sign of respect.

The three members of Omega Force that submitted to attending the formal reception for the Senator they had rescued were unceremoniously dropped off near a service entrance, well away from the main entrance to the hall where people were being announced as they entered. Far from feeling snubbed, the trio couldn't have been happier with the arrangement; getting their pictures in the local press wasn't exactly in line with their policy of keeping a low profile.

Entering the hall, Jason asked Lucky to scan for Chief of Staff Kross and was rewarded with the synth pointing towards a corner or the enormous hall near one of four bars that were serving drinks. Jason blended in well with the native Eshquarians, Doc was also no problem, but poor Lucky drew stares and gasps as he tried to quietly shadow his Captain towards the far corner for which they were headed. "Don't worry, Lucky. We'll only stay as long as we absolutely need to, and then we're gone. This isn't a social call," Jason said to the obviously uncomfortable synth.

"Do not concern yourself with me, Captain," he said quietly. "I will remain inconspicuous as you and Doc conduct business." Jason has his doubts about how inconspicuous he could be in a setting like they were in, although he had shifted the color of his armor panels to a muted black that looked quite formal against the burnished silver of his "skin." Kross saw them approaching and turned to dismiss most of the people he had been talking to, save for one man. He was tall and thin, almost severe looking, and had white hair and a prominent pointed chin. It seemed like the white hair was a natural coloration, or lack of, rather than a result of advanced age.

"Gentlemen," Kross said smoothly, "welcome. I see not all of you made it."

"The rest of the crew was a little under the weather after such a long flight," Jason said blandly, knowing full well the politician would see right through the lie.

"Of course," he agreed. "May I introduce our mutual friend and your current employer: Mr. Crisstof Dalton." *I'll be damned... a normal sounding name for once.* At the mention of his name, Crisstof Dalton placed his right hand on his chest and bowed slightly.

"A genuine pleasure to meet you, Captain Burke," his rich, deep voice seemed to hang in the air. "And you as well Dr. Ma'Fredich and Lucky."

"If you don't mind my saying, you seem quite familiar with us Mr. Dalton," Jason said smoothly, hiding the alarm he was feeling.

"Please, call me Crisstof... And do not be alarmed, I've been tracking your exploits for some time now, but not for any nefarious purpose," Crisstof said. "I believe we can be mutually beneficial to each other in the future, but for now let us get acquainted, settle up our account, and discuss the possibility of discussing another job you can do for me soon." *This guy is smooth.*

Soon, Kross left the four of them to talk quietly at the far end of the hall while the reception went on around them. Jason got the impression Crisstof was what he would call a "trouble shooter:" someone who found ways to accomplish things when official channels either broke down or were unavailable. He practically confirmed this when he explained why Omega Force had been hired to get the Vongaard family off Corran instead of any number of military units that were probably not only better equipped, but already on the payroll.

"You see, Corran is being subjugated by her sister planet, Kellaan. Kellaan shares an orbit very similar to Corran, in fact they overlap each other in some places. Kellaan was settled by the Corranians nearly a millennia ago when the technology was still quite primitive. There wasn't regular commerce, just a steady stream of settlers and refugees that wanted to escape the pollution and overcrowding of Corran's cities." Crisstof paused to take a long drink of a clear something that smelled like a distilled spirit before continuing.

"After the last planetary war on Corran, the two worlds lost contact with each other and set off down two very different social evolutionary paths. When they finally were able to communicate and visit after the technology caught up, there was a constant tension between the two.

"In recent years, an increasingly vocal contingent within the Corranian government has been advocating the more totalitarian, militaristic methods of the Kellaanians," he paused to take another drink.

"Let me guess," Doc filled in the silence, "the movement caught on and before long were advocating a takeover by the Kellaan government."

"Correct," Crisstof confirmed. "Through creative manipulation of the media, and in turn the population, they were able to convince people that it was in their best interest. This put the opposition in a dangerous place; if the Kellaanians actually attacked then they would be in serious danger. The Kellaan regime doesn't allow much in the way of dissenting opinion."

"So as soon as the attack and blockade happened you hired us to extract Senator Vongaard," Jason finished. Crisstof simply nodded as he looked out over the crowd.

"Senator Vongaard is crucially important if we're to ask the ConFed Starfleet to step in. As the most respected member of the opposing minority, he would be the obvious choice to approach the

71

council to plead his case. The Eshquarian government, while sympathetic, isn't a voting member of the Confederated Systems. Not only could they not petition the council on behalf of Corran, but any active assistance would be a violation of the treaty they entered.

"We're spinning this to look like the Senator escaped by his own ingenuity, and the story being told by the agents you left behind mostly confirms that," Crisstof finished his lengthy history lesson and leaned back.

"I guess I'll ask what we're all thinking," Doc said. "What's this next job about?"

"Ah... If you're open to the possibility, we'll discuss that tomorrow in a more secure locale," Crisstof said with a smile. "What I will promise you now, however, is that this job is in line with your code, your ideals. While it won't be strictly legal, it will help a lot of innocent people if you can pull it off." Jason opened his mouth to answer, but was cut off by a little girl's voice screeching in delight.

"Lucky!!" They all turned and saw that Seleste, Senator Vongaard's youngest daughter, was almost at a full run before she flung herself into the arms of a very surprised battlesynth. Only his preternatural reflexes allowed him to bend quickly and break her headlong rush into him by picking her up.

"Seleste," he said, seeming genuinely happy to see her. "How are you enjoying your party this evening?"

"It's great! But where's Crusher?" She asked.

"He is off protecting the others right now as I stand watch over Captain Burke and Doc," he answered with a wink. Once he placed her back on the ground he noticed the attention he had garnered and moved back a step further from the light of the table lamp. He was saved from further scrutiny as the Senator and the rest of his family approached the table. Out of respect for him, many of the partygoers turned away to give them their privacy. The tale of their harrowing escape had been spreading and everyone was full of sympathy. *Or the closest thing to it the political class can manage.*

"Forgive me, Captain," Vongaard said with a smile. "She got away from us as we were getting ready to leave."

"No apologies necessary, Senator," Jason said, returning the smile. "I'm sure it made Lucky's evening."

After Senator Vongaard had collected his errant daughter and departed, the others agreed that it was a good time to adjourn their own deliberations as well. The three members of Omega Force agreed to meet with Crisstof the next day and then made their way around the perimeter of the ballroom to the side exit they had come in through. *At least they didn't make us sneak in through the kitchen.*

Once outside, they stood in the cool night air and looked around. So far as they could tell, there was no sign of the vehicle. "Fucking typical," Jason quipped. "How far is it back to our rooms, Lucky?"

"Two-point-one-seven kilometers," he answered without hesitation.

"Walk?" Jason asked. When the others nodded they set off down the side street, letting Lucky and his impeccable sense of direction (and active sensors) lead the way.

When they walked into their suite, there was evidence that there had been what could be called a struggle. Either that or a bomb had gone off in the room. "What. The. Fuck?" Jason asked to nobody in particular. "I'm assuming there is some sort of rational explanation for this."

"Look, Captain," Kage began, holding a rag to his nose that looked to be soaked in greenish blood. "I know this looks bad, but almost all of it was an accident." Jason held up a finger, demanding silence as he took in the rest of the room. One of the sofas was completely upended and a set of enormous feet, that could have only have belonged to Crusher, were sticking up in the air from the other side. Another large chair was smashed flat and there was broken glass covering much of the floor.

"Where is Twingo?"

"He's in the bathroom... in his room," Kage said. "But he's probably wanting to just sleep it off," he finished hurriedly. Jason stomped out of the room as Doc and Lucky rushed over to check on Crusher. Crunching over more broken glass, he went into the indicated bathroom and found Twingo unconscious, beat up, and laying in the shower stall with a wet rag on his head. After checking to see that he was still breathing, Jason decided to leave him where he was and walked back out into the common area. As he entered he saw that Lucky had Crusher sitting up on the one couch that wasn't flipped over.

"Ok, Kage," he said calmly. "I'm going to go out on a limb and say this *didn't* happen because three platoons of hardened marines charged into the room. So... start talking." He leaned against the door frame to Twingo's room and crossed his arms over his chest.

"Hmm, where to start..." Kage said, looking for support from anyone in the room. "You knew the bar was fully stocked, right? Ok. Well we started drinking after you guys left, and then we started to get bored. We knew you'd be mad if we went walking around outside, so we started playing drinking games from our own homeworlds."

I can already see where this is going…

"It started off tame enough, but then Crusher said we couldn't handle the games his people played, so Twingo challenged him to play what he called 'Stollanari Arm Wrestling'. He had Crusher make a fist and told him to pull it towards him with all his strength while he held onto it with both of his own hands. If he could get his fist out, he won."

"Then what?" Jason prompted.

"Well, Crusher starts pulling towards himself, almost lifting Twingo off the floor," Kage continued. "Then, Twingo just lets go and Crusher punched himself in the face as hard as he could. Twingo yelled, 'You won!' But then Crusher came after him, that's what happened to that chair," he pointed at the flattened piece of furniture, "and Twingo's face… and body." Crusher was sitting on the couch glaring at the smaller, four armed alien out of the eye that wasn't swelled shut as he recounted the night's events.

"That explains *one* chair," Jason said, still angry, but suddenly trying hard not to laugh. "Crusher, you actually beat up one of your own crewmates?" Jason was stunned.

"No, no, no," Kage interjected. "He tripped and fell chasing Twingo... but he is *really* fast, so Twingo sort of got caught up under him on the way down." Jason winced at the thought of being smashed to the floor underneath the hulking warrior.

"Fine. So they broke the chair playing... What was it? Stollanari Arm Wrestling?... why is the floor covered in glass?"

"Oh... that. Crusher claimed that the crest on his forehead was the hardest substance in the known universe... I didn't believe him, so I hit him with one of the empty bottles to see for myself," Kage was still slurring his words badly and wobbling on his legs. Jason knew he didn't have long before the diminutive alien passed out. "So, after a few more bottles, I wanted to try something more solid. I hit him with one of the supports from the broken chair... but I missed and *accidentally*," he stressed the word to Crusher, "hit him in the side of the face. He stumbled and fell back. That's what flipped the couch over."

"So why are you hurt?"

"I slipped in spilled booze and hit my face on the floor trying to check on him. After he started snoring I figured he was fine," Kage finished.

"Crusher... is this what happened to the best of your recollection?" Jason asked, now trying very hard not to laugh. Crusher simply nodded, still glaring at Kage. "Alright. We have a meeting tomorrow about another high paying job with the same client that hired us this time. You two: go to bed. Doc, could you check on Twingo please?"

"Of course," Doc was already moving towards the doorway as the other two stumbled off to their respective rooms. Lucky was standing in the middle of the common area seeming somewhat stunned.

"So this is how they were having fun?" he asked, bewildered.

"They thought so at the time. I've been there more than once myself," Jason said as he punched a few commands into the touchpanel on the wall by the bar. A few moments later a trio of cleaning bots rolled in through the service entrance of the suite and began addressing the mess. Even they seemed taken aback by the amount of damage. "Just clean up the glass and fluids," he said to them directly. "I'll worry about the furniture later." He got a couple soft beeps in reply and they set to work. Jason walked around them and made his way to the bar, he had been so focused on business during the reception he had declined to have a drink himself. Now he wanted one very badly after seeing the carnage from his misbehaving crew.

After more than a year of working in space Jason's gastrointestinal system could handle about anything he threw at it, but that didn't always mean he liked the taste. He discovered that a simple smell test could narrow things down quite a bit, so he set about sniffing all the bottles of brown liquid, looking for anything resembling whiskey. He hit pay dirt with a decanter of a light brown liquid that had a nice vanilla/smoky aroma and tasted like a fine Canadian whiskey. *Now that's more like it.* He poured a liberal shot in a short glass over ice and leaned back, watching the efficient little cleaning crew finish up their task. He looked up as Doc walked out.

"He's fine. Going to be very sore and very hungover tomorrow, though," Doc said as he made his own way to the bar and started shuffling though bottles as well. Now that they were alone, the dam broke and Jason broke into near uncontrollable laughter. It was apparently infectious as Doc also giggled, then started laughing so hard tears were coming from his eyes. Lucky watched the two with the same bemused expression he usually had when he simply didn't understand the behavior of his biological friends.

"Were you planning on any sort of discipline?" Doc asked when he could finally catch his breath. Jason thought on it for a moment. Omega Force wasn't a military unit, the glue that held it together was mutual respect, trust, and a sense of purpose. If, as Captain, he began dispensing punishment haphazardly he would quickly create an Us versus Them (or Us versus *Him*) mentality. But beyond that, he considered each crew member his friend, and his family, so he had no desire to impose meaningless "punishment" for something he would have likely participated in himself.

"No," he said, "I think they've suffered enough already, and if not they certainly will tomorrow." He took a slow drink from his glass, savoring the flavor. "Besides, these guys have been cooped up on a small ship, practically on top of each other, for months on end. Add the stress of dangerous operations and then getting locked in this room when we finally do make it planetside somewhere... I can understand the need to blow off some steam. In the grand scheme of things, if all we got from a drunk Galvetic warrior is some bruises and a broken chair, I'd say we came out on top. Wouldn't you?"

"When put that way, yes... I would," Doc chuckled. The two finished their drinks and discussed what the new job might be while Lucky made rounds to each room to check on his fallen comrades. After another drink apiece, Jason and Doc went to bed while Lucky, per his usual habit, stood guard in the middle of the common area. Jason always felt like he was taking advantage of the synth when he stood watch while the others slept, but Lucky assured him he would be "awake" anyway, so he may as well do something useful with his time. In truth, he took the time to sift through the events of the day and give each incident, each interaction, a level of scrutiny he wasn't able to as it happened. It allowed him to continue to grow and find how he fit into this new world as a free-thinking being.

The next morning Jason walked out and found that Doc had taken the liberty of ordering a veritable buffet from room service and had it stretched out along the bar. When he smelled it, his stomach growled in anticipation and he made his way directly to the food with only a wave of greeting to Lucky and Doc. The others were nowhere to be found.

"Good call on breakfast, Doc," Jason said as he grabbed a plate. "I didn't eat much last night."

"I don't think any of us did. You want me to rouse the others?" Doc replied.

"Nah. The smell should start breaking through their stupor pretty soon," Jason answered between bites. As if on cue, Crusher shuffled out of his room holding his head in one hand and growling softly. "Hungry?" Jason asked brightly.

"Yes," Crusher said simply, but instead of walking to the bar he came to stand directly in front of Jason and drew himself up to his full height. "Captain. I apologize for my actions last night. I will accept any punishment you deem necessary." His rigid, formal stance let Jason know he needed to do something more than wave him off, so he stood as well.

"Very well. I accept, and appreciate, your apology Crusher," Jason said. He actually didn't feel it was necessary, but he knew the big warrior would feel cheated without some sort of penance. "I have no intention of 'punishing' you. You're my crewmate and my friend, and you're a free man to do as you will. But I will ask that you refrain from excess for the rest of the time we're on Eshquaria, I need you clear headed and watching our backs until we're back on the *Phoenix* and flying offworld."

"Yes, Captain," Crusher said. He didn't quite bow, but he did nod deeply. His gaze also sneaked over to the bar laden with food, the smell must have been driving him crazy. Jason smiled.

"Go get some food," he said lightly, slapping Crusher on the shoulder. And just like that, all was forgotten. It was simply amazing how quickly his injuries from the night before had healed and Crusher wasn't pumped full of medical nanotech that worked to heal his body like the rest of them were.

Kage was the next to emerge looking only slightly worse for wear. When he and Crusher saw each other they immediately started laughing, which was a slight relief for Jason. Although it seemed like harmless fun the night before, much like he had taken part in countless times in the service, it wouldn't take much to create turbulence within the tight-knit crew. When Twingo stumbled out, however, everyone began laughing raucously. Sometime during the night he had managed to make an attempt at changing clothes, with varying degrees of success, and looked like he had been dragged behind the *Phoenix* during an unpowered landing.

"What?" The small, blue alien asked indignantly, his ears laid flat against his head.

"Your pants are on backwards," Crusher said from his seat at the bar. His comment only increased the laughter at the engineer's expense. Twingo looked down and could only laugh himself. He shrugged and made his way over to the buffet and began loading up a plate, still a little unsteady on his legs.

"Ok, gentleman, and I use that word in the loosest possible terms, we have some decisions to make before we get called to this meeting with Crisstof," Jason said, getting everyone's attention. "This guy seemed to be on the level from what we could tell, and we were paid very well for picking up the Senator and his family."

"I hear a 'but' coming," Kage said.

"But," Jason continued, "that job was a little more risky than he originally let on, so we're going to have to keep that in mind when he pitches this next one to us. We squeaked it out, but we almost ended up on the business end of a destroyer's main guns."

83

"So we have no idea what this job is?" Twingo asked.

"No," Doc said. "All he would tell us was that it wasn't 'strictly legal', but no specifics. From what I could tell, he wasn't all that comfortable talking at all in the surroundings we were in. Lots of ears in that room last night."

"I concur, Doc," Lucky spoke up. "He seemed to want to say more, but stopped himself short each time."

"Let's also get something else out of the way while we're all here," Jason said. "I know you all had a good time last night, or at least started out to, and it got a *little* out of hand. Does anybody have any grievances to air before we press on? Once we leave this room, it's buried and done with." Nobody spoke and Jason was met with three very sheepish looks that threatened to break into spontaneous laughter at any moment. "Alright then, let's finish eating and get cleaned up. I want us packed and waiting for Crisstof's call within the hour." They all began to eat with more of a purpose and made their way to their respective rooms to get cleaned up and changed. Jason had no intention of staying on Eshquaria another night; either they would be flying out on another job, or they would just be flying out.

Chapter 4

The call came three hours later to tell them that there was a vehicle waiting in front of the building. Jason marshaled his crew out the door, the room looking as they had found it... minus one chair. They walked out into the bright Eshquarian sunlight and towards a long, black ground vehicle. *Apparently government vehicles are the same the galaxy over.* They all piled in and were soon off. Jason was glad to leave the suite behind before someone presented them with a bill for the damages.

The vehicle drove past all of the shining government buildings, past the more mundane looking service buildings, and even past the squat, ugly utility buildings. They pulled up to a pre-fabbed style building that looked like it might be used for vehicle maintenance or storage and pulled inside through one of the large roll-up doors. Just when Jason was about to ask what they were waiting for, the floor in the stall began to lower, taking the vehicle with it. The elevator took them down at least a couple hundred feet to a large, well-lit chamber that was filled with large, well-armed security personnel.

Omega Force submitted to another litany of scans and questions before being allowed to proceed on towards a large set of blast doors. Once inside, they were directed to board a waiting open-air car that appeared to be on a mag-lev track. The car whisked them away through a tunnel until they arrived in another large chamber that was also teeming with armed security personnel. The crew disembarked and were led into a small but well-appointed conference room. Jason shrugged and gestured for everyone to grab a seat and wait for whatever was about to happen. As usual, Lucky declined and remained on high alert.

"Welcome to our off-site meeting location, gentlemen." The voice came from behind them. As they turned, they saw Prime Minister Colleston walking in trailed by Crisstof and a half dozen security personnel. "I trust the trip wasn't too taxing?"

"Not at all, Mr. Prime Minister," Jason said respectfully. "Your men have been nothing but professional. I am curious about the cloak and dagger routine, though." The Prime Minister paused while his translator implant tried to chew its way through the term "cloak and dagger." As it did, he smiled faintly.

"You can never be too careful, Captain," he replied. "While the citizens would never know it, these are perilous times for Eshquaria, as you're about to find out. For security reasons, there are some things that I must omit, or be intentionally vague about, but I will try to answer all your questions to the best of my ability."

Over the next hour and a half, the Prime Minister, and mostly his advisors, briefed the crew on the current state of affairs in their system. Eshquaria and her surrounding worlds maintained their sovereignty even as their neighboring systems submitted to more and more ConFed oversight, trading off internal control for the security the ConFed fleet offered. Eshquaria was unique in one way: its main export was some of the most advanced weaponry in the quadrant. Eshquarian warships were immensely powerful and, due to the money coming in from exporting, plentiful. The end result was that they were able to handle their own security needs, and as the chief exporter to the ConFed government of capital ship weaponry, they were largely left to their own devices.

Being somewhat isolated politically, Eshquaria also maintained robust trade treaties with a host of other systems to keep a steady flow of critical infrastructure and other supplies coming in. Corran had been one of these systems. When its sister planet, Kellan, had inexplicably initiated hostilities towards the planet, a major ally and food supplier had been lost to Eshquaria. The Eshquarian intelligence services suspected another player must have been involved, but was so far unable to prove it. The fact that the ConFed council had refused to intervene in a timely fashion was also suspicious, but didn't necessarily prove anything.

After the elimination of the Corran-Eshquaria trading route, another threat had popped up. Pirates and raiders had been harrying freighters up and down the shipping lane that moved raw materials from the Concordian Cluster to the Eshquarian System. There was no pattern or apparent logic behind the attacks, and recently they had moved into hitting passenger ships. This latest development had grabbed the public's attention and had prompted them to start pressuring their government representatives to do something about the attacks. This, in turn, put enormous pressure on Prime Minister Colleston's administration to do something, anything, to put a stop to it.

"So, that's where we are currently," Crisstof was saying. "All efforts to find a base of operations or leadership for these raiders has been ultimately unsuccessful. The ConFed council refuses to step in: their stance is that since Eshquaria is so adamant about remaining independent, then it is their responsibility."

"They've also made it clear that the delivery schedule for weapons contracts is to be strictly adhered to," Colleston added. "Any slip in deliveries or milestones is grounds for withheld payment, something we can't afford given the loss of the Corran supply chain."

"The obvious answer is that some element within the ConFed government is behind these attacks, trying to destabilize Eshquaria to the point they won't be able to remain independent," Jason said.

"We thought so as well," Colleston confirmed. "But again, we've been able to confirm nothing. We also can't establish a motive for ConFed interference; with their aggressive ship building schedule, any delays by our weapons contractors will do nothing but harm them economically and politically."

"Are there any other interested parties that would benefit from hurting Eshquaria economically? Or is it possible that the attack on Corran and these raids are simply coincidences?" Doc asked.

"I'm sorry to say, we just don't know," Crisstof volunteered. "These raiders are not only better equipped than they have any right to be, but thus far have been able to give our intelligence operators the runaround. We know they're using some of the local criminal element, but there are also some fairly advanced ships that will pop up now and again using tactics that are more in line with military training than a ragtag group of smugglers and pirates."

"We don't know much, do we?" Jason asked to nobody in particular. "And now to the crux of this discussion: what do you want from us? Although I think I can already guess..."

"We need to know what the root cause of this rash of attacks is, Captain," Colleston said. "We know this isn't the natural ebb and flow of the normal, reckless attacks that happen up and down the space lanes from time to time. This is gaining momentum and it's becoming increasingly dangerous to ship passengers and goods. We want you and your crew to find out what is causing this sudden uptick. My own intelligence service has come up with nothing actionable, so Crisstof has suggested we try a different approach and send in someone who isn't affiliated with the Eshquarian government, someone who would more naturally fit in with the criminal element."

"Send a group of mercenaries to catch a group of mercenaries, right?" Kage asked.

"I meant no offense, I realize that you're team is...unique... but you are technically guns for hire, are you not?" Colleston said.

"That we are. But we're not assassins," Jason answered. "We can try to find any leadership that may exist, if these attacks are even centrally coordinated, but we will not kill a politically inconvenient target for any amount of pay nor will we bombard any position where there may be civilians. Speaking of pay, what are we looking at for compensation on our end? This could end up being a very long job."

"Let us hope not," Crisstof said. "But the compensation would be a base rate of fifty-million credits, plus an additional ten-million for each ringleader you find and capture, or kill. Assuming there are leaders, of course." Twingo and Kage both made choking sounds at the sum of money being offered; it was more than triple what they made on the rescue mission to Corran. "The money will be funneled through me, the same as before," he continued. "It is important that your involvement not be traced back to the Prime Minister's office, or the Eshquarian government at all."

"Understood," Jason said, trying to keep his own excitement in check at the prospect of such a big payday. "How much time do we have to prepare?"

"You'll be taken back to your ship from here, after that we'd like you to launch out as soon as you can. Your intel package will be delivered to you there and Crisstof will coordinate any services you may need from us to prepare your ship," Prime Minister Colleston said as he stood up, indicating the meeting was over. "Good luck, gentlemen, and good hunting." He turned and left through the same door through which he had entered. Once he had left, the remaining security personnel ushered the crew, now including Crisstof Dalton, through the other exit and to the waiting rail car that would take them back to the government compound.

*   *   *   *   *

Jason and his crew sat at the bottom of the *Phoenix's* cargo ramp, bored to tears. It had been four hours since they had been dropped off and had yet to see any sign of their intel package or Crisstof. Twingo was leaning against the ramp and bouncing his foot, making odd clucking sounds with his mouth, completely oblivious to the increasingly hostile looks he was getting from his crewmates.

"Someone is approaching," Lucky said, the only one immune to being bored and annoyed.

"About fucking time," Jason muttered as he stood up. As expected, Crisstof entered the hanger with an officious looking little Eshquarian in tow that could only have been a government official.

"Gentlemen," Crisstof said loudly as he approached. "We're clear for uplift. The plan is that we head to a location with less prying eyes watching us and do all the preps and briefs you'll need to get started."

"So you're coming with us?" Doc asked.

"Indeed. I'm greatly looking forward to a ride in this ship," Crisstof said with a smile.

"So what's he for?" Jason asked, pointing to the smaller man without actually addressing him.

"I am from the Office of Internal Accountability and Audits," the man said by way of introduction.

"I'll bet that makes you popular," Twingo said with a laugh, already walking up the ramp to begin prepping the *Phoenix* for flight. Ignoring the engineer, the official pushed on.

92

"I'm here concerning some stolen furniture from a suite you and your crew were guests in recently. While we encourage guests to enjoy themselves, which is why we provide a fully stocked bar, we don't allow people to simply remove any items they may like." Once he had finished Jason simply stared at him. *He can't be serious.* He looked over at Crisstof, who only shrugged and smiled.

"Doc," he asked. "Did you steal any furniture?"

"No."

"Kage?"

"Hell no, that furniture sucked."

"I see. Since Lucky doesn't use furniture I guess that leaves only one possibility," Jason said. He then raised his voice, "Crusher! This guy says you stole some furniture... is that true?" A bellowing roar issued forth from the cargo bay and a seemingly irate Crusher came stomping down the ramp.

"Who accuses me of stealing?!" he roared as he reached the bottom. "You!! Was it you?" He pointed at the small government official, coming at him with malice in his eyes. Even in the enormous hanger the sound of his bellowing was uncomfortably loud and quite terrifying. The man was backpedalling as fast as he could.

"Would you like to settle up the account now?" Jason asked blandly as Crusher was still coming towards them.

"I... I... I think maybe there was a misunderstanding..." The man looked far beyond terrified as he then turned and actually sprinted from the hanger, fumbling with the door as he did. Crisstof looked like he wanted to follow, but stood his ground, although he did pale noticeably. As soon as the door to the hanger slammed shut Crusher stopped to stand by Jason. Both were silent a moment before Crusher snorted, then Jason let a giggle slip out, and soon both were laughing uncontrollably. This went on a moment more before Crisstof, who regained his composure, spoke up.

"I take it this isn't the first time you guys have pulled that little act," he said.

"Oh, no... it's one of our favorites," Jason said as he wiped the tears from his eyes. "Best way to not have to pay our bar tab."

"I almost couldn't walk that slow," Crusher said. "I thought maybe the little weasel was going to stand his ground." Crisstof simply shook his head in amusement.

"I'm technically your liaison while you're here, so I could have sent him away when his office contacted me. But I wanted to see how you'd handle something you couldn't shoot your way out of. I must say," he said with a chuckle, "you didn't disappoint. So what actually happened to the chair?"

"What chair?" Crusher and Jason said in unison. The high-pitched whine of the *Phoenix* going into her pre-engine start sequence cut off any more conversation within the hanger. Jason jogged over to the controls and started the main doors opening while the rest of the crew walked up the ramp and into the ship. *What the hell? I'm the Captain and I have to run to go open the doors...*

Walking onto the bridge, Jason was pleased to see everyone in their place and the ship about ready to get off the ground. Hopping into the pilot's seat he asked for an update, "Give it to me."

"Reactor is up, emitters are up, and all primary flight systems are coming up," Kage said as his four hands flew over his controls. "We're ready to roll out, Captain."

"Very good," Jason said as he nudged the jog control that managed ground taxiing back a tad. The *Phoenix* began to roll slowly backwards out of the hanger, powered by the inductive motors in the landing gear. It was a useful feature to be able to move the ship on the ground, or in a hanger, without having to have the engines up. Able to observe their progress on his holographic heads-up display in front of him, Jason kept the speed at a crawl; he'd be damned if he was going to ram the trailing edges of his wings into a building because he was too impatient to wait a few minutes.

The gunship backed out into the midday sun, gleaming dully in the bright light. Jason nudged the jog control to the left as the nose cleared the hanger, bringing the ship about to point out towards the taxiway. He maneuvered them over into a well-marked staging area and had Twingo begin a series of power-up tests on the main drive. The ship groaned as opposing gravimetric fields warped the air around it from the main drive running up and down at low power to check out the emitters and plasma conduits. Everything was green on his board, so Jason nodded to Doc to call for launch clearance. Operating out of established, heavily populated areas had its advantages, but one of the drawbacks was the barrage of procedures and permissions to do something as simple as taxi out to the launch area.

After an irritating amount of back and forth on the coms, they were finally granted clearance to depart and given a vector up to their first transfer orbit. Eshquaria was a planet with heavy commerce traffic, so they didn't typically allow ships to just lift and fly out at any random vector they wanted. Instead, the controllers kept close watch and directed all ships up through a series of transfer orbits, much like a European roadway roundabout, that kept proper intervals between ships and minimized the chance of a collision or drive field overlap.

Crisstof could have probably got them clearance to leave via one of the military launch windows, but being discreet was the name of the game for now.

Since the *Phoenix* was so small compared to the cargo freighters coming and going, they were bumped out rather quickly and given their final send off as Jason steered them onto a course that would lead them towards the edge of the system and pushed their velocity up. "Twenty minutes until our jump point," Jason said to their guest. "How about some coordinates."

"Of course," Crisstof said. "He walked over to Kage and handed him a small, handheld data pad that had a set of jump coordinates on the display. "It's only a seven hour flight. Our destination is a ship of mine that has a large enough hanger deck that we can do any modifications and refits to your fine vessel you deem necessary after your final briefing." Jason wanted to press him further, but decided he could wait another seven hours to find out what all the skulking about was for. After the short flight through real space to their jump point he hit the control to engage the slip-drive, meshing them out of the Eshquarian system.

The *Phoenix* flew back into real space with a flash and turned onto a course that would bring them on a leisurely approach to the ship that hung thousands of kilometers ahead of them. They were in the middle of nowhere, drifting in interstellar space. Even if an entire fleet was looking for them it would be nearly impossible to find them in the vast nothingness that existed between star systems. Crisstof's ship

97

looked to be a fairly modern frigate-class vessel that gleamed a bright white under the flood lights that illuminated her hull. The *Phoenix*, by comparison, was a tiny patch of black on more black as she had no external floods to light up the exterior, just some small marker lights on the ends of the wings and stabilizers.

The entrance to the hanger was on the top of the hull, directly in front of the bridge. A landing pad, complete with chasing marker lights, indicated where Jason should land. He cycled the landing gear, fought down a mild case of nerves, and edged the gunship over to match speed with the frigate. He then crabbed them directly over the landing pad and descended to a flawless touchdown. The crew of the frigate activated the grav plating on the pad, holding the gunship secure.

"*Gunship-class vessel, Phoenix. Secure systems from flight operations and we'll bring you in. Welcome aboard the Diligent,*" a voice said over the coms. Jason and Kage began shutting down the primary flight systems, starting with the engines. Once they, and the reactor, were secured and at minimal power, the platform they were on began to recess into the hull, taking them down into the hanger deck. When the lift stopped, a small hovering bot with strobing yellow lights appeared before the canopy and began to drift slowly away. It was obvious that Jason was supposed to follow it, so he nudged the taxi-motor controls and the *Phoenix* rolled slowly off the landing pad and into the interior of the ship.

Once parked in a spacious service bay, the crew went about doing the final shutdown and headed off the bridge. "Nice landing, Captain," Kage said once the others had filtered out.

"Thanks," Jason said. "I didn't think Crisstof would take to kindly to me dinging his ship. It looks pricey."

"That it does," Kage agreed. "So who do you think this guy is? He's not with the Eshquarian government, and this ship has to be insanely expensive to operate."

"Hopefully all will be revealed shortly," Jason said, standing up and stretching. "In the meantime, I'd appreciate it if you would keep your instincts in check and not try to find the answers by breaking into their computers."

"Sure thing, Captain," the excitable little alien said as they walked through the ship towards the cargo bay. When they arrived, the crew, and Crisstof, were standing around the rear pressure doors.

"What's going on? Why is the ramp still up?" Jason asked.

"That was my suggestion, Captain," Crisstof said. "I thought that you'd like to be the first one off the ship."

"We don't really stand on ceremony or tradition all that much here, Crisstof," Jason said with a smile. "I have the job because I suspect nobody else wanted to put up with the hassle."

"Nevertheless, my captain does stand on such ceremony," the older man continued with a smile. "I'd like for the two of you to get off on the right foot as equals, it may be important that you can work together and respect each other mutually as the rulers of your respective domains." Jason didn't see why that would be necessary, but it was a simple request so he didn't push the issue. He smacked the controls to open the doors and drop the ramp and was surprised to see a humanoid female (a stunningly attractive one, no less) with jet black hair and an impeccable uniform of some type standing at the bottom. There was also a retinue of officers standing at attention off to her right, also dressed to impress. He looked down at his own utilitarian clothes, and then over at the ragtag bunch that made up the rest of Omega Force. *Shit.*

He walked down the ramp with the touch of swagger he had begun to adopt as they established themselves as "outlaws." As usual, Lucky and Crusher flanked him to either side and slightly behind in an impressive display of potential violence. Remembering his customs and courtesies from his few times on U.S. Naval vessels, Jason paused at the foot of the ramp and straightened slightly, but not actually coming to attention. "Captain," he addressed the woman standing in front of him. "Requesting permission to come aboard." There was a barely-perceptible raise of a single eyebrow as she regarded the group standing in front of her.

"Permission granted, Captain Burke," she said in an emotionless, but not unfriendly voice. "Welcome aboard the *Diligent.*"

"Thank you," Jason said as he stepped onto the deck, followed by the rest of his crew. Crisstof moved up to stand with the two captains and nodded in respect to the woman.

"Jason," he said familiarly, "may I introduce Captain Kellea Colleren. Kellea, this is Captain Jason Burke of the *Phoenix* and commanding officer of Omega Force. They've agreed to help us out with our little problem."

"Hopefully they'll have better luck than we've had," she said in a tone that indicated she doubted they would. With that she turned and walked away towards a hatch in the far wall leaving the others rushing to keep up. Crisstof did a sort of jog/skip to fall in beside her. The two began having a hushed conversation, believing they were out of earshot of the rest of the group. Jason smiled to himself, there was no way they could get far enough away on the hanger deck to avoid Lucky's hearing.

They all filed through the hatch and followed a series of non-descript passageways until they arrived in a utilitarian conference room, obviously built for ease of maintenance rather than comfort. At Captain Colleren's gesture they all seated themselves, with the exception of Lucky, who never sat in chairs. "This briefing is for the benefit of the newcomers," she began, "For the rest of you it will be more of a rehashing of things you should already know.

"I'll just say for the record that I don't agree with this new approach. I don't feel that hiring a group of outside...contractors... is going to deliver any better results than our own efforts have." She said it in such a matter-of-fact way that Jason was a bit taken aback, normally when someone was openly insulting they tried to soften it with a pseudo-apology. *Looks like it's going to be one of those... a pissing contest with some self-important officer who wasn't able to get the job done on her own.* Although he carried the title "Captain," Jason's prejudices were still very much in line with his former enlisted life in the USAF. Too often officers with no experience, or little intelligence, simply got in the way of themselves and the people who were trying to perform the mission. He decided to head things off now before a pointless territorial dispute started.

"Hold up," Jason said, making certain it didn't sound like a request. "Just so we're clear, we were hired by Crisstof," he said, pointing to the man in question, "I don't know any of you, nor do I feel the need to answer, or explain myself, to you. We're more than happy, and capable, of doing the job at the rate we've agreed upon. However, if that becomes an issue, we'll happily be on our way." The cold stare coming from Captain Colleren gave Jason the creeps, he'd seen a similar look from a rattlesnake in a zoo on Earth.

"Let's step back from this for a moment," Crisstof interjected. "Kellea, the *Diligent* has been out here for almost six months with almost nothing to show for it save for a large fuel bill. Jason, I hired Omega Force to try and shake things up, not replace my own people. The two of you will need to work with each other instead of against." Captain Colleren nodded respectfully to Crisstof in feigned acquiescence, but Jason could see that her eyes told a completely different story. But, a job was a job.

"I apologize, Captain," he said. "We'll do what we've been hired to do, and to the best of our ability, and then we'll be on our way."

"Of course, Captain," she replied. "Getting back to the matter at hand... as Crisstof said, we've made very little progress in trying to sniff out any type of central leadership behind the attacks on Eshquarian shipping lanes. Normally I would say this is because there simply isn't any, but the attacks are far too well planned to be coincidental." Over the course of the next two hours Captain Colleren and her staff deluged Jason and his crew with a compressed version of all the intel they'd been gathering. As the briefing droned on he once again was thankful he had upgraded his neural implants; the information flowed over him and the bio-machinery in his head categorized and filed away everything in a way that he'd be able to recall later at will.

One of the more useful aspects of the briefing was the ship and crew profiles the *Diligent* crew had been able to compile, and he was beginning to see why they had been running into problems. "I may see an issue already," he said, trying to gently broach the subject.

"Please," Captain Colleren said, indicating he should continue.

"You've been using the *Diligent* to gather this intel and try to establish contacts?"

"Of course," she answered. "Well, the *Diligent* and often the various shuttlecraft that you probably saw on the hanger deck when you arrived."

"I suspected as much," Jason said slowly. "First off, I'd like to compliment you on running such an impeccable ship. I could see from a hundred kilometers away how clean and well maintained she was. In fact, if I didn't know better I'd say the *Diligent* was a military vessel."

"Thank you, I think," Colleren said confusedly. "I'm not sure I see where you're going with this, Captain."

"Look again at the ships you've been tracking," Jason suggested. "Try and view them in comparison to the *Diligent*."

"I'll be damned," she said after a brief moment. "That docs make sense."

"Am I missing something?" Twingo asked.

"Probably," Jason smiled. "And you're not going to like what it means when you figure it out."

Chapter 6

"No! I will not be a party to this!" Twingo was almost in hysterics in the hanger bay where they all stood on the deck, looking the *Phoenix* over.

"Be reasonable, Twingo," Doc said soothingly. "It's all just going to be cosmetic anyway, you can change her back when we're done."

"Captain! I can't believe you're asking me to do this... you want me to deliberately damage my ship?" Twingo asked in a wheedling voice, changing tactics.

"I'm not asking, Twingo," Jason said forcefully. "She's too clean. You saw those other ships, we'll never fit in landing a mint condition DL7 in the middle of that. If we can't fit in, we can't execute our mission. By this time tomorrow I want the hull dinged and damaged, some blast marks added, and corrosion evident in all the right places. None of this has to be real, it just needs to look real."

"How do I fake a hull dent?" Twingo asked indignantly.

"I don't know. I'm not an engineer," Jason shot back. "Just get it done." He turned to walk away, wanting to end the conversation and get his crew to work. "Oh, one more thing... it would help if she didn't run all that well. Try to arrange it so she smokes a little bit and sputters for effect when we start landing on these backwater worlds." With that he hurried up the ramp, leaving an apoplectic Twingo spluttering on the deck.

"You know," Kage said from behind him, making him jump. "This isn't a bad idea, but we shouldn't just stop at the ship."

"I'm listening," Jason said as he crossed the *Phoenix's* cargo bay.

"We're all a tad too clean to really fit in with a bunch of pirates and smugglers. We should dirty ourselves up a bit, maybe some fake tattoos... Oh! I'm going to get one of a Galvetic skull on my chest," Kage said as he warmed up to his idea.

"Probably want to check with Crusher first," Jason replied. "I'm not sure if he would find that offensive or not. It's not something you want to find out the hard way."

"Good idea," Kage agreed fervently. Jason had to concentrate on keeping a straight face; skull tattoo or no, the diminutive little Veran wasn't likely to intimidate anybody.

Twingo and a crew from the *Diligent* worked through the next twelve hours straight while Jason sat on the bridge and went over the data Crisstof's people had provided and tried to formulate some sort of plan that wouldn't leave them out there for months on end chasing ghosts. As he poured through the dossiers and after-action reports from previous attacks, a plan began to form in his mind. One of the main advantages Omega Force had was the fact it wasn't hampered by departmental or governmental regulations and rules. He felt the main approach taken so far was fundamentally flawed in that it would always be a group of outsiders looking in and the criminals they were after had made a career of sniffing out and dodging their kind. So acting as an "investigative unit" simply wouldn't work, they'd burn a ton of fuel and putter around out in the Concordian Cluster until Crisstof finally became bored and dismissed them.

Or...

"*Diligent*, this is Captain Burke on board the *Phoenix*," he said into his personal com unit.

"*Go ahead, Captain,*" a cheery female voice said back.

"I'd like to set a meeting with Captain Colleren and her staff prior to our departure. I'm making some changes to our plans and she'll need to know about them," he said as he scrolled through the intel images on the terminal screen.

"*I'll inform the Captain of your request and let you know when, and if, she's available,*" the disembodied voice said.

"Of course. Thank you, *Phoenix* out." Jason terminated the link and walked off the bridge, heading for the galley.

He was in the middle of eating when word came back that Captain Colleren would see him in an hour. He had time to go get cleaned up and grab Doc before heading out. He decided to let the others finish up their preparations; he'd brief his own crew once they were off the *Diligent*. Now that the mission was taking shape, the excitement began to settle into Jason's gut and, as he always was, he was anxious to get to it.

Fifty minutes after he had spoken with the *Diligent's* com officer Jason and Doc were seated in the same, nondescript conference room they had been in before. They only had to wait another four minutes before Captain Colleren, her first officer, and Crisstof walked in and also sat down. "Ok, Captain Burke," Colleren began, "you mentioned something about wanting to change the plan?"

"Yes," Jason began. "Our original plan of poking around on some of the smuggler's moons and remote spaceports simply won't work."

"Oh?"

"Think about it… these types of people already live in a society in which they don't even trust each other. A group of outsiders showing up asking questions will only cause them to batten down the hatches, so to speak. We're going to have to present ourselves as the real deal, and that means actually hiring ourselves out to these people," Jason said. The idea of undercover work wasn't exactly farfetched, but in this case it meant taking an active role in attacking commercial and private shipping vessels. This was where he was going to have to talk very fast to sell the idea.

"You're talking about taking an active part in these raids," Crisstof said. "I'm not sure that's something we can get behind. The risk of collateral damage is too great and I'm certain the Eshquarians would not approve."

110

"True, but you've already tried it your way. Sitting around in seedy taverns will not get you the information you want. I'm convinced we're going to have to go all in to crack this nut, and that means we have to be available to make runs if we're approached."

"So what's your plan?" Captain Colleren asked.

"We're going to need seed money," Jason said. When he saw the confused stares looking back at him he went on, "I'm going to need some 'stolen' cargo to try and sell when we find someplace promising in order to gain a level of credibility. Something from a verifiable theft would be preferable."

"So you want to commit a crime before you even start?" Crisstof asked incredulously.

"No, I just want it to look like I did. There's got to be something of value on this ship that you can report as stolen. By the time we get someplace to try and sell it, it should disseminate through most local law enforcement databases. It has to look real though, these guys are smart," Jason finished.

"If they're so savvy what makes you think they won't see through your deception?" Crisstof insisted.

"They're smart, but they're also greedy. That's why they're in that line of work," Doc spoke up for the first time.

"The more I think about it, the more I like it," Colleren admitted. *I bet that killed her to say that out loud...* "But I want to be clear that I won't be turning over anything that could be used to further these attacks on civilian vessels."

"So we're all onboard with this?" Jason pressed, wanting to seal the deal. The lone holdout, Crisstof, looked around the table helplessly.

"It would appear so," he said. "Captain, do we have anything on board that would suit our purposes?"

"I'm sure we can come up with something," she said. "My First Officer, Commander Bostco, will assist you with that. Now, if you'll excuse me, I have something else I must attend to." Jason noticed an effort on Bostco's part not to smile as she left the room. The Commander was a taller being than an average human and sported an impressive shock of distractingly bright orange hair, a wide, flat, almost simian face. He also had an easy smile, at least when his Captain wasn't around, and Jason had taken a liking to him immediately when they had met.

"That was great," Bostco said. "She rarely has to backtrack on one of her plans."

"Is she going to be upset for long about that?" Jason asked as he and Doc followed the Commander into the passageway, leaving Crisstof in the briefing room.

"Who Captain Ice Princess? If so she'll never show it," the orange haired alien laughed.

"I'm sensing she's difficult to work for," Doc stated.

"Nah, not really. She is just entirely focused on her job and *only* her job. But, she's easily the best Captain I've ever served with. She's saved our asses plenty of times and never comes off a mission empty handed," Bostco said as he led them through a series of passages they'd never been through. "I did like your plan though, Captain Burke. Crisstof is sometimes too unwilling to take risks for the greater good. He wants to play it safe and treat everything like a passive police action. That's why you got so much push back on what should have been an obvious course of action."

"That explains some things," Jason admitted. "I had wondered why they were so resistant to what amounts to basic investigative work. I had thought that's why we were hired in the first place." Bostco simply shrugged, flashing his infectious smile and leading them through a secure door into a large cargo bay. The large storage area was packed with palletized cargo containers of all shapes and sizes, many bearing the crest of one government or another.

"So what do you think would be good?" Bostco asked as he grabbed a tablet computer from a holder by the door and brought up the manifest.

"Something that would seem plausible to steal, but something that's fairly rare and traceable," Jason answered.

"We obviously can't hand over crates of actual armament that could be used against civilians later on. Parts for specific makes of starships are also out," Bostco mused to himself. "Oh! This might be something; focusing rods for infantry beamers." Jason had learned that "beamer" was slang for a laser emitter. Beamers were lasers, blasters fired plasma bolts, but Jason, true to his Earth heritage, preferred weapons that fired solid metal slugs.

"I thought you said no weapons," Doc said.

"The rods aren't the whole weapon," Jason answered for Bostco. "It's a critical piece, but it's not even the most expensive part of the weapon. The emitter source and power supply are high-cost items, but without the more rare focusing rods to polarize the light and let only the proper frequency pass to the lens, the other parts are useless." Bostco simply nodded in agreement at Jason's explanation. Doc also nodded, he was continually surprised and impressed at how quickly Jason was able to integrate into his new surroundings. Sometimes he forgot that only two short years ago the human had been wholly unaware of the galaxy beyond his own star system.

"Do you think that will work?" Bostco asked.

"I think so. It would be something that we could claim we were stealing for another buyer, and then they backed out, so we had to run. It would explain how we came by them and why we suddenly appeared with them," Jason said.

"There are eight full crates of these rods," Bostco said, reading off the manifest, "and they come from a planet called Essoc. It's an average ConFed world that isn't all that far from the Concordian Cluster. Seems believable, but how are we going to enter the theft into their database so it starts to propagate out?"

"We'll take care of that," Jason said with a smile, pulling his com unit out to call Kage and get him started breaking into Essoc's criminal tracking database.

Jason and Doc followed Commander Bostco through the bowels of the *Diligent* back to the hanger deck. The two members of Omega Force weren't prepared for the sight that met them; the *Phoenix* had completed her transformation from sleek predator to dilapidated smuggler's scow. "What a piece of junk!" Jason exclaimed, quoting one of his favorite movies at a most fitting time. Twingo, who had never seen Star Wars, didn't understand his Captain's glee nor why he was smiling ear to ear. The comment snapped the engineer's last frayed nerve and, after giving Jason an evil glare, he stomped up the ramp and into the cargo bay. Even Doc gave him an odd look, but said nothing.

The *Phoenix* looked to have buckled hull plates, energy weapon scorching, and severe corrosion issues at first glance. It was all cosmetic, however, even down to the crumpled hull panels. Twingo had manufactured warped and scorched plates and affixed them to the outer hull with a nano-adhesive, once the signal to the molecular machines ceased, the plates would just fall off. The rest was simply creative application of colored coatings.

When they reached the ship they could see Crusher nestled in one of the main landing gear assemblies, using the two inboard wheels as a sort of hammock, snoring away. "He got bored halfway through the modifications," Lucky explained as he walked up to the small group. The synth was covered in paint and grease, evidence that he had helped out extensively in the work.

"It's not really his specialty," Jason said with a shrug. "Lucky, I'd like you to meet Commander Bostco, Captain Colleren's First Officer. Commander, this is Lucky, one of my crew."

"It's an honor to meet a genuine battlesynth, sir," Bostco said, seeming to be somewhat star struck.

"Is there such a thing as a non-genuine battlesynth?" Lucky asked.

"Actually, you'd be surprised. People fab up robots, or try to model androids after you guys. The fakes are easy to spot though, they just never move quite like the real thing," Bostco answered.

"Quite interesting," Lucky said. "In any case, it is a pleasure to make your acquaintance Commander Bostco." The Commander beamed as he shook Lucky's hand.

They waited for another twenty minutes or so before a large door opened up in the aft bulkhead and two *Diligent* crewmembers pulled two hover carts through loaded down with the crates holding the focusing rods. They traversed the length of the hanger deck and, at Jason's direction, loaded them up into the *Phoenix's* cargo bay. Once the loading and securing was complete, the crewmembers left and Jason followed them down the ramp to the deck. He was greeted by Crisstof and Captain Colleren.

"Good luck, Captain," Crisstof said, extending his hand. "I know you'll prove me right in hiring you." Jason just nodded and shook the older man's hand. He was surprised when Captain Colleren stepped forward and offered her own hand.

"Be careful, Captain, these are dangerous people. If you get yourself in too deep or need backup, we'll be in the area ready to assist."

"Thank you, Captain," Jason said as he shook her hand, enjoying how soft it felt after being stuck on a ship with all males for months on end. "I appreciate both the advice and the assistance." With a final nod to both, Jason turned and walked back up the ramp, hitting the controls to close the ship up as he headed for the bridge.

He walked directly to his seat and clicked on the intercom, "All right boys and girls, we're about to get underway. Get everything secured and ready for flight." He was anxious to get out of the *Diligent* and into space. He fiddled with the nav computer, studying the way-points Kage had programmed in for their slip-jumps, waiting for clearance to begin taxing out.

Jason saw a red, strobing light reflected off the wall and listened as the *Diligent's* com officer gave them clearance to leave. One of the small, hovering bots that had greeted them when they had first arrived flew in and, again, hovered in front of the canopy, now slowly pulsing a green light. He did one final check to make sure everyone was on board and looked at the aft video feed to ensure the space behind the *Phoenix* was clear before rolling his ship out of the servicing bay. He followed the directions of the bot in front of his ship as he taxied backwards at a crawl, not wanting to take any chances within the confined hanger bay.

The hovering bot steered him so that his nose was pointing forward in relation to the *Diligent* and guided him towards a different platform from the one they came in on. It made sense to Jason, it kept an aft to fore flow to the hanger deck that would be advantageous during hectic flight ops. Once they rolled up onto the platform, the bot flashed a yellow strobe three times and then flew off; *"standby."*

With a jerk, the elevator began lifting the *Phoenix* up to the launch deck, which was actually the top of the *Diligent's* hull. They cleared the electrostatic barrier that kept the atmosphere in the hanger bay and stopped. *"Gunship Phoenix, you are clear to bring primary flight systems online and launch when ready. Good hunting, Omega Force, Diligent out,"* the voice of the *Diligent's* com officer came over the ship's intercom.

"You heard the lady," Jason said. "We seem to have worn out our welcome. Twingo, bring the reactor up and get the engines online. Kage, start aligning the nav system."

"Copy."

"Copy, Captain."

Jason felt power start to pulse through his ship as the reactor ramped up and fed the grav emitters of the primary drive and the other flight systems. In under five minutes the ship was ready to launch. Jason did one more check of his instruments and crew and then nudged the *Phoenix* off the platform. He cycled the landing gear up and began to drift away from the *Diligent* on thrusters in a tangential course before throttling up the main drive and turning towards their first jump point. Twenty minutes after they had left the *Diligent's* deck, and all their systems had come online and checked out, the *Phoenix* meshed out of real space and was racing towards the Concordian Cluster and its next mission.

*   *   *   *   *

Since Crisstof was footing the bill for their operational costs, as well as their contract fee, Jason didn't bother with trading speed for fuel economy and had the *Phoenix* cranked up to eighty percent of maximum slip-space velocity. The blistering speed would put them at the edge of the Cluster within twenty hours, well ahead of their support vessel for this mission; the *Diligent*. Captain Colleren was flying in a well established shipping lane and was keeping their speed comparable to a like-sized cargo hauler. The result was that the *Diligent* wouldn't enter the Cluster for an additional eight days after the *Phoenix* did.

With such a short flight, the crew had little time to do anything but prepare for their first attempt at contacting someone associated with the raiding parties that had been plaguing Eshquarian shipping. They started by cutting back, and in some cases eliminating, their hygiene regimens; Jason's wild, course hair stuck out in places and a full day's worth of beard was already visible. Crusher's "dreadlocks," which were actually sensory organs, were now splayed about his shoulders instead of pulled back neatly. The other's didn't "dirty up" in such an immediately visible fashion, but they made up for it by creating a wardrobe that looked like it hadn't been updated, or cleaned, in years. Kage, who had shown himself to be a fairly talented artist, had adorned Lucky with threatening looking symbols and phrases. Jason had to laugh at the effect; it looked like the synth had just come out of a supermax prison.

Their first stop was a small moon, Felexx, that had been terraformed in the hopes that it would become a resort world. But, despite the stunning views the moon offered, the climate never stabilized enough for people to want to visit. As a result, the major investors had pulled out of the project and largely left it to whoever wanted it. That mostly being people who would rather not be interfered with by local or ConFed governments. The moon had a stable nitrogen/oxygen atmosphere thanks to the processors pumping out air, and gravity, while light, was also solid. The issue came from the atypical orbit the moon had assumed once the terraforming had begun, as well as a distinct wobble that had resulted from the process. For reasons the project scientists were not able to fully explain, the moon's orbital apogee increased and that shift in orbit was thought to have caused the polar axis wobble. As soon as it became apparent Felexx would never be a suitable resort location, the company involved abandoned it and over the next few hundred years it was settled by enterprising traders as well as bottom feeding criminals. It made for an exciting mix.

The *Phoenix* swung into a wide orbit around the host planet and began chasing Felexx as it crossed the terminator and into the light of the primary star. Jason chose the lesser developed of the world's two spaceports to make landfall. The procedure was absurdly simple; broadcast an all-channel announcement on the com that you were attempting to land, and then wish for the best. This didn't necessarily mean others couldn't also try to leave at the same time, it was just a friendly heads-up. With no traffic control system, or controllers, ships could be seen on the sensor display coming and going at random vectors, often jumping to slip-space while still quite close to Felexx. *This should be all kinds of fun.*

Once Kage broadcasted their warning on the local com channel, Jason took a quick breath and plunged the gunship into a steep entry dive, spiking the hull temperatures almost immediately. "Take it easy on your entry vector," Twingo shouted over the intercom from engineering. "Our new panels aren't hanging on by much."

"Too late now," Jason replied. "I'll keep that in mind next time."

They couldn't fully bring up the navigation shields without interfering with the *Phoenix's* "costume", and coming in hot with the combat shields raised might give the locals the wrong idea. He did reduce his speed dramatically, however, and decreased the friction burn over the hull. The canopy soon cleared as they pushed into the lower atmosphere and Jason got his first good look at the surface of Felexx. It was rather pretty, it seemed such a waste for it to be little more than an unimportant trading depot. He steered onto a new course that would take them directly to the spaceport and watched the rolling green hills pass underneath them.

If the traffic above Felexx was disorganized, the spaceport itself could only be described as utter chaos. Ships came and went with no regard for how their flight path affected others, and the landing pad seemed to be a system of first come, first served as pilots just touched down where they could fit their ships on the tarmac that lined both sides of the main taxiway. Jason just shook his head as he tried to find a place near the outskirts of the complex that would accommodate his gunship. The less eyes on her the better; even though they had disguised her, there was still no doubt that she was a warship and not one of the light or micro freighters buzzing about the spaceport.

Jason swung the shabby looking *Phoenix* in a low, wide loop that gave much of the chaos a wide berth, the number four engine blowing a steady stream of smoke in an artful touch by Twingo. He settled the ship non-eventfully on a broken section of tarmac and went about putting the ship's systems in a standby mode that would allow them to lift off quickly if needed. "Crusher, Lucky... you're with me. Doc, you and Twingo get the cargo ready to move," Jason said as he vacated his seat. "Kage, you know the drill; monitor all the com traffic and keep me up on anything that sounds interesting." He walked off the bridge to a chorus of affirmative responses as his crew set about getting ready to start the operation.

After stopping by the armory so he and Crusher could arm themselves, Jason walked to the rear of the cargo bay and opened the ship up as he settled his plasma sidearm in its holster at his hip. When the ramp lowered enough, they saw a timid looking being waiting for them at the bottom. It was short, wide, and covered with a sleek, black fur. It also had large, bizarre looking eyes that sported three pupils of varying shapes and sizes, experience told Jason it was likely this alien saw over a much more broad spectrum than his eyes naturally would.

"Can I help you?" He asked as he walked down the ramp. The alien looked Lucky and Crusher over before answering.

"Yes," the being said, his deep voice seeming to indicate he was a male. "I'm the dockmaster for this section of the facility. I was just wanting to welcome you to Felexx and inquire as to the nature of your visit." The small alien didn't look like he served the spaceport in any official capacity, and Jason had encountered any number of scams trying to shake a few credits off of them when they first arrived someplace.

"Let me guess... landing fees?" Jason asked sarcastically.

"What? Oh my, no!" The alien exclaimed, taken aback. "If the port manager thought I was charging fees for something like landing I'd loose my franchise. I'm simply here to expedite any business you might have by pointing you in the right direction or facilitating meetings with the right people." Although still skeptical, Jason decided to give him a chance.

"Ok. I tell you want, we have a load of somewhat specialized cargo we'd like to offload," he said. "If you can point me in the right direction to sell it there could be some credits in it for you." At the mention of payment the alien perked up and gave Jason the location of three different buyers who might be interested in moving small arms components. After sending him on his way, the trio locked the ship back up, armed the defensive systems, and made their way to the main terminal so they could hire a ground vehicle to take them around the town that surrounded the spaceport.

The first two were a bust; the instant the merchants caught wind that the items were illegally obtained they abruptly ended the meeting. The third, however, seemed to be far less squeamish about moving items that may have been stolen. He instead called another contact of his, who arrived shortly afterwards. The newcomer unoriginally introduced himself as "Mr. Black," an obvious alias, so Jason in turn introduced himself as "Mr. Smith." Black was concerned about the potential traceability of the items, so he insisted on a sample. Jason had already anticipated this and removed a small, cigar sized tube from his pocket and handed it over. Inside, the well-padded tube was one of the rods from the crates they were hauling. The shady trader took the crystal rod and moved over to a microscope, explaining he wanted to check the clarity and structure of the rod. Jason wasn't fooled; he was looking at the micro-etching on the side of the item that gave the name of the manufacturer and the specific lot number. This was exactly what he was wanting. Mr. Black would probably go through his own back channels and hopefully discover the "theft" that Kage had carefully planted in as many databases as he could. After that he would hopefully give them a nudge in the direction they needed to be going.

The trader, a male of a species Jason couldn't readily identify, handed the rod back and told them he'd ask around if there was any interest. They thanked him and gave him the com codes where they could be reached. Not in any hurry to get back to the ship, the three found a tavern within walking distance and decided to stop in for a drink. "So, what do you think?" Jason asked his friends.

"About what?" Crusher answered with a question as he sipped from a bottle of ale. Jason just rolled his eyes and looked to Lucky.

"I cannot give definite odds on how successful we will be with this gambit, Captain," the synth said. "If the trader does as we hope and finds out that the rods are indeed stolen, and worth a lot of money, his greed may override his caution and it could be the first step we need."

"Yeah," Jason said, frowning, "there are a lot of 'ifs' with this plan. More than I would normally like. But these guys are too smart for us to just stumble onto. If we're going to make inroads the first move will have to come from them." They sat in silence over another drink while they pondered their next move. Many of the locals were giving the new comers some not-so-friendly stares, but nobody was foolish

126

enough (or yet drunk enough) to walk over and challenge the menacing looking trio. Right as he was about to suggest they leave, Jason's com unit beeped with an incoming message. "That didn't take long. He wants to meet again, this time to check the rest of the cargo." He replied telling the "merchant" to meet at the ship in one hour. Crusher expressed concern at this.

"Do you think it wise to have them meet us at the ship?" He asked.

"Honestly, can you think of a more easily defended position? If they're up to something, I'd rather have the *Phoenix's* defensive systems backing me up than trying to flee with a bunch of heavy cargo crates," Jason answered. Crusher conceded the point with a nod and a shrug and rose to leave.

"Let's get out of here before one of these idiots does something they'll regret," he said loudly, looking at the bar patrons meaningfully. Almost all of them quickly averted their gaze, refusing to meet his intense stare. The three left the bar without incident and flagged down another ground vehicle for hire to take them back to the spaceport. Jason was apprehensive about this part of his plan; if it didn't bear fruit he would have just given away the one bargaining chip he had in the stolen weapons parts.

Felexx's host planet was moving across the sky as they reached the terminal and began their walk back to where the *Phoenix* was parked, casting everything in a gloomy light. When they reached the ship and dropped the ramp, they saw that the others had already gotten the cargo straps removed and had slid the crates back closer to the rear doors. Jason was also pleased to see that one of his crewmembers had the foresight to activate the more formidable ground defenses they rarely used, as evident by the pair of articulated plasma cannons that were flanking either side of the cargo bay entrance. The stunners that were located throughout the ship were good, but if someone was wearing armor or a personal shielding device, they'd be next to useless. The rear-facing guns were also powerful enough to deal with any ground vehicles that may prove problematic.

It was almost an hour to the second when four figures approached the rear of the ship, hands clearly visible although two were obviously armed. Crusher and Lucky stood on either side of the ramp where they could cover the entrance and also be covered by the ship's cannons, the former in full body armor. Jason was standing right at the foot of the ramp as they approached and held up a hand when they were within earshot. "That's close enough," he yelled across the distance. "Only two of you need to come any closer. Your armed escort is free to watch from there." After a brief conversation amongst themselves, the trader Jason had met earlier and one other approached.

"Mr. Smith," the trader said, addressing Jason by the fake name he had given. "It seems you're in luck. I was able to find a buyer for your merchandise, but not nearly at the price you were asking."

"Well that is unfortunate, Mr. Black," Jason said, using the obviously fake name the other had given as well. "How much less are we talking?"

"Half."

"Have a good evening, gentlemen," Jason said, turning his back. "Come on guys, pack it up."

"Hold on!" Mr. Black shouted. "Aren't you willing to negotiate?"

"I am," Jason said. "But not from a position of being offered half my asking price. That tells me you don't take us seriously... I find that insulting." The trader gave Lucky and Crusher a nervous look and continued.

"You have to understand, Mr. Smith, those items are marked. Trying to find a buyer willing to overlook that wasn't easy," he said. "Maybe there's some room for a trade to sweeten the deal?"

"I'm listening," Jason said, turning back to fully face him.

"I can offer you up to seventy-five percent of what you want, in exchange for a small service from you; a simple transporting job," Mr. Black said.

"How simple?"

"Twenty crates delivered discreetly to another spaceport further into the Cluster. Nothing dangerous loaded in them, just something that a contact of mine would greatly appreciate having moved." This was along the lines of what Jason was hoping for; a smuggling job in exchange for the rods he had in his cargo bay would put them in just a little deeper and that much closer to what they were after. He kept his face blank and pretended to think it over.

"Eighty percent of asking price and you have a deal," he said after a few moments.

"Let me confer with my client and I'll let you know," Mr. Black walked away towards his other two men who were waiting and pulled out a personal com unit. Jason didn't think this was anything more than a stalling tactic, but it did make him nervous; from what he'd learned there was very little in the way of law enforcement on Felexx, but he didn't want to be the unlucky sap that walked right into a sting operation meant to snag the small time smugglers that infested the settlements on the moon.

"He wasn't happy, but he agrees," Mr. Black said. "But, your deadline is tight... I hope your ship is fast."

"Fast enough, I'm sure," Jason said. "If the deadline is tight, I'd suggest we get moving on trading out cargo and, of course, our pay."

"Tomorrow morning," Black said. "It will take some hours to get the shipment packaged and ready. We'll be here at planet-rise."

"Looking forward to it," Jason replied, turning his back on the four and walking back up the ramp into his ship.

Chapter 7

The crew of the *Phoenix* was up and about well before a heavy wheeled vehicle lumbered across the tarmac and came to a halt near the rear cargo ramp. Black and two others hopped out of the front and waved to Jason and Lucky, who were standing at the top of the ramp. Jason nodded and indicated to Crusher and Twingo to start unloading the crates they had been carrying even as Black's two cohorts began unloading twenty smaller containers from their vehicle. The trader was acting even more nervous than he had yesterday, and that made Jason nervous in turn.

It took an additional thirty minutes to completely swap cargo and for Jason to accept payment for the weapon frequency rods. Black looked like he wanted to leave as quickly as possible, "We're all square here. Look, I don't know you, and I don't care to... but a word of advice: do *not* try to tamper with the containers, or swap them out, or do any of the other little tricks you smugglers like to pull. I also can't stress enough that you be on time for your drop off." He handed Jason a data card, "The coordinates are on here. It's not a prepared field so don't be concerned that you're not landing at a proper port." That made Jason even more nervous than he already was.

"Even if the cargo isn't dangerous, your client might be," he said. "I'm not sure I'm thrilled with the idea of landing my ship in a place with no security."

"I can promise you my client could care less what thrills you and what doesn't," Black hissed. "Just do what you agreed to do, and you'll be on your way. He'll have no interest in anything else you have." Jason shrugged and turned to walk away. Mr. Black, relieved to be done with the conversation, practically ran to his vehicle and wasted no time speeding away. As he did, Jason also broke into a run as he moved through the cargo bay, pausing to close up the ramp and pressure doors. Something was wrong, he could feel it.

"Kage!" he called into the intercom, "Get us ready for flight, now!" As he ran onto the bridge his fears proved to be founded.

"We have four small ground vehicles speeding towards us," Kage said as the main drive was coming up. "It's not likely they're heading for some other ship."

"How long until we..." Jason's sentence was cut off as a blast rocked the *Phoenix*. "Holy shit! These guys are loaded for bear!" Jason jumped into his seat and began feeding power to the main drive even as the reactor was coming up to power. The gunship lifted smoothly off

133

the tarmac and Jason pulled it into a tight turn to bring them about and start putting distance between them and the ground assault. Two more blasts reverberated through the ship and a flashing warming lit up on Jason's display.

"They just took out one of the inertial stabilizers," Kage said tensely. "Bringing the shields up." Three more rapid blasts hit them, but all they felt was a mild buffeting as they hit the shields harmlessly. By then they were accelerating up and away from the spaceport and were quickly out of range.

"Keep your eyes on the sensors," Jason said. "I don't want to find out they have air support the hard way by taking any more shots."

"Got it. What the hell were they carrying on those ground cars? That first shot burned a hole right through the forward emitter baffles," Kage said. Jason cringed at the news. *Twingo won't be happy about that.*

"I don't know what they had, but they knew who we were, what we were carrying, and when we'd be picking it up," Jason replies. "That was no coincidence, our shady trader was trying to get out of there as fast as he could."

134

"Yeah... here we go again, huh?" Kage said with a nervous smile. "We'll be in orbit in three minutes. Slip-drive is ready when you are."

"Very good," Jason answered. "Go ahead and find out where we're going," he said as he handed Kage the data card, "and plot us a jump out of here."

Once they had a jump point, Jason wasted no time in getting them out of the system. Felexx may have been lawless, or at least very close to it, but he had no doubt that the little exchange at the spaceport would be noticed by someone. It was only when they were in slip-space and on their way to the drop off did Jason call Twingo on the intercom and check in. Oddly enough, instead of the usual huff, or full-on assault of profanity, Twingo simply informed him that repairs to the damaged stabilizer were already underway and that it would be operational again within the hour. The rest of the damage was superficial so he didn't worry about it.

His next task was to get Lucky and Crusher to scan their cargo and make sure it was safe; or at least safe as far as they could tell. The cargo bay was fairly secure, but it did sit above and between the nacelles that housed their main engines; a well placed bomb could seriously ruin their trip. With the crew going about their own tasks, Jason accessed the data card he had given Kage from his own terminal. Along with detailed jump exit points, orbital entry vectors, and landing coordinates, the card contained very specific information on how they were to make contact once they meshed in-system. It was a clever method of embedding a burst transmission within their transponder's normal "pinging." Only someone who was aware of the specific harmonic the burst was carried on would be able to clearly intercept it and even then, they would need the proper encryption algorithm to decode the signal. To everyone else it would appear as a miniscule burp of static on the carrier frequency.

They had set a velocity that was eighty percent of what a comparable-sized micro freighter would be able to achieve, so it would put them at their destination in a little over thirty-six hours as well as giving the *Diligent* some time to catch up. Or at least catch up as far as Felexx. Jason had instituted a policy of com silence now that they were digging deeper into the criminal underbelly of the Concordian Cluster. He had no idea who may be monitoring their transmissions and he was taking no chances by sending, or receiving, anything that could blow their cover. With nothing else pressing to do, Jason went to grab a meal, shower, and some rack time. He made an announcement to the rest of the crew to do the same when they could.

"Meshing in-system in twenty seconds," Kage said. Jason just nodded. Everyone was well rested, the ship had been repaired during the flight, and they were ready to meet whatever came next head-on. Their destination, the planet Oorch Prime (pronounced Ork), was one of the ubiquitous small rocky worlds orbiting a medium sized star that seemed to be innumerable in that part of the galaxy. Not all supported life, but Jason was shocked to find out how many did; it was far more than he would have ever guessed. He was also surprised, and disappointed, at the rather mundane appearance of most of the species he had encountered. It seemed life wanted to evolve around a few specific paths, most were bipedal, mostly hairless bodies, and featuring a comforting bilateral symmetry. Doc, a geneticist by trade, had tried to explain why this was, but the lecture had just confused Jason even more. Suffice it to say, Jason Burke, homo sapien, had little trouble fitting into this world. There were the more exotic beings like Crusher and Kage, but for the most part he walked freely among the space-faring cultures with hardly a second look.

The *Phoenix* burst into the Oorch system and turned onto a course that would lead them to Oorch Prime, the forth planet out from the primary star. "Start squawking," Jason told Kage, indicating he should begin the embed signal that would alert their contact they would be arriving soon. Oorch was like most of the habitable planets in the Concordian Cluster; it didn't have an advanced, indigenous species, so almost all civilization was from the colonization boom that happened a few hundred years in the past. This normally left for sparsely populated planets, at least by most standards, so there weren't a lot of strict regulations controlling entry and exit of ships. A traffic control computer checked the transponder code the *Phoenix* was broadcasting, verified there were no open law enforcement actions tied to it, and simply logged it. The only time a pilot would talk to an automated system or live controller was if they planned to approach one of the four large cities that dotted the planet.

Since Omega Force had no intention of landing near a city, they proceeded to slip into an equatorial orbit and began to slow their velocity to smoothly enter the upper atmosphere without a word to the ground controllers. Jason remembered Twingo's admonishment about slamming into the mesosphere at high velocity, so he pulled back even more and let the gravimetric drive work its magic as the *Phoenix*

137

descended in a smooth, controlled arc towards a largely unpopulated area.

Their landing site was literally in the middle of nowhere; a field with tall grass that wasn't within detection range of any sizable community. As Jason walked out of the armory into the cargo bay, having donned his body armor and grabbed his weaponry, he saw that Crusher had grown inpatient and had already opened up the ship. He debated calling up to the bridge and telling Kage to launch the twins, but decided he would keep a low profile for the time being. When he walked down the ramp he could see Lucky and Crusher taking up watch positions on either side of the ship and could also see Twingo's lower half sticking out of an access panel near the number four main engine to make certain the damaged stabilizer was back to full operational condition. There was an alert tenseness that everyone shared, but only Jason, Lucky, and Crusher seemed to enjoy it. They stood silently as they awaited their contact.

It was nearly two full hours later before Kage called over the com and informed them they had an aircraft closing on their position. The strain of remaining on high-alert for so long had tightened the muscles in Jason's neck, so he was glad for something to be happening. Soon they could hear a far away, high pitched whine of an atmospheric engine as the aircraft grew closer. "There," Crusher said, pointing to the northeast. Jason turned and let his enhanced eyes focus farther away until he could just make out a moving speck against the clear sky.

"Ok, guys," he said. "Let's be alert."

"I am always alert, Captain," Lucky said without a trace of humor. Crusher turned to his friend and cocked one eyebrow, but said nothing; Lucky's penchant for stating the obvious annoyed the big warrior to no end.

It took the aircraft another fifteen minutes to traverse the distance and circle the gunship in a slow, wide loop. Jason could see the four engines (two in front, two in the rear) angle downwards and the craft settled into a low hover before lowering its landing gear and touching down. The engines weren't the typical turbines that were found on most atmospheric vehicles. Instead, they seemed to employ some sort of ionic airflow system in which electrostatic fields accelerated air through the motor at high velocity and created thrust. While not as powerful as jet turbines, they were significantly quieter and cleaner.

As soon as the aircraft touched down, a ramp dropped down in the rear and eight beings, all concealed head to toe in black clothing, disembarked with four hover sleds and made their way towards the *Phoenix*. The black-clad person in the lead stopped in front of Jason as the rest of his crew went up the gunship's ramp without pausing. Jason gestured for Crusher and Lucky to stand down and turned to face alien in front of him. "You didn't tamper with the containers in any way?" it asked in a distinctly masculine voice.

"Of course not. None of my business what's in it," Jason replied, hoping to strike up a conversation with him.

"That's good." That was all the answer Jason was going to get. Within a couple minutes all eight of them were crossing back to their idling aircraft and loaded the containers into its hold. A few seconds later a *whoosh* came from the engines and the ship lifted smoothly into the air and flew off the way it came.

"I guess that means no tip," Jason quipped.

"It also means that our only lead just flew off into the sunset," Crusher growled.

"I wouldn't be too sure, my gargantuan friend," Twingo's voice came from the top of the cargo bay. He was looking at a spot on the hull directly to the right of the entrance of the cargo bay.

"What have you got," Jason asked, moving up the ramp. Twingo simply pointed to a spot on the hull, but Jason wasn't sure what he was supposed to be looking at.

"Very clever," Lucky said. Still not seeing anything, Jason was trying to figure out a way to ask without coming out and saying he had no idea what they were talking about.

"Quite," Twingo agreed. "The question would be: why?"

"Who knows?" Crusher asked. "Should we get it off?" This infuriated Jason; even Crusher knew what everyone was looking at.

"That's not my call," Twingo said. "Captain?" They all turned and looked at him, and he stared back helplessly.

"Ok, fine," he surrendered. "What the hell are you guys looking at? And I want Lucky to answer me."

"It is a tracking device, Captain. Do you see the slight discoloration on the hull? The device is capable of mimicking the ship's coloration and texture," Lucky said. Jason asked him to answer because the synth seemed incapable of sarcasm, and he certainly would never call his Captain's intelligence into question.

"Wait," Jason argued, "we pull trackers off our hull all the time. They never blend into the ship's skin so well."

"Those are deep space trackers, Captain," Twingo explained. "This is only good for short distances, and not for very long; maybe three or four days tops. It's coverage is probably only good for this quadrant of Oorch itself."

"So they weren't wanting to keep track of us much further than it takes us to leave," Jason mused. "This could be useful. Leave it there for now. Let's close her up and get out of here." He dropped his rail gun off at the armory, kept his sidearm, and made his way to the bridge. "Get ready to liftoff," he said to Kage as he walked over to where Doc was manning a com station. "Find us a small spaceport on this side of the planet, arrange for berthing and pay for it, if they require it."

"So we're staying?" Doc asked, somewhat surprised.

"Yes. This is the only lead we have right now. They left a tracker on our hull, I'm going to park somewhere on this planet and see if we can't get them to come to us," Jason replied as he flopped down into the pilot's seat. Kage had the main systems online and transferred control back over to his station as he sat down.

"Head southeast," Doc said. "I'll have us a landing slot by the time we get there." Jason lifted the *Phoenix* smoothly off the turf and accelerated gently towards the spaceport. He had no doubt the tracker was meant to either verify they were leaving after the drop off or to ensure they weren't going to try and track the other aircraft back to their base of operations. In that respect, it was good the spaceport lay along a different heading. He hoped that if they parked and put out some feelers that they were looking for work, this particular group might come to them. It was weak, almost paper thin. But, for the time being, it was all he had and he wasn't thrilled about that. This job had all the potential of turning into a very long and drawn out goose egg. *Glad we negotiated an upfront fee.*

The spaceport was smaller than most they'd been to, but it was larger and much more organized than the one they'd left on Felexx. They entered the traffic pattern as directed and circled the spaceport, waiting for clearance to begin their approach. After traffic control had given their blessing, Jason came about sharply and began a steep, nose-up descent and followed the glide slope Kage had sent to his station. At five-hundred feet he cycled the landing gear and touched down with barely a bump to announce their landing. Following the indicating arrows that came up on his display, he taxied the gunship off the landing pad and to their assigned docking berth, which was basically a large section of tarmac with a number painted on it. He braked smoothly to a stop, leveled the ship, and then put the main drive into standby. Having no idea what to expect, he was going to leave his ship in an "alert" state, able to take flight at a moment's notice.

"Ok, boys," Jason announced over the intercom. "We're parked. Keep the ship ready to launch immediately if needed. Once you're ready, meet me in the galley and we'll go over the plan."

"We have a plan?" Kage asked. "That's a nice change of pace."

"Shut up."

*   *   *   *   *

The next two days passed uneventfully for Omega Force, and that wasn't a good thing. Twingo took the time to enlist their help in performing various repairs and maintenance actions on the *Phoenix*, but boredom was setting in. This was a non-issue for Lucky, who stood stoically by Jason's side as he aimlessly went about trying to make a contact that could get his crew some work. Doc took the time to read and, since they had access to wideband communications at the spaceport, catch up on some research. Crusher and Kage, however, were becoming stir-crazy and that had proved to be a volatile combination in the past. Jason hoped he could find something soon before they began to break things.

It was late into the third day on Oorch when they received a visitor. Jason and Twingo were up on the ship's backbone working on a glitch in one of the Twin's launching cradles when Lucky called up that someone was coming. Jason stood up, stretched his back out, and walked down towards the starboard wing where they had parked the service platform they were using to get up onto the ship. He reached around to the small of his back to situate the plasma pistol riding in his waistband and then made his way around to the rear loading ramp where Lucky and Crusher had already intercepted their visitor. After much cajoling, Jason had convinced Crusher that a simple verbal challenge should precede him throwing people to the pavement when they approached. This time he stood in front of a plain-dressed man, casually holding a large blast rifle, but otherwise making no threatening moves.

"Can I help you?" Jason shouted as he approached.

"I'm simply here to satisfy a curiosity, Captain," the man said. "We assumed you'd have been well on your way from Oorch days ago, yet here you are." He was an unassuming looking sort, not too imposing, but the way he moved and carried himself alerted Jason that this was a dangerous person. He couldn't hazard a guess as to the other's species, especially in the Concordian Cluster where there were no indigenous intelligent life forms.

"Is there some problem?" Jason asked. "You say you had assumptions about our intentions, but I have no idea who you are."

"I represent certain interests on this planet that don't like to have attention drawn to themselves. Attention such as an obvious smuggler's ship, that was recently used in a covert delivery, being parked in a busy spaceport on our doorstep," the man said more forcefully. "Is there some reason you aren't lightyears away from here?" Jason stared at him for a moment, making it obvious he wouldn't be intimidated.

"During the excitement of picking up your cargo we were hit with some powerful weapons fire while still on the surface of Felexx," he said slowly. "We're affecting repairs here, at a proper facility, rather than have it break on us in interstellar space. So now I have a question; why the interest in what we're doing at all? We've made no overt moves that would--"

"That's hardly the point," the man interrupted. "We leave nothing to chance. Nothing. Now, is there any other reason you're dithering here on Oorch?"

"We could use a job," Jason said, deciding to try and feel things out. "Our delivery service was a one-time gig. I've got a thirsty ship and a crew with expensive tastes, we were poking around here to see what other jobs we could kick up."

"There are better opportunities for private contractors out of Felexx. Why not go back there?"

"The same reason we're making repairs now; I don't think we'd be welcomed back. Protecting your cargo has cost us any potential employment there," Jason said. "So now we have no choice but to push further up the Cluster and see what else we can find."

The man looked from Jason to Crusher and Lucky, then back. Without warning, he reached into the front of his jacket. He froze at the warning snarl from Crusher, who had raised his weapon within a split-second. "That is not advisable," Lucky said, moving around to cover him from the other side. The man wisely stayed absolutely motionless, but Jason did see that he didn't panic or show any real fear. *I was right, this guy is one dangerous individual. I'm sure of it.*

"If I wanted you harmed, you'd have never seen my face," he said calmly. "May I?" he asked Crusher. When Jason nodded once the big warrior lowered his weapon slightly, but Lucky was still behind the man and to the left. He continued his hand motion and withdrew a small, personal com unit from the inside pocket of his jacket. He tossed it to Jason with a flick of his wrist. "There's a slim possibility we might have some need of your services again. After seeing it up close, something tells me this ship is a lot faster than it appears," he said in a deadpan voice. "Keep that com unit on you. If I call, you won't have much time to be ready. If you don't hear from me within the week, get into your ship, take off from Oorch, and never return."

147

The man left quickly, disappearing around a utility building and out of sight. Jason watched him go, turning the com unit over in his hand. It was a standard, commercially available unit that didn't appear to have anything special about it. "Get everyone together in the galley," he said to Crusher. "We' need to be ready if this guy calls." He had no idea if this person was even connected to the rash of attacks they'd been sent out to investigate, but as of right then he didn't have any other credible lead. The Eshquarian Intelligence Service had been of shockingly little help when it came to trying to find them even a starting point. For all he knew they were just out there committing petty crimes that were unrelated to the harassment of shipping lanes.

As the crew filed into the galley area he wrapped the com unit in a towel and then put it in a drawer. He was certain it wouldn't be chiming within the next couple hours, and he was equally certain the unit had been rigged to allow someone to open a channel and spy on them without alerting them. It was a fairly standard trick they'd employed themselves on occasion. Once they were all seated he started.

"As of right now, we're condition 'red'," he told them. This was a prearranged signal that meant they no longer had the freedom to openly discuss their operation, no matter where they were. While they were "red" they would completely live their cover story. Between the tracker on the hull and the suspect com unit Jason couldn't risk someone mentioning their real purpose and giving them away. It wouldn't mean just a failed mission; it would likely mean their lives.

When everyone nodded they understood him, Jason took the com unit back out of the drawer and slipped it into his pocket. Pocketing the unit would be the expected action and would arouse the least amount of suspicion.

"We had a visitor today," he began. "Someone who works for the people we delivered those crates to. He says there's the possibility of more work, but we'll see."

"Good," Crusher rumbled. "We're tired of sitting around here doing nothing. We either need to find a job or move on." Jason suppressed a smile, for some reason the role-acting aspect of their job intrigued Crusher to no end. He would develop a whole different persona to wear like a costume during operations that required them to appear as something they were not.

"You know the reality of the situation," Doc said, picking up on the cue. "We can't afford to burn fuel just *looking* for work. We need something definite that pays."

"He's right. In the shape we're in now, we're going to have to do some things that we may not like if the money is good," Jason said, continuing the charade. "For now, just stay alert and stay ready. Twingo, get her back up to full operational status; the call could come in at any time. Other than that, let's split into normal watch shifts and get to it." *I hope at least someone is listening if we're going through all the trouble to playact.* In his pocket, the com unit discreetly closed the

149

open channel that had been transmitting their conversation to an outside party.

Despite the contact from the mysterious man, it was another five days on Oorch before anything happened. Jason had begun to worry that they were just going to run the clock out and be forced to leave empty-handed. But, on that fifth day the com unit chimed. It was a text-only message giving planetary positioning coordinates and a local time. He knew what it meant; where to be and when to be there. He had been in the galley eating at the time, so he activated the ship's intercom from there; "Gentlemen, we're wheels up in thirty minutes. Prepare the ship for flight."

Kage must have already been on the bridge, Jason had no sooner finished speaking when he could feel the main drive starting up. During startup, if standing in the middle of the ship, the engines created a disorienting effect as the coils formed gravimetric fields before the shielding was at full strength. He wolfed down the remainder of his sandwich in two bites before jogging up to the bridge to prepare. "Crusher, Lucky," he said as he walked onto the bridge, "get to the armory and get ready. I have no idea what we're flying into, so I want you armed to the teeth." The two marched off the bridge eagerly as Jason began going through his preflight checks.

Eleven minutes after he received the message, the *Phoenix* rose easily into the early evening sky and flew north to their destination. It was a three hour flight since they were required to keep their speed subsonic the entire way, but it gave the team a little more time to get ready for whatever would be meeting them. It turned out their destination was another open field in the unsettled grasslands of Oorch. Jason had to assume there was not satellite surveillance of the planet given the casual way their contacts conducted business out in the open. It seemed they were more concerned with being away from the cities than from electronic eyes above them.

Jason eased the gunship around and gently landed at the designated site, not at all surprised they were the only ones there. He kept the engines running and had everyone stay at their stations, it seemed to be the usual games, but he was taking no chances.

Thirty-five minutes after they had landed, a pair of the unique VTOL (Vertical Take-Off and Landing) aircraft, of the type that had met them earlier, descended and landed behind the *Phoenix*. Jason jumped out of his seat to head back to the cargo bay. "Be ready to get us out of here if I give the word," Jason said as he left. He jogged back to meet up with Crusher and Lucky, who were already at the rear pressure doors waiting for him. He nodded to the pair, opened up the doors, and lowered the rear ramp. Waiting for them at the bottom was the man who had approached them at the spaceport, a contingent of well armed guards, and two men with their heads covered. What made it strange to Jason was that their hands and feet were unbound; these apparently were not prisoners.

"Very good, Captain," the man said as he approached. "We didn't have to wait on you. That is very good indeed."

"We're nothing if not punctual," Jason said. "Am I to assume this is a passenger charter?"

"Something like that," was the reply. "This ship has facilities in which to secure two passengers?"

"We have a brig, but it's only a single cell," Jason said, frowning.

"Not a cell, these two are not prisoners. Their faces are covered for your protection. You will have no contact with them nor will they interact with any of your crew. Two of my men will accompany them, as well as their administrator, to provide for their needs and insure their privacy."

"We can accommodate them," Jason said. "Where are we taking them?"

"You'll find out once you're airborne. Once away from Oorch you will maintain com silence and be given your destination by one of my men. The imperative part of your job is to get them to their destination without attracting any undue attention, I've checked your ship's registry; you won't have any trouble getting to where you're going. You'll be paid five-hundred thousand credits for this task," the man finished, looking around the interior of the cargo bay. Jason whistled softly.

"That's a lot for a passenger transport," he said. "We're not taking them to the other side of the galaxy are we?"

"No," the man smiled humorlessly, "It is well within range of your ship. As I said, I suspect it is much faster than its appearance would indicate."

"She'll get the job done," Jason said. "I never got your name."

"Nor will you. Do this right and you'll be well compensated. Mess up, and you'll beg me for a quick death."

"Oh please," Jason scoffed as Crusher growled at the threat. "We're doing this because you're paying us. We could care less who you are or why you want these people moved. You can take your melodramatic threats and shove them. As you can see, we're far from helpless." The man looked like he was about to push back but stopped as one of the hooded figures raised a hand. That was all it took for the man to back down and assume a more submissive posture.

"So you say, Captain," he said. "Just remember your instructions." With that he turned and walked back off the ship, leaving only the hooded men, two armed guards, and one well-dressed man that was slight of build and appeared to be somewhat distressed at the aggression that had been on display. He came forward and offered his hand in greeting.

"Hello, Captain," he said in a servile tone. "My name is Dowarty, I'm the administrator for... um, them... and I'll be handling the details of their care."

"Very well, Dowarty," Jason said, wiping his hand on his pants. "If you and your charges will follow me, I'll show you to berthing and you can get them settled. You two," he said to the armed guards. "I'm not going to try and disarm you, but I expect a certain level of respect on my ship. You threaten any of my crew, or the operation of the ship, and you'll be put down. My deal is to keep them safe and anonymous, I don' think you were part of the bargain."

"Stay out of our way, and there won't be any trouble," one of the guards said indifferently. Jason just nodded and led the group out of the cargo bay after raising the ramp and closing the rear doors. He led them up to one of the crew berthing bays, one that remained unused since they only normally had six crewmembers, and showed the guards how to operate the door. He crooked a finger to Dowarty, indicating he should follow them out. He showed the sniveling little administrator where the galley was, how it worked, and a host of other things he would need to know for the flight.

After returning Dowarty to berthing, he went up to the bridge, stopping to give Twingo the assumed-to-be-bugged com unit to be incinerated. The crew and the ship were ready as he walked onto the bridge and hopped into the pilot's seat. "Computer," he said, "I want our new passengers closely monitored. If any one of them raises a weapon, threatens any of the crew, or tries to access any part of the ship other than the galley or the starboard berthing bay I want them incapacitated. Non-lethal only."

"Acknowledged."

"Ok, let's get out of here," he said to the bridge crew as he fed power to the main drive and lifted off the surface of Oorch. Soon after, the *Phoenix* meshed out of the system towards their first "dummy" jump-point. Once in slip-space, Jason keyed the intercom, "Passenger Dowarty, please come to the bridge."

A few minutes later, the administrator shuffled onto the bridge, "Yes, Captain?"

"We'll be needing our destination now," Jason said.

"Oh! Of course," Dowarty pulled out a small tablet computer and began searching through menus. Jason rolled his eyes as he waited. "Here it is... set your course for Solic-2. Your coordinates for landing will be provided once we achieve orbit."

"Of course," Jason said evenly. "That will be all." The Solic System wasn't too far away, and it was still considered part of the Cluster. This was the good news. What wasn't good news was that Solic-2 was fairly notorious for having an overreaching, almost abusive approach to local law enforcement. He was beginning to see why they had needed an unknown ship, but he couldn't imagine why any criminal operation would risk even having a presence there at all. Solic-2 and Solic-3, both habitable worlds, were closely aligned with the ConFed government, but their small populations disqualified them from membership or from having a seat on the council. They were sympathetic to the ambitious ConFed Council, however, and ConFed fleet ships navigating the Cluster often congregated in orbit over the two worlds.

This instance was no exception; no less than four ConFed cruisers were in orbit over Solic-2 as they made their approach. The specifications for the ships began to scroll across Jason's right-most multi-function display, and they were impressive. The third largest class of ship in the fleet, cruisers were a potent mix of firepower and speed, the type of ship that would be dispatched to make the ConFed's presence felt. The ships that patrolled the Concordian Cluster, making stops and waving the flag at various worlds of port, naturally gravitated to the planets with the most sophisticated and developed settlements. That and a predilection for treating ConFed captains like celebrities.

This wasn't uncalculated on the part of the leadership of Solic-2. The planet had become wealthy due to the heavy deposits of rare elements found in its crust, but fielding and maintaining a fleet to protect that wealth was difficult and cost prohibitive despite the lucrative ore trade. So, they created an environment that brought their protection force to them; no organization or planetary government in its right mind would risk raiding, or illegally mining, on Solic-2 when a ConFed cruiser or destroyer could make orbit at any time.

The *Phoenix* slid into orbit squawking clean codes that identified them as a micro-freighter. They declared no freight needing to be inspected and awaited their turn to begin entry. The decaying orbit they were in let the gunship slide under one of the ConFed cruisers at fairly closer range, so Jason asked Kage to train the optical sensors on it and project the image up on the main canopy. The tiny spec of light resolved itself into a sleek warship as the sensors zoomed in on the ship that was flying above them in a parking orbit.

"That's one big ass ship," Kage said. "Hope we never have to tangle with one of those." Jason snorted.

"It'd be a short fight if we couldn't run." The DL7 was a uniquely powerful ship, but there was no feasible way it could go toe-to-toe with the weaponry a ship like the cruiser could bring to bear. Luckily, the comparatively tiny gunship could outrun nearly all the larger mainline ships.

After another three orbits, they were cleared to land and swooped in for an uneventful touchdown at a smaller spaceport that was outside of an industrial district. Judging by the number and size of the cargo haulers coming and going, Jason figured it must be one of Solic-2's logistical hubs. Not wanting to risk a misunderstanding with the security guards on board, Jason called down to Dowarty over the ship's intercom. "Dowarty, we're on the ground," he said brusquely. "You're clear to disembark whenever you're ready."

"Thank you, Captain," Dowarty's voice came over the bridge speakers. "We've alerted our contacts here to dispatch transportation. I'll inform you when we're ready to leave your ship."

"None too soon," Jason muttered after the intercom had clicked off. He let his breath out noisily. "This isn't working," he announced to the bridge crew, which was everyone.

"No kidding," said Crusher.

"Not a chance in hell we're finding what we're looking for this way," Twingo chimed in.

"Alright! I get it," Jason said, heading off any more disparaging comments thrown his way. "Any ideas?"

"We don't seem to have a plan, as such," Doc began, "but I don't see the benefit in abandoning one haphazard approach to adopt an equally haphazard one just for the sake of doing something different. We really haven't been at this all that long yet."

"I'm getting the feeling you have more to say," Jason prompted.

"These passengers are not prisoners; they're being protected, not guarded. If they're really a couple of higher-ups in an organization, it may be in our best interest to see how this plays out," Doc said.

"Yeah, but what organization?" Twingo asked. "We could be escorting around a pair of drug-runners or weapons buyers. The Cluster is full of criminal 'organizations.' The chance we've stumbled upon the right one seems slim."

"You two have anything to add?" Jason asked Lucky and Crusher. Lucky just shook his head negatively.

"We're just bored," Crusher grumbled. Jason was sympathetic to the big warrior, sitting around on a cramped ship accomplishing not a whole hell of a lot had to be torturous for him.

"I understand. I'll try to get us some action soon, otherwise we're never going to get off this job," he said.

"Should we try to contact Crisstof?" Kage asked. "The *Diligent* has to have gotten into the Cluster by now."

"Absolutely not," Jason insisted. "No transmissions of any kind. We're keeping our cover airtight until we know something definite, or we need rescued. Whichever comes first."

"Probably the second one," Crusher mused sourly.

"I agree," Lucky said. Jason turned to look at them, an acerbic retort on the tip of his tongue when the intercom interrupted him.

"Captain," Dowarty's voice came over the speakers once again, "we're ready to depart if you'd care to escort us down to the boarding ramp."

"Of course, Dowarty. We'll be there momentarily," Jason said, indicating to Crusher and Lucky to follow him. They found their five passengers standing outside of the crew berthing bay they'd occupied during the flight to Solic-2. With a simple nod, Jason led them aft and into the cargo bay so they could be on their way. When he lowered the ramp he saw a long, sleek-looking ground vehicle hovering a foot off the ground. Jason had noticed some time back that the affluence of a population could be determined by their ground transportations. Wealthy, wasteful societies utilized repulsors and grav generators to whisk them along in complete, isolated comfort. More pragmatic worlds still used the efficient, reliable wheel, something that seemed to be the first technological leap every civilization made. Unless one counted turning grain into alcohol as a technological feat.

"I've been asked to extend our thanks to you and your crew, Captain," Dowarty said as the others walked down the ramp and climbed into the vehicle. "Your professionalism and promptness was greatly appreciated. So much so, in fact, that we're tacking on an additional fifty thousand credits to your payment."

"We aim to please, Dowarty," Jason replied. "To be honest, this has to be the easiest money we've ever earned; nice, quiet passengers and no exchange of gunfire."

"Yes, of course," the slight man smiled indulgently. "Would you be willing to stay on Solic-2 for a bit longer? My employers may want to leave... quickly... and would prefer not to try and arrange transport in a hurry."

"I'll bet. I'll tell you what, for another twenty-five thousand credits we'll stay parked right here, ready to launch, until you feel comfortable releasing us."

"Hmm," Dowarty pretended to think it over, "It would simplify things. Very well, Captain, twenty-five thousand it is. We'll be in touch." He handed Jason another handheld com unit before turning and walking down the ramp towards the waiting vehicle. Instead of gliding away hugging the ground, it lifted off and climbed away into the sky. *Cool. They must be important. And in a hurry.*

"Let's grab something to eat," he said to his friends, indicating with a finger to his lips that they should still be in character while waving the new com unit at them. They nodded and followed him out of the cargo bay as the rear pressure doors slid noisily shut. *I wish Twingo would fix those damn things.*

Once he had gathered the crew in the galley (and secured the almost certainly bugged com unit) he began his brief. "I've had a change of heart, something tells me we're in the right place, or at least someplace that can lead to the right place.

"I'm convinced our passengers weren't a couple of underlings. The casual appearance had me fooled, but I think they were major players, which is why they needed to be smuggled onto the planet. What I can't figure out is why they're here at all. From what I've heard, this place is not receptive to any sort of criminal element, much less organized crime."

"I'm inclined to agree with you," Doc said. "The impression I got from that group was similar. How do you want to play it?"

"For now, we wait," Jason held up a hand as Crusher and Kage let out simultaneous moans of disgust. "Stay with me, we just took twenty-five large to sit here for a bit, so we're not going anywhere no matter what. I did that to give the impression of cutthroat mercenaries that are only in it for the money. Hopefully that translates into a job that gets us in touch with the people we're after."

Jason's instinct proved to be correct; the com unit started beeping about twenty hours after they made landfall. It was a message on the screen and not a person-to-person call, all it said was, '*Meet at Sparks Lounge, Perlick District in 3 hours. Dress casual, do NOT draw unwanted attention.*'

"What'd I tell you?" Jason asked Crusher smugly as the warrior read the message over his shoulder. All he got was a low growl in response. "Go get dressed, Crusher. Something that makes you look like a tourist. Tell Doc he's coming too," he said over his shoulder as he walked back to his quarters to get ready. Or at least he tried to, he ran smack into Lucky as he turned down the passageway that led to

163

the Captain's quarters. The battlesynth showed no intention of moving. "Can I help you?"

"Am I to understand you are leaving the ship to meet a contact with only Crusher and Doc to accompany you?" Lucky almost managed to make it sound like an accusation.

"Yes," Jason replied, reminding himself that despite his appearance, the synth had a full, complex range of emotions. "It's not because I don't want you there, but I need you here. The safety of the ship, and the other two idiots, are as important as my own safety. That's why I need to split you and Crusher between the two teams."

"I see," Lucky said in a manner that indicated he still wasn't convinced. "I will protect the ship and the remaining crew, but I am submitting a formal protest at not being added to your own protection detail."

"Lucky, this is Omega Force; we don't do anything formally," Jason said, patting the synth on the shoulder as he tried to squeeze by. (Since Lucky refused to move, he had to suck it in to make it around him.) The truth was that Lucky simply drew too much attention, his kind were so rare that wherever they went, he was gawked at and, inevitably, approached. Once a group of people from Helderan Prime actually wanted to pose for pictures with him while the team was in the middle of an operation. While Galvetic warriors were also rare, with a set of fitted clothes, Crusher didn't look quite so exotic on some of the more cosmopolitan worlds.

Chapter 8

As soon as they were ready, Jason had Kage call for an aircar to pick them up and deliver them to the Perlick District, a swanky part of the city that was well north of the spaceport. The car was quite cramped and the ride consisted mostly of arguments over personal space.

"Stop touching me," Crusher said.

"I can't help it," Jason snapped. "Get on your own side."

"I'm all the way against the door as it is. Would you like me to get out while we're still hundreds of feet in the air?"

"Actually, yes, that would be great."

Doc, who was sitting in the front with the driver, simply smiled at his good fortune at having jumped in the front of the vehicle when he saw how small it was. He was sure Kage knew the *exact* volume of the aircar's interior when he had called for it.

Despite the bickering coming from the back seat, the ride was smooth and uneventful. The aircar swung easily down onto a busy landing area and let them out before rising back into the air and zipping off to another pickup. The three smoothed out their clothes, Doc being the only one who felt even remotely comfortable in the casual civilian attire. Crusher in particular kept pulling and adjusting the billowing jacket he wore that was made of some type of shimmering synthetic material, obviously in some state of distress at being forced to wear anything with sleeves. Jason wore a black on black three-piece suit that had been a "gift" from a crime lord he had later set up to take the fall for an ambitious escape, and theft, they had pulled.

The lounge was three blocks away from where the aircar had dropped them off, so the three set off to try and get to the place first. Past experience had made Jason always want to arrive first to these meetings in order to perform a little casual recon before a client or contact showed up. It reduced the possibility of them filtering in too many of their own people posing as customers and it also gave his team a chance to commit the layout, and exit locations, to memory. More than once that had come in handy as contract negotiations devolved into a bar fight. That trend was another reason Jason preferred Crusher over Lucky as backup in those types of situations; while Lucky was an incredibly powerful soldier, Crusher was a natural (if somewhat over-eager) brawler.

"This is the place," Doc said as they approached a sleek high rise building. Sparks Lounge seemed to take up the entire ground floor of the building and was readily identified by the obnoxious sign that was made up of swirling holographic, incandescent motes that would coalesce to form the word "Sparks!" before exploding outward. Jason rolled his eyes at the gaudy effect before leading the way into the establishment.

"Subtle," Crusher mumbled as he passed under the animated sign and followed Jason in. The interior was just as slick and trendy as the exterior, as were the patrons. More than a few stopped to stare at Crusher, who was blotting out the light from the entrance, before assuming a studied, bored expression and turning back to their drinks and conversations. Jason wove through the crowd, scanning for any sign of someone paying a bit too much attention to them, while making his way back towards a secluded booth. As far as he could tell, they had arrived before their contact.

At exactly fifteen minutes before their scheduled meeting time, Dowarty, escorted by two enforcers, walked in and looked about. He spotted them almost immediately and made his way over to their table. Jason was struck by how confident the man was as he crossed the crowded bar area, quite the opposite from his passive, servile attitude while onboard the *Phoenix*. *Maybe he likes to strut around when the bosses are away.* It did add a level of credence to the theory that they had been carrying some high-ranking bosses on the flight out there.

"Captain!" Dowarty greeted as he approached. "How good to see you again so soon."

"Likewise," Jason said in a non-committal tone. "Please, have a seat. All of you."

"Just me, I'm afraid," the small man said as he sat down. "My associates don't much care for sitting, or talking, while on the clock. Now then, at the behest of my superiors, I'm here to offer you another job. Should you decide to take it, the pay will be quite substantial. Assuming you succeed, of course."

"Of course. Another ferrying job for your hooded passengers?"

"Oh no, I'm afraid not," Dowarty said, actually sounding apologetic. "This will be quite a bit more dangerous and will likely involve the exchange of hostilities."

"About time," Crusher said quietly, watching the two enforcers carefully. Dowarty smiled indulgently, if not a bit condescendingly.

"Indeed," he said before turning back to Jason. "This would normally be handled by one of our regular crews, people we've vetted thoroughly and trust. However, time is of the essence and we simply have no way to reposition one of our own crews in time, so my boss wants to see if you guys are any good. They have, of course, been tracking your movements since you've entered the Cluster... can't be too careful when it comes to new faces coming around peddling stolen wares, after all. There is also the additional factor that you don't really know who it is you're working for, so if you get caught it would be impossible for you to turn on them.

"This will be a simple grab and dash. The only thing unique is that it will be from a ship that's underway. Is that something your crew and that worn-out ship can handle?"

"Not an issue," Jason replied evenly. "Of course, we usually like to work for people *we've* thoroughly vetted and trust. Can't be too careful when it comes to working for new people, after all. What assurances do we have this is on the level? I'd rather not fly into a trap."

"I'm authorized to offer you none. This is a take it or leave it proposition," Dowarty answered. "You'll receive an upfront payment as a show of good faith, but that is all I can give you. I'm sorry, Captain, but my employers are paranoid individuals. I'm sure you understand."

"I can relate, if that's what you mean," Jason agreed. "I'm assuming you don't want to go over the details here in a bar..."

"Of course not," Dowarty gave him that same smile he gave Crusher. Despite the assumed mannerisms of a boot-licking underling, Jason got the distinct impression the little man was looking down his nose at them. He slid a memory chip across the table. "This contains all the information you'll need, including the access codes to receive your initial payment. If you take the chip, and agree to the terms, we'll know by your ship lifting off at a precise time. If not, no harm done; there's no way to glean anything from the information on that chip.

"However, and I can't stress this enough, if you decide *not* to take the job... walk away. If you accept the initial payment and run, if you warn the target in an attempt to get a higher fee from them, or if you try to alert the authorities in any way; my employers will hunt you down and blow your ship out of the sky with you in it. This is not a threat, Captain, but a standing policy for all those who work for the people I do. I hope you'll take that seriously... for your sake."

"We're professionals. As I said on my ship: there's no need for theatrics or melodramatic threats," Jason affixed the little man with a cold stare. "We'll look over the details. If we decide to take the job, you'll know. If not... you'll probably never see us again. Now, is that everything I need to know?"

"Yes. Yes, of course it is, Captain," Dowarty again assumed the role of the subservient nobody. "Thank you for your time." With that he rose from his seat and made a hasty exit with his two guards close behind. Jason flagged over a server and ordered a drink, indicating for the others to do the same. He palmed the memory chip and slipped it into his pocket.

"We'll stay here a bit," he explained. "You never know who is watching and I'd rather not be seen leaving with them. We may be unknown, but I doubt the same is true of our little friend there."

"He seemed to swing between cowering in fear and outright threats. I found that a bit odd," Doc said.

"I noticed that too. It's not that unusual for someone in his position to try and bully someone he thinks is of lower standing, I'm sure he gets pushed around all day and wanted to see what it felt like to do the pushing," Jason said as their drinks arrived.

"Maybe," Crusher said. "Still a little strange that on the flight out he was a glorified butler and once we're here he's calling us out to meetings and arranging contracts."

"Let's not think too much into it," Jason said. "He only delivered the chip, he wasn't out here negotiating terms. But, this may be an inroads to what we're looking for. Anyway, let's drink up and get back to the ship. I want to go over this tonight and see what we may be potentially getting ourselves into."

The three finished off their overpriced drinks and got up to leave. As they were walking out, Jason could see that the crowd had become thicker and more intoxicated since they had arrived. They almost made it to the landing pad to catch an aircar back to the spaceport before there was an incident. Apparently Sparks was in an entertainment district that was frequented by young, wealthy citizens of Solic-2 that had more money than sense. As Jason approached the last remaining car on the pad an obnoxious, nasally voice called out.

"Excuse you, that is our car!" Jason turned and gave the driver an inquiring look, who simply shrugged and shook his head. Ignoring the obviously drunk catcaller, he went to pay the driver and get in. "I *saaaid*... that is *our* car! Are you deaf?" Jason turned and saw four stumbling, very young men making their way towards them.

"I'm only going to say this once," Jason said irritably. "If you four morons walk away now, I'll let you."

"Let us?!" The speaker laughed hysterically. "There's four of us, and two of you." Jason frowned and looked around. *Can they not count?* Then he saw that Doc was already on the other side of the aircar, obviously intent on grabbing the front seat again. He was sadly shaking his head at what was about to befall the four dullards who had made their way quite close at that point. "Now... get out of our way. We're taking this car," the speaker was slurring his words and weaving badly. Jason looked to Crusher, who had an amused look on his face as he watched things play out. Jason sighed at the inevitable.

"Why don't you idiots sit here, sober up, and wait for the next one? I'm really very busy," Jason said in a reasonable tone. He had no desire to hurt any of the misguided fools. The "leader" stepped in close to him and poked him in the chest.

"Why don't *you...*" That was all he got out as Jason, lightning fast, reached with his right hand, grabbed the offending wrist from underneath, and wrenched it back and over with enough force to throw the boorish dimwit to the tarmac. He howled in pain and grabbed his arm, nearly sobbing. With his enhanced strength, Jason probably could have torn the arm from its socket, but he wasn't going to maim some kid who'd only had too much to drink. He was, however, going to teach him a lesson in etiquette.

"Steppen!" One of the others squealed. The group, having lost its leader, and its bluster, milled around, unsure what to do. Crusher decided to make the choice for them; he lunged forward and let loose with a deafening roar that left Jason's ears ringing. The remaining three decided it was every man for himself and bolted, leaving "Steppen" rolling and moaning on the ground. Jason could hear Doc laughing out of his right ear. He could hear nothing out of his left ear save for a loud ringing.

"I *really* wish you'd give some sort of warning before you do that," Jason said to Crusher irritably. Crusher just smiled and shrugged. Jason leaned down to the still moaning youth. "Tough night, huh? You'll be fine... you just need to learn some manners." He stepped over him and into the car, waiting for Crusher to get in on the other side. Once they were all in, the driver, also chuckling, whisked them away and back to the spaceport.

*   *   *   *   *

"This is a lot more complex than your simple smash and grab," Kage quipped as the rest of the crew sat around the table in the tiny meeting room directly aft of the bridge on the port side of the command deck. They were going over the information on the chip and weighing the options available to them. The room had a standalone computer that mitigated the risk of malicious software making its way onto the ship's main computer.

"You can say that again," Twingo said. "This is absurd, Captain. We're supposed to run this ship down, unseen, board it, and try and find a box of antiques to steal?"

"I'd hardly call last remaining artifacts from the Talisian Empire a box of antiques..." Doc began before Twingo waved him off.

"Whatever, Doc. No matter who it used to belong to, it's still just a box full of old crap now."

"The point isn't what's in the box," Jason reminded them. "This is a means to an end. We steal the box of old crap, garner favor with whichever eccentric crime boss wanted it, and maybe we get closer to wrapping this mission up. Or at least providing some useful intel."

"Do we even have the technical ability to pull this off?" Lucky asked quietly.

"Yes," Twingo said, reluctantly. "Our countermeasure suite is more than able to hide our approach to a civilian luxury yacht like that," he indicated to the sleek ship slowly rotating on the display. "We just slip in under low power, override one of their emergency airlocks-- that's your job, Kage-- and we're in. But how do we find the item?"

"The chip contained detailed layouts of the ship's interior, including the likely location of the box," Jason said. "Oddly enough, it also had the ship's duty cycle rotation. Whoever put this together has been on board that ship and has been planning this for some time."

"Either that or we're flying into a trap," Twingo muttered.

"Or that," Jason was forced to agree. "But, we don't have any other promising leads right now. Nobody said this was going to be easy, we are being paid a lot of money for this."

"Weren't we supposed to be helping out the little guy when we all signed up for this outfit?" Twingo asked, trying a different tactic. "Why are we out here risking our collective asses to help out the Eshquarian government? They're one of the richest systems in this part of the galaxy."

"There are innocent people on Eshquaria as well, Twingo," Jason asserted weakly. The feisty little engineer did have a point; Omega Force had formed with an overarching mandate to help out the people who didn't have the ability to help themselves. An ultra-wealthy system of arms manufacturers didn't really fit into that ideal. "But beyond that, we all know that the money Crisstof Dalton is paying us will go a long way in making sure we can keep helping out the little guy. All that loot we stole from The Vault... that huge fortune was squandered because we've been forced to change our identities, and the *Phoenix's*, multiple times.

"We're going to do this our usual way. We'll take off at the prescribed time and make the intercept, but if we don't like the way it looks… we bolt. As a precaution, we'll not be cashing in the advance bonus just yet. So, if there's nothing else… grab some food and sleep and get ready. We launch in twelve hours." They all stood to leave when Jason put his hand on Kage's shoulder to stop him. "I want you to transcribe the data into the ship's computer manually. I know it seemed to come up clean, but I don't want to take the chance of plugging that chip into our systems." The small Veran grumbled, but went to work immediately. Jason smiled as he left him to it. His species had an especially evolved cerebral cortex that could process and store the information as fast as a computer, and Kage had the added benefit of a slew of exotic neural implants to help him out.

Jason saw Doc was on the bridge, immersed in something on one of the displays and looking like he didn't want to be disturbed. He walked down the stairs to the main deck and saw Lucky and Twingo walking together towards the engineering compartments and Crusher sitting in the galley getting ready to eat. He walked over to grab something himself and join his friend.

"So what do you think, Crusher?" Jason asked as he programmed the processor for what he wanted.

"Seems easy enough," he rumbled, sitting with a tray of his usual bland (although nutritious) fare. "Which means it will go to hell the minute we step foot on that ship, if we don't get blasted on our initial approach." Jason grabbed his tray and walked over to the table.

"That's what I love about you, Crusher: your eternal optimism."

"I do what I can, Captain," he said with a short, barking laugh.

"That you do..." Jason replied thoughtfully. "You know, I've been around warriors for most of my adult life, or at least people who considered themselves warriors, and I can't recall a single one who behaved like you."

"In what way?"

"A lot of them are uptight assholes," Jason began. "Well, that's maybe unfair to most of them... I guess what I'm trying to say is that when you're not bashing in some poor bastard's head, you're one of the most polite people I've ever been around." While he said it he realized, if taken wrong, how wildly offensive it sounded. Crusher looked over Jason's head, chewing slowly.

"On my world, there are thousands like me. The warrior caste of my people has been developed into what we feel is the perfect soldier, but that process wasn't without its problems," Crusher put down his food and looked to be willing to open up a bit. Jason sat stock still with rapt fascination as he began, Crusher rarely talked about his past, or his lineage. "The first few generations were physically impressive, and had the aggression and mindless courage to be good cannon fodder, but they were hardly a cohesive fighting force. Not only that, but they were a danger to the very population they were supposed to be protecting.

"The next phase was much more successful; even more improved physical prowess but with a sharper intellect and a capacity for empathy. As the warrior caste became more and more powerful, we developed our own culture and way of relating to each other as well as members of the other castes. At first I think it may have been driven by self-interest; our government would have forcibly exiled us had we posed much of a threat to the others."

"You talk about your kind like I would expect Lucky to describe his; versions and modifications and such," Jason said.

"In a way you're right. It took much, much longer, but our scientists improved us by trial and error much like his designers. Anyway, when it got to the point that fights between us usually ended in at least one fatality, we began to adopt an almost formal way of relating to each other. It keeps the bloodshed to a minimum," Crusher smiled slightly and continued eating. Jason also continued with his meal and thought about the hulking alien's tale. He wasn't sure if he should feel sympathetic or not; Crusher was made to be exactly how he was with no choice to be anything else despite the obvious mental capacity for so much more. But, then again… being raised from birth to be a soldier, and coming from a long, long line of soldiers, would he choose to be anything else?

"That's why I like it so much here," Crusher said again, startling Jason a bit. "Although I'm still a warrior, the choice is now mine as to what I fight for. But what about you? Were you not a warrior among your own people? Do you see yourself as a... uptight asshole, was it?" Jason spit out some water laughing at that last bit.

"I was well trained, yes, and I was put in harm's way more times than I can remember... but my role was primarily to save lives. I guess I never tried to figure out exactly where I fit in."

"You certainly have a warrior's spirit, and you're crazy enough to let it make decisions for you," Crusher said with another rare smile. "I like that." From him, there was no higher praise.

"Thanks, I'll take that the compliment I'm sure you intended it as," Jason said as he stood up and placed his tray on the counter. "I'm hitting the rack for a few hours of sleep. Good talk."

"Sleep well, Captain."

*   *   *   *   *

The *Phoenix* was pushing up through the thermosphere of Solic-2 exactly on schedule, thus entering a tacit agreement to perform the job they'd been tasked with. Jason still had no intention of unnecessarily risking anyone's life, so if it looked impossible without major bloodshed, he would call it off no matter the consequences.

"Everything's green," Kage said. "Slip-drive is primed and ready to jump on your command. Coordinates are already programmed in." Jason looked down at one of his displays and saw the nav system had their pre-designated coordinates already plugged in. They were slightly different than the set that was provided by Dowarty and would allow them to jump in at a distance and reconnoiter the surrounding space before committing fully. They were relying on the *Phoenix's* speed in real space to get them in position when they needed to be there.

"Looks good," Jason replied. "Standby for jump." He hit the flashing green button on his lower right console and felt his ship build power and mesh smoothly out of the Solic System. "Stay sharp everyone. This is a short jump, we'll be meshing in soon and from there we go dark. I'll be in the armory getting ready." He stood up and nodded to Doc as he walked off the bridge. He snuck through engineering as quietly as possible, smacking Twingo in the back of the head as the engineer was bent over inspecting something. He shuffled out of the area, laughing, as the short alien blistered the air with implausible threats to his anatomy. *He must be in a good mood, he didn't throw anything that time.*

As they always were directly before an operation, Crusher and Lucky were already in the armory getting ready and discussing the pros and cons of different types of weapons. Jason greeted them both and then went to his own full-length wall locker and opened it up. Inside, hanging on a rack, was the improved armor he had designed and built with the help of his crew. His original protective gear had been designed by Deetz, the treacherous synth that had wanted to sell Jason into bondage when they had first met. It had been serviceable, but the more he learned about what worked and didn't he began to make improvements on his own. This armor, while still lightweight and providing excellent range of motion, had more coverage and had powered shields. The energy shields only covered the hard plates of the armor, and weren't especially powerful, but they did nicely when deflecting energy weapon fire.

Crusher wore a similar setup, but only a chest protector; no pauldrons or arm guards. For some reason the enormous alien had a huge aversion to sleeves or gloves. Jason knew there was a good joke in there somewhere, but his own fierce self-preservation instinct kept him from saying it aloud. Even a good-natured, glancing hit from the warrior was enough to cause serious damage.

Lucky, of course, was ready for combat at all times. He was just there for the company. Jason put on his base layer pressure suit, the black, active over suit, and finally his armor, sans helmet. When he looked up he saw that Crusher was regarding him with a raised eyebrow. "You know, Captain, we could maybe have Twingo build you a miniature tank to roll around in during ground ops."

"Kiss. My. Ass," Jason said as he finished his preparations. "The first time you take a shot to the arm I don't want to hear any crying--"

"Crying?"

"--about how much it hurts. I don't have millennia of selective breeding and genetic manipulation to make me invincible. It's actually the exact opposite; evolution has been a cruel mistress when it comes to humans and our natural weapons. My body isn't up to the punishment."

"I think your body is fine, Captain," Lucky spoke up helpfully. Both Crusher and Jason just looked at him for a long, uncomfortable moment and then turned quickly back to sorting gear. "What?"

"I'll be on the bridge," Jason said as he headed for the door. "It'll only be a couple more hours before it's show time."

Once back on the bridge, he had little to do to occupy his mind but watch the timer count down to zero. But, he was the Captain, so he would set a good example by staying at his post and not roaming about the ship because he was bored. Kage was busy setting up his scripts and intrusion routines he would use to bypass their target's security and Doc was scouring through research documents he had downloaded on Solic-2 regarding the item they were supposed to steal. So Jason sat quietly and mentally prepared himself for the upcoming op and let the drone of the *Phoenix's* engines relax him.

The *Phoenix* meshed into the Careechi System just inside of the heliopause, well short of their suggested jump point. She ghosted into the system, going dark immediately and listening intently with her passive sensor array to anything that might be out there. Jason had no doubt that his client, or clients, really wanted the item they had been commissioned to steal, but he also didn't trust them any further than he could throw Crusher, which was not at all. The star system was along the outer boundary of the nebula the Concordian Cluster was nestled against. The surrounding space was full of both incredibly beautiful views and deadly traps of radiation and gravitational anomalies. The effects of these unpredictable conditions had created a unique wonder among the planets in the Careechi System, which was void of habitable worlds. Of the four gas giants orbiting the primary star, two had orbits that would occasionally bring them quite close to each other (close being a relative term when dealing with planets the size of protostars). The result was the smaller of the two passing behind the larger and having its atmosphere interact with the charged particles trailing its bigger sibling. The visual effect of this interaction was breathtakingly beautiful, and a much sought after vista.

Their target, a large, luxurious, slip-capable yacht, would be arriving to enjoy the view within the next four hours if their intel was to be believed. She was the pride and joy of a wealthy shipping magnate, although Doc's research had turned up some unscrupulous dealings he had initiated that led to his vast fortune. It was thin, but Jason needed to cling to something so he could tell himself he wasn't actually robbing an innocent person. While the yacht was fast and graceful, it was built for looks more than defense. This was something Omega Force hoped to exploit.

The yacht arrived almost a full hour after it was scheduled to, but it was there. More importantly, it was alone. The intel they had been given indicated that it would be since Careechi was an utterly useless system for anything other than the view and the mark foolishly felt extra security would be unnecessary. He was known to bring lady friends out to Careechi-3 for dinner and drinks when the orbits would properly intersect, and his mate was out of the area on business. *Powerful men are the same the galaxy over. Wonder what sort of prenup you'd need when you owned a private star fleet.*

Jason guided the *Phoenix* to intercept the yacht's course well behind it; he would mask his approach by hiding in the gravity vortex of the other ship's engines and employing their own countermeasures. They were several thousand kilometers behind the ship, which appeared as a slightly brighter dot against the stars, when he throttled up ever so gently and began to slowly close on it. He would get close enough to hide in the small sensor blind spot created where the engine fields overlapped, and then he would pace the yacht around Careechi-3 until the party on board had run its course and night hours started.

He hoped the booze was flowing; passed out passengers wouldn't notice an armed boarding party rifling through their prized possessions.

"We're on," Jason said, interrupting the tense silence on the bridge. "They should all be asleep by now. Kage, mask our approach as best you can until you can get into the computer and shut the external sensors down."

"Copy," Kage replied nervously. Jason didn't think anything of it; the jittery little Veran was always a bundle of nerves during a mission and he always came through. He pushed the throttle up smoothly and quickly closed the remaining gap between them and the yacht. When they were within visual range, he rolled the ship over a full one-eighty and synced his optical implants to the external sensors so he could see through the hull. He slowed to match speed with the other ship and began gradually closing the interval until they were underneath and inverted in relation to the yacht's orientation. He let the computer guide him as he lined their ventral hatch up with an auxiliary airlock on the other ship's belly.

"Extend the cofferdam," Jason ordered. "As soon as you have connectivity you're clear to start. If we have to boogey, call it out."

"Gangway extending," Kage said absently. "Contact. Beginning entry..." A glazed look came over the Veran's face as he tied his neural implants into the *Phoenix* and attempted to override the security measures on the yacht's airlock. The DL7 gunship had an extendable, pressurized apparatus that could be deployed from the drop-hatch in the cargo bay and allowed them to mate up to almost any size airlock. Most standard airlocks had an inductive, low bandwidth connection that allowed for minimal data transfer without needing a hard connection, Kage planned to use this to gain access to the ship's main computer and shut down the security subsystems as well as open the airlock. They'd done it before, and it was much preferable to blowing the hatch with explosives for a variety of reasons, the fact that massive, hull-breaching explosions tended to alert the crew not among the least of them.

It was nearly two full minutes before Kage spoke again, "I can open the outer airlock hatch without activating an alarm. You'll have to get me a remote connection for me to handle the ship's internal security measures."

"We can do that," Jason said, moving to walk off the bridge. "Open the drop hatch and shut off the gravity in the cargo bay."

"Copy."

The ventral "drop hatch" was a design consideration meant to make it easy to ferry ground troops into a hot landing zone without risking the ship by opening up the main cargo hatch. It was a small, circular, iris-type hatch that had been fitted with a pressurized

188

cofferdam to allow ship-to-ship transfers. Since the hatch was on the *Phoenix's* belly, and they were entering the yacht from *its* ventral side, Jason had opted to kill the artificial gravity in the cargo bay to avoid the disorienting shifts. He wasn't all that savvy at zero-G operations yet, but just maneuvering around in his own cargo bay shouldn't be an issue. Besides, Lucky had a full set of maneuvering repulsors and ionic jets built into him, if it got too bad he could always just grab a hold and hang on for the ride.

He went back into the armory to collect his two crewmates that would be joining him and grab his helmet and weaponry. He opted for a simple plasma carbine with a formidable stun setting as well as an electrostatic stun sidearm, all contingency items; Jason wanted to slip in and out without being detected if at all possible. His helmet had originally been a dull, black affair with no visor; the sensors built into the helmet fed directly into his neural implant and provided him a full field of view in multiple spectrums while eliminating the weak point of a transparent visor. In the tradition of his spec ops background, he'd had Kage paint a stylized skull's face on the front, complete with improbable fangs and an evil glare.

"Time to make some money," he said with a smile as he opened the blast door that led out into the cargo bay. Jason made a grandiose "after you" gesture to his friends, who had no idea the gravity had been turned off. Crusher stepped through forcefully and ended up launching himself end-over-end into the hold.

"You little shit!" He exclaimed. He flipped himself over and hit the far wall in a crouch before pushing back off towards the floor in an impressive display of acrobatics. Jason activated the relatively weak mag-locks on his boots and strode carefully out into the bay, laughing out loud. Lucky, always unflappable, walked calmly out to the middle of the cargo bay without so much as a stumble. Jason turned the remote link box over in his hand and made sure it was actively connected to the ship's computer. Satisfied with the winking green light, he called up to the bridge, still laughing to himself inside his helmet.

"Kage," he said, "we're ready for you to open the hatch whenever you want." Almost immediately a large, circular section of the deck began to rotate and recess into the floor. After it sank about five inches, it sectioned itself into four curved quadrants and disappeared into the ship, leaving a gaping hole that led to the yacht they were flying in formation with. Jason peered over the edge and saw that the other ship's hatch was hanging open and the inside of the airlock was dark, all good signs. He slid over the edge and entered the flexible tunnel head first, wanting to be properly oriented when he was within the artificial gravity of the yacht.

Once he was in the other airlock, he looked around for the access terminal to interface with the remote link he carried. It took only a moment to locate it since it was the only control panel in the small chamber. He was standing in an auxiliary lock that was meant more for maintenance than anything else, but it would serve their purpose just fine. He stuck the box against the edge of the panel like he'd been told and watched, fascinated, as tendrils composed of nanobots threaded out and disappeared into the panel, creating hard circuit paths within the guts of the control panel itself. It would then allow Kage to work his magic via the wireless link between the box and the *Phoenix's*

190

computer. It was all very much over Jason's head, but he'd seen it work enough times before to trust the process.

After planting the remote link, he turned and hopped back through the still-open outer hatch, drifting down towards his own ship until Lucky grabbed him and pulled him through, back into the cargo hold. They would wait there until Kage was able to break into the other ship's computer; if he was unable to, or was caught in the process, Jason wanted them all inside the *Phoenix* so they could make a run for it the instant they were detected. The process sometimes took as long as thirty minutes, so the three members of the boarding party kept a loose grip on the edge of the hatch opening and floated in place, watching for any sign that someone on the other side of the airlock's inner hatch was trying to come through.

Nearly ten minutes ticked off the mission clock before Kage called to the team. "*Intrusion successful. You can open the inner hatch from the control panel in the airlock. I've also taken control of the security and internal sensor subsystems, they'll give no warning to the bridge crew and I'll also be able to put up the security personnel positions on your HUDs. Happy stealing,*" the little Veran said as he signed off. Jason drifted back into the yacht's airlock and, after verifying on his floating heads-up display that there were no security guards roaming in the area, popped open the inner hatch and pulled himself through. He scanned in all directions, in a combination of thermal and light amplification, to clear the area of potential hostiles. He trusted Kage implicitly, but he always cleared any room he entered. He leaned over the open hatch and waved the other two through. Lucky was the first to pull himself silently up through the open hatch, then Crusher.

They found themselves standing in what appeared to be a general maintenance area in one of the engineering bays. Having planned the mission out already, no signal was given as Crusher moved to the exit and covered the austere maintenance passageway beyond with his stun rifle and Lucky moved to cover another, smaller entrance to a series of crawlways that led to the engine emitters. Jason closed the inner airlock hatch as quietly as he could and locked it. He could have Kage pop it open when they needed it again and leaving it open would be an obvious sign of intrusion were someone to stumble upon it... not to mention it led straight into his own ship. A thrown explosive device into the *Phoenix's* cargo bay would cause some serious problems.

Leap-frogging forward, the three ghosted up the passageway, covering every hatch and branch as they made their way forward. Most of the aft part of the yacht was made up of engineering, crew quarters, and storage. The luxurious forward and upper decks, well away from the hum of the engines and reactor, housed the owner's stateroom and the entertainment areas. The service passageway they were in spanned the entire length of the ship, conveniently providing access for the crew and as well as a trio of would-be thieves.

Crusher, being the one currently in the lead of the column, held up a closed fist to indicate a stop; they were at the set of stairs they would take to the upper decks, this was where it became interesting. The big warrior turned around and smiled broadly, obviously enjoying himself immensely. Despite the potential danger, Jason found himself smiling back in his helmet. After slogging around on barely-developed worlds and playing the role of a glorified delivery service, this was the most fun they'd had in weeks. Crusher waved Jason up to take the lead. "You're the one with the display showing the

192

location of the guards," he whispered. Jason didn't respond, he simply went to the hatch and pressed the pad to open it. The door slid silently away revealing a curved stairway leading to the deck above. Leading with his sidearm, he began to ascend the steps, followed by the other two.

They emerged into a well-appointed room that seemed to be just a sitting room as all there was were sets of curved couches surrounding a circular table. Jason switched back to thermal mode on his display and called up a false-color overlay since the ship was on night-hours and the lighting was dimmed down to almost nothing. The view was disconcerting at first because it didn't include the shadows of objects and tended to throw his depth perception off just a bit. He led them out of the room and deeper into the living quarters of the yacht. Their ultimate target was the main salon that was amidships and one deck above them, but to access it they would need to go forward into the galley, then up, and back aft again. He just hoped Kage was able to keep the internal sensors tied up until they could grab the loot and backtrack the convoluted path back to the airlock.

They were in the galley when, all of the sudden, the overhead lights came on and they heard a sharp, startled gasp. Turning quickly, Jason took aim and fired, his sidearm coughing once as it fired an electrostatic charge at the target. A woman with pale green skin and long black hair, wearing nothing but a night shirt, went down without a sound. The pistol delivered a stunning charge of electrical energy that overloaded the nervous system and put the average-sized being out for at least a few hours. The person then woke up with little recollection of what happened and a near-debilitating headache.

"Good shot, Captain. Truly you saved our lives from this dangerous warrior," Crusher whispered.

"Shut up," Jason answered. He walked over to the pantry, grabbed a bottle of what was probably a very expensive wine, and handed it to Crusher. "Empty most of that out, *without* drinking it, and spill a bit on her shirt. Take her out to one of the couches we passed and lay her on it and place the bottle nearby. When she comes out of it she won't remember that she didn't actually suck down a bottle of wine and pass out. Then move as quickly and quietly as you can to catch up, we're pressing on."

With Crusher carrying the unconscious woman out to the sitting area, Jason and Lucky climbed a narrow, spiraling stairway that led from the galley to an area just forward of the main salon, obviously meant for the serving staff. The salon was dimly lit with side accent lights and was luxurious beyond anything Jason had ever seen. Along the aft wall was an expansive display case that housed a veritable treasure trove of unique and exotic items, many of which were probably illegal to own as a private collector. He knew the item they were after was a priceless cultural artifact that should be turned over, but to him it was a way deeper into an organization that had been, hopefully, running attacks up and down the Cluster's shipping lanes. For the moment, the latter was of greater value to him.

He motioned to Lucky to post up and stand watch. The battlesynth, able to move with astonishing stealth for his stature, made his way quickly to an area that enabled him to cover the entire room and remain somewhat hidden. As he made his way to the display case he saw another, large shadow move against the forward bulkhead; Crusher had made his way up to them and was now covering the forward passageway. Looking the large glass case over, he thought it seemed straight-forward enough to open, but he would not be so easily fooled. "Kage," he said, his com transmitting on an open channel. His video feed was also being linked back to the ship so the other three could see what he saw.

"*Working on it, Captain,*" Kage confirmed. "*The case is tied into the ship's main security protocols, but it operates under its own subroutine. This may take a moment.*"

Jason knew his code slicer was working as fast as he could, and far faster than anyone else he had ever met. Cajoling him or distracting him with pointless words of encouragement wouldn't help them out, so he remained silent. It wasn't long before there was a *pop-hiss* and the glass raised into the ceiling. His displays warned him momentarily about an increase in argon gas concentration in the room and he realized that the case had been filled with the inert gas to help preserve the items. He called up an image he had been provided by Dowarty and began comparing it to the items in the case. Several seconds later he was lifting an absolutely ancient looking wood box out with the reverence it deserved. The case was exquisite, and when he opened it he knew he had the correct item; nestled inside, carved from colored gems the size of his fist, were what looked like a pair of four-winged hummingbirds in breathtaking detail. The statues were thousands of years old and were literally priceless.

Closing the box, he motioned Crusher over and told Kage to close and re-purge the display case. Crusher came forward, removing a padded bag as he did to place the box into. Once Jason slid the box into it, the bag formed itself around the item, squeezing out the air and inflating a series of bladders to pad it. He took the bag and motioned for the big warrior to turn around and kneel, then slipped it into the pack he was wearing. Once the item was secured and they were on the move, his adrenaline really started pumping, this was the most exhilarating part of a job: the getaway.

They moved quickly though the galley, stopped to make sure their wayward party girl was still out, and slipped back into the service passageway without attracting any more attention. Jason risked a slight compromise of stealth for speed as he moved quickly towards the cramped engineering bay.

Then, without warning, the ship lurched slightly and there was an noticeable pitch change in the engines. *"Captain! The ship is powering up to break orbit! You've gotta hurry!"* The frantic call over the coms was from Twingo. The trio didn't waste time looking about and broke into a flat out run.

"Kage, pop the inner hatch! Keep the *Phoenix* in formation with the yacht until we're back through!"

"Copy, Captain," Kage said. *"You don't have much time though."*

They burst through the hatchway and noticed that the inner airlock hatch was just swinging up and open. Jason frantically motioned his guys through as the yacht's engines continued to build power as it climbed up out of orbit with the *Phoenix* clinging to it like a parasite. Lucky hopped through the opening head first, followed by a headlong dive by Crusher. Jason slipped into the airlock, keyed the hatch closed, and began to disconnect the remote link box from the panel. "Are you out of their system, Kage?"

"Yes, Captain! Please hurry!"

He pulled the box off and noticed the flexible cofferdam was swaying wildly beneath him as his ship struggled to hold formation while flying though the gravitational wake of the bigger vessel. He tucked his arms in and dove through the tunnel and flew into his ship's cargo bay, careening wildly off the ceiling and spinning towards the walkway that led to the upper hatch. "Close up the outer hatch and disconnect us before it rips the gangway off!" Jason shouted as he grabbed for some purchase on the railing he had hit. He looked down and saw that the drop-hatch in the floor of the cargo bay was rising back into place.

"Outer hatch closing! Gangway detaching now, Captain!" Kage exclaimed. After a moment more, *"We're drifting free. It looks like we're still undetected, they're pushing up out of orbit and heading out of the system."*

197

"Restore gravity to the cargo bay," Jason ordered once he had climbed up onto the small walkway in front of the crew entry hatch. A second later he planted firmly to the grating as the artificial gravity was restored. He walked down the stairs to the cargo bay floor, pulling his helmet off as he went and sporting an ear-to-ear smile. "Now *that* was fun!"

"Yes it was," Crusher agreed, returning the smile and laughing out loud as the three made their way back into the armory to stow their weapons and put the purloined box in the ship's safe.

"I must admit, while I do not condone stealing… that was quite exhilarating," Lucky said as they were stripping off their armor and clothes. Crusher laughed sharply and slapped the synth across the back with enough force that it would have sent Jason flying into the opposite bulkhead. Lucky barely budged.

"There you go!" He exclaimed. "You're starting to catch on now. As for the stealing… I'm sure that guy deserved it." Jason smiled as Crusher tried to rationalize a petty theft into a somehow honorable action. He tossed his gear on the bench he had claimed as his own and pulled on a clean set of utilities he normally wore while shipboard. He then headed towards the exit, only to be stopped by a reproachful glare from Crusher.

"I'll clean it up later," he said, trying to put as much sincerity as he could into his voice. When the giant simply crossed his arms and intensified his glare Jason pressed on. "I swear! This time I'll come back down and put everything away. I'm the captain, I should be on the bridge in case that ship comes about and opens fire."

"Do you have any idea how sensitive my sense of smell is?" Crusher asked in a deathly quiet, and terrifying, whisper. Jason mutely shook his head that he didn't. "Then allow me to enlighten you. It's over one hundred times stronger than your own... so, the next time you leave your sweaty undergarments in the armory to ferment and kick up an unholy stench, I *will* respond in kind." At that point Jason waffled on his decision to leave. He looked at the offending pile of clothes, and then back again at the glowering Galvetic, and then back again to the clothes. He decided that backtracking would weaken his position, tenuous as it was, so he turned and wordlessly left the armory. Once he was out of earshot, he asked the computer to give him a double-beep over the intercom when they meshed into slip-space to remind him to clean his mess up. He may be proud, but he wasn't crazy; he had no desire to know what Crusher's idea of "in kind" was.

"How did everything go?" Doc asked as he walked onto the bridge. By his crew's relaxed posture, Jason knew that they must still be drifting freely away from the other ship.

"Went great," he said as he swung up into his seat. "As long as Kage was able to spoof the internal sensors to mask our actions, I think we're free and clear."

"Oh please," Kage said indignantly. "That security suite was five years out of date ten years ago. I was even able to trick the logger into tracking the drunk girl's actions as being real, without the part where Crusher carried her to the couch and peeked up under her shirt."

"I don't think she was actually drunk before I shot her," Jason said, deciding to ignore the second part.

"Technicalities," Kage shrugged. "Drunk or not, she's going to have a raging hangover from that stun shot." They fell silent as they watched the optical sensors' magnified view of the yacht still accelerating out of the system.

"She came up out of the well pretty slow," Twingo said. "I'm guessing the captain had orders to ease them out of the system after the partiers had all gone to bed. Not a bad life... slip-space in for a view while you dine and drink, go to bed, then wake up back on your own world."

"Yeah," Kage laughed, "great. Except for the part where a group of badass mercenaries breaks into your ship and pilfers through your priceless collection of rare artifacts, pours out your vintage wine, and shoots your lady friend." Jason laughed as the yacht meshed out of the system in a flash of slip-energy.

"There they go," he said. "Give me the engines, we're out of here. The delivery schedule is a bit loose so…"

"Coded burst transmission coming in, Captain," Doc said frowning. "It's to us specifically, but it's addressed to the auxiliary com node." Jason also frowned, not many people knew the link address for that slip-transceiver.

"Who is it?"

"Decoding now, it's text only," Doc said distractedly. "It appears to be the *Diligent*. Captain Colleren is demanding that we rendezvous with them at the provided coordinates."

"She's demanding, is she?" Jason asked acidly.

"I'm just reading what is says, Jason," Doc said, almost apologetically . "We are working for her, after all."

"No, we're working for one Crisstof Dalton," Twingo said irritably. "We're supposed to be working *with* Kellea Colleren." Jason held up a hand to cut him off before he could really get wound up.

"Are we close, and is the location sufficiently discreet?" Jason asked.

"We're eight hours away, and it's in the middle of interstellar space with no systems or shipping lanes in the vicinity," Doc confirmed.

"Fine. Send no reply, but plot a course to take us there. Maximum slip speed, I want to be very early in case this is a trap."

"That cuts us down to six hours, give or take, depending on how well the engines are running," Kage offered, ignoring Twingo's spluttering at the suggestion his engines weren't running at optimum efficiency.

"This had better be fucking important," Jason said after letting his breath out explosively. "Give me a plot and crank this pig up... let's see what the good captain has that is pressing enough to risk blowing our cover." Twingo's jaw jutted out, indicating he was less than pleased at the casual insults being bandied about regarding his ship. But he turned to his console and began giving the ship instructions nonetheless.

"Engines ready, Captain," he said.

"Plot is entered, ready when you are," Kage confirmed. Jason smacked blinking drive engage and climbed up out of his seat as the *Phoenix* accelerated hard out of the system and meshed out of real space. A soft *beep-beep* sounded over the intercom, causing everyone but Jason to scan their displays in confusion.

"Where are you going?" Kage asked.

"To clean up the damn armory," Jason snapped. The three remaining crewmembers on the bridge just looked at each other and shrugged.

Chapter 9

The *Phoenix* hung motionless in space, her drive down to minimum power and all running lights extinguished. She was just a darker patch against the black of space. Jason always felt uncomfortable this far out between star systems. If something went wrong, there would be nobody coming to help. He thought back to his first extra-vehicular activity while they were deep in interstellar space, he had thought it would be like the NASA films; well lit with stunning views. The view was indeed stunning, but it was so dark that he couldn't even see his hand in front of his face until Twingo had turned on the external flood lights. The experience left him with a firm understanding of just how alone they were when drifting between the stars.

His thoughts were interrupted by a beep from his console and he saw that a ship matching the *Diligent's* profile had just meshed into the area. It coasted to a stop and held position exactly in the pre-arranged coordinates. Jason watched the sensor display for a moment, his face a mask of calm. Underneath he was seething at the interruption to his operation, if this visit ended up being nothing more than a tug on his leash, it would not go well for the standoffish captain aboard the other ship. He reached over and engaged the main drive and nodded to Kage, who pinged their transponder once to identify them, and began a slow approach to the much larger frigate.

"Gunship-class vessel, Phoenix: come along side as directed and prepare to be boarded through your port airlock. Diligent out." At the terse message the bridge crew looked at each other in alarm; something was very wrong.

"Crusher, Lucky; get your asses to the armory and gear up! Meet me at the port airlock, and bring my gear," Jason shouted over the intercom. "Doc, you're flying. Don't run into anything." He didn't wait for an answer as he launched himself out of his seat and ran off the bridge. The fact that they weren't taking them aboard their ship, and their use of the phrase "prepare to be boarded" gave Jason the sinking feeling this was anything but a social call. He ran down the stairs from the command deck, spun around grabbing the handrail and running forward on the main deck to the forward airlock and waited for the other two.

A moment later Lucky came into the sparse room the airlock was in, followed seconds later by Crusher, the latter carrying Jason's shipboard weapons and light body armor. Jason wasted no time getting his gear on and verifying his weapons were ready for action.

"What's going on?" Crusher asked.

"The *Diligent* meshed in and more or less demanded we come to and prepare to be boarded, their words. I don't think this is going to be a friendly conversation," Jason said grimly. "Doc, Kage! Bring the weapons online, but don't go active yet. Monitor the discussion here, if it goes sideways get us the fuck out of here at any cost, light the *Diligent* up with the main guns if you have to."

"Copy, Captain. Let's hope it doesn't come to that."

"This seems serious," Lucky said calmly. Already Jason could feel the battlesynth powering his own arsenal as a precaution, the air in such close quarters humming with energy. Crusher smiled fiercely at Lucky and nodded, engaging the power supply on his own plasma weapons.

"Let's talk first," Jason cautioned. "This may be a misunderstanding, or it may not. I want you two on either side of the hatch, I'll be in the middle and back out of your way to clear your shooting lane. Match force for force, don't shoot unless you see me draw down or dive out of the way." The two warriors turned and moved to either side of the airlock hatch and waited. A few long minutes later he could hear the pressurized gangway banging against his ship's hull and anchor itself.

"They're requesting we open up, Captain," Kage said over the intercom.

"Open it up," Jason said simply, every nerve tingling in his body. With a hiss and a jerk, the inner airlock door began to slide into bulkhead. Standing in the hatchway, looking quite angry, was Captain Colleren herself along with a visibly armed Commander Bostco and another armed crewman flanking her. Crisstof could be seen looking worried and pallid behind the trio. They remained just a step back from the hatch opening.

"*Captain* Jason Burke, we're here to take you into custody. Will you and your crew come willingly?" She asked simply.

"What in the fuck are you blathering on about, *Captain?*" Jason retorted with equal insult in his inflection. "Explain yourself before I tell my crew to engage the engines and fly out of here, whether you're back onboard your own ship or not."

"You were hired to gather intelligence in order to plan a lawful interdiction of a certain criminal element. You were not hired to run wild through the Cluster as a part of that element," she said hotly. "Since you disappeared, without giving any status reports, we've heard nothing but news of shootouts, assaults, drug running... and this ship popping up in some of the most brazen attacks the Cluster has seen yet." Jason, a little confused, just stared at her as if he couldn't believe how dense she was.

"No shit, genius. That's why you called us; to gather the intel you were too incompetent to gather yourself. It's called being undercover, operational security precluded the ability to file status reports with you people," Jason said insultingly. "How the hell is it you're so bad at this? Did you really think we'd just land and walk into a bar and the ringleader of this operation would come introduce himself to the new faces?" Captain Colleren was turning red and appeared apoplectic at the human's barrage of insults.

"We don't operate this far outside of the gray line, Captain," she said through clenched teeth, showing the first bit of emotion Jason had ever seen from her. Perhaps it was this loss of control that led to her next mistake; "Take him." Bostco and the other crewman came forward, weapons raised and pointed at Jason's chest. He could see quite plainly they were simple stun rifles, so he almost felt bad for what was about to happen.

"We don't want any trouble, Jason," Bostco said as he stepped forward slowly. "Just call up to your..." An ear shattering roar cut him off as he cleared the threshold of the hatch. Crusher slammed his palm down on the stun rifle and clamped the other massive hand around Bostco's neck and yanked him off the floor, slamming him hard against the opposite bulkhead. The roar distracted the other crewman so Lucky grabbed the stunner out of his hands and broke it in half like it was a twig, showering the room, and the crewman's face, with sparks.

Jason hadn't stood idle during the exchange, he roughly grabbed Captain Colleren, spun her around, and wrapped his arm

208

around her throat in a vise-like choke hold. He could feel her reaching for a weapon so he dug the end of his plasma pistol into her temple. "This is *not* a stunner," he snarled into her ear. She was struggling to breath, but Jason wasn't stupid enough to let up and risk her going for her weapon. He saw Bostco trembling in utter shock and terror as Crusher held him off the floor by his throat. The other crewman had fainted, so Lucky turned and aimed one of his arm-mounted plasma cannons directly at Crisstof, who seemed to be at least somewhat in control of himself.

"What's it going to be, Crisstof? My crew is listening in right now, any further aggression and they have orders to turn our guns on the *Diligent*. We're too close for your shields to come up and save you," Jason said.

"Please, everyone! Stop this! There's no need…"

"Oh yes there is, you piece of shit… you boarded *my* ship with an armed party with the intent to take me by force. I'll drop all of you and do it with a clear conscience. This is *not* a stalemate; start talking, and fast, or bodies start hitting the floor." Crusher punctuated Jason's words with another snarl and a snapping of his jaws that was straight out of a nightmare. He felt Colleren squirm a bit so he dug the pistol in harder until she went still.

"Please!" Crisstof pleaded again. "Let's defuse this misunderstanding. Let's you, I, and Kellea find someplace to talk about this where the threat of death isn't imminent." Jason stared at him a hard moment before releasing Captain Colleren and shoving her towards Crisstof before she could turn and draw on him. When she spun she saw that Jason already had his weapon raised and trained on her head.

"Your men go back to your ship. We talk in my galley with Crusher present. Lucky stands guard at the airlock, which we'll leave open as the *only* show of good faith at this point," Jason said calmly. "Understand your situation is still not good. I view this boarding as nothing more than an unprovoked assault, which we don't take kindly to."

"I agree to your terms," Crisstof said, his arms raised, palms out, in a calming gesture. Jason couldn't miss the death stare that Captain Colleren sent his way. *I do have a way with the ladies...*

"Very well. Crusher, gently lower and release Commander Bostco. Lucky, wake up the other one."

"He appears to have urinated himself—"

"--that's fine, Lucky," Jason interrupted, closing his eyes and shaking his head. "Just get him up. He can walk in wet pants." Bostco went and picked his fallen comrade up, gave Jason an unfriendly glare, but quickly exited the airlock as Crusher saw the look and gave another growl. The other crewman seemed to be almost walking under his own power when they were halfway down the gangway. After holstering his sidearm and handing his plasma rifle to Crusher, Jason gestured for the remaining two members of the *Diligent's* crew to follow him. He was supremely confident nobody would do anything stupid while Crusher had two weapons pointed at their backs.

Once they were seated in the galley, Jason began, "As you can see, we're not a helpless, soft target despite only being six people on a tiny ship. My crew will not allow you to take me into custody for doing what you essentially hired us to do. If you want to fire us, that's up to you, but any further attempt at an arrest will be met with a violent response. Is that clear?" When they nodded he continued, "Good. Captain Colleren, I sincerely apologize for physically assaulting you. In a way, you can look at it as a complement; you were one of the most dangerous people in the room and needed to be neutralized quickly."

"I'm flattered," she said in a tone that indicated she was anything but.

"Captain Burke," Crisstof began. "I'm afraid I own you an apology. I let Kellea convince me you had gone rogue and needed to be neutralized before you could do any more damage. It seems you still feel you're working towards our mutual goal, but I am somewhat appalled by your methods."

"Speaking of," Jason said, holding up a hand. "What are you talking about, specifically? We've mixed it up a little bit, and I emphasize the word little. To be honest this has been one of our more tame jobs so far." Captain Colleren wordlessly handed over a tablet computer with a series of reports from various local law enforcement agencies and a collection of images. The first thing that stood out was that the supposed actions were on worlds that they had yet to visit within the Cluster, the other was that the included images of one of the suspected ships bore a striking resemblance to the *Phoenix*. "Twingo! Get down here," Jason yelled over the intercom. He held up a hand to silence the other two as the engineer hustled down the stairs. When he arrived Jason handed him the tablet with an enlarged image, "What is that?"

"Hmm, it's a Jepsen Aero Mk XII rapid transport," Twingo said. "Looks to be in pretty bad shape. Too bad, that's actually a rare ship these days."

"So that ship is not the *Phoenix*?" Jason pressed.

"The *Phoenix*? Hell no," Twingo scoffed. "It looks similar if you're ignorant and don't see very well, I'll admit, but this is a high-speed courier ship. They were sometimes used as executive transports as well. It's a Jepsen, so it has some design cues similar to our own DL7, but this thing is a butterfly compared to a heavy gunship."

"Thanks, that's all I needed," Jason said, grabbing the tablet back. Twingo just stood there until Jason turned and gave him a pointed stare.

"Oh. Yeah," he stammered, "I'll just be on the bridge if you need me." Crusher rolled his eyes and shook his head as Twingo strolled off.

"Anyway," Jason continued. "Can we agree that the ship in these law enforcement alerts is not my ship?" When Crisstof and Captain Colleren nodded mutely he continued, "For now we'll treat the existence of this ship as a wild coincidence, like Twingo said; all Jepsens will look similar at a distance. So... why is this particular ship so special?"

"It isn't especially so, Captain," Kellea Colleren spoke up, managing to look somewhat abashed at her armed incursion into his ship on such flimsy evidence. "It has been involved in the continuation of the raids in the Cluster, but it hasn't been involved in some of the more serious actions. While we assumed incorrectly that you had been involved, there is something you may not be aware of; the raids are not only happening at greater frequency, but they've taken a disturbingly violent turn."

"Please, go on," Jason prompted, not at all sure he wanted to hear what was coming next.

"These raiders have moved on from attacking lightly crewed commercial freighters and have concentrated almost entirely on passenger starliners," Crisstof said quietly. "While this wasn't unheard of, there have been a number of civilian deaths. The political climate on Eshquaria is of growing concern to us, the population is demanding action on these attacks and now the Prime Minister's opposition is coalescing around a certain few vocal representatives."

"What is the opposition demanding?" Jason asked, wishing not for the first time the job didn't include so much political intrigue.

"For now, only action. They aren't being specific about what action that should be, content to let Colleston face the brunt of the public backlash alone. For now," Crisstof answered. "Colleston has dispatched a few small patrol fleets from the Eshquarian System, but they're too few and far between to make much of a difference. His fleet advisors warn that these attacks may be designed to draw Eshquarian forces away from the homeworld and leave them vulnerable to attack."

"That makes no sense," Jason said with disgust, rising quickly from his seat and startling the other two. "If the goal is to attack Eshquaria you don't give them months to put their forces on alert by harassing their commercial fleet with a ragtag bunch of wannabe pirates. The change in tactics to attacking passenger ships is the main clue here; this is a terroristic action, it's meant to drive the Eshquarians onto a particular course of action. The trick will be to find out what that is."

"Easier said than done," Captain Colleren said. "They're a fiercely independent bunch, and often unpredictable. Besides, I can't imagine any major power wanting to disrupt anything on that world; nearly all of them are supplied with Eshquarian weapons, at least in this quadrant of the galaxy."

"Ok, so is this an internal or external push?" Jason asked rhetorically.

"Indeed," Crisstof agreed. "We could be looking at a power grab within the government."

"Wait," Colleren said, holding up her hand. "They're a republic; any power grab would have to be geared towards rigging an election, one way or another. This is an off cycle, Colleston isn't up for reelection for another three years. If someone tried to mess with that they'd have a full blown, planet-wide insurrection on their hands. I can't imagine that would benefit anyone."

"All I'm taking away from this discussion is that we desperately need more intel," Jason said, staring at the ceiling and worrying at his scalp. "Are we still on the job?" Crisstof and Captain Colleren looked at each other sheepishly before answering.

"Yes, Captain Burke," Crisstof said. "For now, you're still our inside team. But things have taken a dangerous new turn, we need you to turn up the heat and expedite the results. Any further civilian casualties may push Colleston into a rash action and until we know what we're dealing with that's the last thing we need." The three stood and made their way back to the airlock, all anxious to get back to what they were doing before the detour. Crisstof nodded to Lucky before entering the gangway and crossing over to the *Diligent*. Captain Colleren paused at the hatch and turned to Jason.

"Captain, I do sincerely apologize for this... misunderstanding," she said, almost displaying genuine emotion as she offered the apology. "I hope this won't affect our working relationship." Jason, never one to be *totally* swayed by a pretty face, wasn't so fast to let it drop.

"No problem, Captain," he said in a deadpan voice. "I'd have regretted putting holes in your big, shiny ship. Tell Commander Bostco and Crewman Piss-pants that we offer our apologies as well." Her eyes instantly hardened again and a not-quite sneer curled her lip.

"I will tell them," she said, turning and storming down the gangway. Jason closed the outer hatch, and then the inner pressure hatch as soon as she made it across.

"His name was actually Piss-pants?" Lucky asked from behind him. Jason closed his eyes and just shook his head. He opened his mouth to answer, then decided against it, turned and walked out of the airlock chamber. "What?"

"Do we really believe that they mistook a light freighter for the *Phoenix*?" Crusher asked as Jason walked back onto the main deck and turned to walk up to the bridge.

"I'm not sure," Jason admitted, continuing up the stairs with Crusher in tow. "It seems unlikely that a few blurry images were all they had to go on. No transponder codes, no markings, no real proof other than a vague shape that their computer still should have been able to resolve as a different model than a DL7."

"Is it possible they're that incompetent that they didn't even run a crosscheck?"

"I'd like to hope not," Jason said as he slid into his seat. "That wouldn't bode well for a successful outcome. I'm going operate under the assumption that Colleren is naive and not incompetent, for now. She seems to run a tight ship, but tactical thinking and the like don't seem to be her thing." He shrugged to himself, "We'll deal with that later, right now we have a drop-off to make and payment to collect. Hopefully this leads to something useful."

"We're clear of the *Diligent*," Kage spoke up. "You're free to maneuver. New plot laid in for the drop-off."

"Thanks," Jason said his hand came down on the control to engage the slip-drive. "Luckily this was nearly on our way, but we're still going to need to make up some time." He ignored Twingo's grunt of disapproval as the ship meshed out of real-space and the slip-drive wound up to its maximum output.

*   *   *   *   *

With an especially bright blast of leaked slip-energy, the *Phoenix* roared back into the Oorch System, the location of their drop-off. Jason turned onto a course for Oorch Prime, confident they were expected, and settled in for the forty-minute flight from the jump-in point to the planet. He was pleased he didn't need to say anything to Crusher and Lucky, they both exited the bridge together to head for the armory to gear up.

The landing was as uneventful as their in-system flight and they settled on a landing pad at the planet's smaller spaceport that was well away from the cluster of buildings that housed operations and security for the facility. Both of these were things Omega Force liked to avoid; mandatory inspections and overzealous cops were never good for business. Kage accessed Oorch's planet-wide data network and sent a one word message to the recipient account that had been provided on the chip Dowarty had given them. Jason then went down and got himself prepped for anything that may, and probably would, go wrong during the exchange of stolen goods for credits. Once he was dressed in his body armor, armed, and had retrieved the case from the ship's safe, he walked out into the cargo bay to meet up with the other two.

It wasn't long before Kage called down to alert them they had a ground car inbound and they had received a reply message telling them to expect company. Jason handed the case, still in its padded bag, to Lucky and told him to remain to the side and out of sight. He then opened the cargo bay up and motioned for Crusher to follow him out to the bottom of the ramp, ordering the *Phoenix* to deploy the rear-facing cannons as he did. A few minutes later a sleek, long ground car pulled up with a deep, subsonic hum. *Must be some sort of performance model.* The door popped up and slid back to reveal a familiar face, although not necessarily a welcome one.

"Dowarty," Jason said, with a nod. "You get around."

"Part of the job, I'm afraid, Captain," Dowarty said. The prissy man climbed out of the car and looked around the grimy landing pad with distaste. "My employer was distressed when you didn't collect your upfront bonus. We were somewhat surprised to hear from you, although you seem to be empty handed."

"All in good time," Jason said calmly. He saw the two bodyguards still in the vehicle, and he was sure Crusher saw them as well, so he concentrated on Dowarty. "We don't like upfront payments as a rule. It makes it impossible to walk away if the target has been misrepresented or has been alerted."

"Prudent, if nothing else."

"So before we start the show-and-tell, I'd say a renegotiation may be in order." Jason had been watching Dowarty closely and didn't miss the flicker of anger in his eyes at the mention of a renegotiation. It was only there for a split second, and it didn't fit with what Jason thought he knew of his personality.

"I see," Dowarty said slowly. "What did you have in mind, and please remember who it is you're working for."

"As far as I know I'm working for you, or a few guys with bags on their heads, so it's not a lot to keep in mind. What I was thinking isn't so outlandish, however. I'd simply like the proposed upfront bonus tacked onto the final payment," Jason said placatingly.

"That seems... only fair," Dowarty said, a slight, relieved smile touching his lips. "I can authorize that myself. So may I see what my bosses paid for?"

"Lucky!" Jason enjoyed the uncomfortable squirming of the armed guards in the vehicle at the appearance of a battlesynth coming down the ramp. Lucky walked up and handed Jason the bag and then moved back and away to cover both him and Crusher. After pulling the bag off of the intricately carved box, Jason carefully handed it over to Dowarty, whose hands were twitching greedily at the sight of it.

"Oh my, my, Captain. You guys actually pulled it off," he said quietly. After opening the box and staring into it lustfully for a second, he motioned for one of the bodyguards to come and collect it. "That box is worth more than ten of you. Treat it accordingly." The offhanded comment startled Jason a bit, he'd never seen the little man puff up and actually threaten anyone like that in their other interactions. "So... should I enquire as to the health of the item's previous owner?"

"You could ask him yourself, if you were so inclined," Jason said. "He never knew we were there. In fact, it's highly likely he doesn't yet know the case is even missing. We left no trace."

"Quite impressive, Captain," Dowarty said appreciatively. Then a small chuckle escaped his lips, which quickly turned into hysterical, almost maniacal laughter. "I wish I could see his face when he goes to show these to someone and they aren't there," he said after he had composed himself. "You've made my employers very happy, and so let me return the favor. We'll pay your asking price, plus twenty percent. The added bonus is for your continued discretion concerning this job."

"What job?" Jason asked innocently.

"Exactly," Dowarty answered with another smile. "Feel free to enjoy the meager entertainment Oorch has to offer, Captain. The community around this spaceport tends to attract a rough crowd, so you and your crew may feel right at home." Without a word of farewell,

Dowarty slid into his vehicle and sped away, disappearing behind another squat, ugly ship within seconds.

"And now we're back to no leads," Crusher growled.

"I'm not so sure," Jason said as he stared at where the car had disappeared, his mind turning over the last few minutes carefully. "Let's call a family meeting. We need to get our shit together and start getting some answers, but for now we'll stay parked here. No point in hurrying off if we've got nowhere to go." The three walked back up into the ship, raising the ramp after them and leaving the aft cannons deployed as a deterrent for any would-be vandals or thieves.

It was the third day since they had delivered the box to Dowarty, and so far no prospect of additional work seemed likely. But they did notice that the ships coming and going at the small spaceport they were at were a little different than your average fringe freighters and scows. There was a parade of sleek, if aging, warships that would land, fuel and refit, and leave again. They ranged from slightly larger than the *Phoenix* to much smaller in size and there was no discernible pattern to the make and model used. All that was certain is that when each ship landed, a crew comprised of what were obviously mercenaries would swagger out and walk with a purpose towards the small town. So, for a lack of anything better to do, all six members of Omega Force tended to gravitate towards one of the more lively

223

taverns come each sundown and see what information they could glean from the crowd of drunken guns for hire.

*   *   *   *   *

"Damn you're big," the drunk slurred at Crusher, using the edge of the table to prop himself up. "Not that being big is the only thing that... matters... you know," he finished between a series of hiccups and burps. Crusher stared at him as a snake would stare at a rodent.

"I'm sure," Crusher rumbled. "Now, if you'll excuse us..."

"Don't turn your back on me while I'm giving you a compliment." Jason watched the fatal mistake take place in slow motion, but was powerless to stop it. The drunkard grabbed Crusher's shoulder and tried to spin him back around to face him. The warrior's huge, clawed hand shot up and enclosed the much smaller hand and yanked the drunk around and up until he was hanging in the air, too shocked to speak.

"While I've appreciated your praise and unwanted attention, I think it's time for you to go," Crusher ground out. Jason, being about seven drinks deep himself, marveled at the warrior's self-control. What he failed to notice, however, was that everyone had stopped talking and was now staring straight at them. The offending drunk, now realizing his position, did the dumbest thing he possibly could; he scrunched up his face and spit right into Crusher's eye. Jason held his breath and waited, wide-eyed. The response didn't disappoint. Crusher tossed his prey in the air and snatched him by the throat before he could hit the ground. He drew him in so he was eye-to-eye and let a terrifying low snarl escape his lips. The drunk, seeming to finally comprehend just how much danger he was in, started to tremble.

"Hey, no offense meant friend..." He got no further as Crusher, in one fluid motion, threw him over two gaming tables and sent him crashing against the far wall, breaking the video display mounted there and finally collapsing in a heap.

"HEY! Nobody throws my crew around!" The shout came from a burly, furred being that looked to be about Jason's height, but wider. The shout drew a raucous laugh from the crowd since Crusher had, literally, thrown his crew around.

"This doesn't concern you, asshole!" Jason shouted back. If some other captain was going to stand up and accost his crew, he'd be damned if he *wasn't* the one to answer back. "Consider that a lesson in manners and tell him he got off lucky when he wakes up."

"Oh shit," Kage said, "not again." Jason felt for him; the small Veran wasn't much of a melee fighter. Or any kind of fighter really. A total of nine beings had started to converge on them, fanning out from their furry captain.

"There's ten of us... *asshole*," he said, as if that mattered.

"That's ok. We'll wait here while you go get some more," Jason said, leaning back in his chair and taking a long drink off his beer in an overt display of contempt. The crowd began laughing again, loving the entertainment for as long as it lasted. The other captain was then in a tough spot; he'd staked out the position that he wouldn't tolerate his men being abused, so he was almost obligated at that point to initiate violence.

"I can't let you get away with that," Furball said hotly.

"Then don't," Jason said with a beatific smile on his face. They were within a few steps now, Captain Furball being wholly focused on Jason. His crew, however, began to take stock of Lucky and Crusher and their alcohol fueled bravado was beginning to wan. Furball looked away momentarily and, just as Jason expected, turned and hurled his drink at him with surprising velocity right for where his head had been as he ducked. He heard some unlucky patron, who hadn't been so alert, cry out in pain behind him. The corner of the bar erupted after that.

Crusher's deafening roar stunned everyone momentarily, giving him time to swing a massive left arm and clear two people out of the fight in one hit. The remaining three on his side froze like prey animals as the Galvetic warrior turned to them.

"The Captain is mine!" Jason shouted, hopping up from the floor to his chair before launching himself headlong across the table. He had no idea what species Furball was, but he was bored, angry, and drunk enough to not care at that point. As per Omega Force's standard operating procedure for bar brawls, Kage and Doc took cover, Lucky and Jason picked their targets carefully, and Crusher went berserk and took on all comers. Twingo, their wildcard, hovered around the perimeter of the fight. Being small of stature, he relied on asymmetrical warfare tactics; always ready with an opportune bottle to break on an unsuspecting head or a random stabbing with a piece of splintered bar furniture.

Furball was strong, but no real match for Jason's human musculature and enhancements. The impact from his dive over the table sent the pair sprawling backwards ten feet and knocking the air out of the alien in a big *whoosh*. He wasn't without skill, however, and managed to get a leg up under Jason and flip him off and over into a tangle of bar stools from the next table. He came down with a vicious

227

forearm swing that Jason barely blocked before bringing his own booted foot back sharply into Furball's head. The alien grunted and went down to one knee, clearly stunned. Jason rolled and turned so he landed in a crouch facing his adversary. While his opponent was still recovering from the kick, Jason pressed his advantage and swung a haymaker and put all his force into it, swinging sharply at the hips and tossing the punch out like a whip. The hit connected with Furball's temple and snapped his head over sharply and, like flicking off a power switch, the alien dropped to the floor in a heap and didn't move. Jason then looked up to see the inevitable results of the rest of the fight.

Lucky had rendered three unconscious with near surgical precision, causing the least amount of damage possible to knock them out of the fight. Twingo had smashed a chair over another one, taking him out, while Crusher had toyed with two others, garnering as much entertainment as possible out of the matchup. By the time Jason had turned back around he was down to the last one, and this guy was by far the biggest member of that crew. The crowd hoped for a good matchup, but were about to be disappointed.

To the frenzied cheers of the other bar patrons, Crusher rushed the lone survivor and clamped down on his upper arms with two massive hands. Before the other could react, Crusher lifted him bodily and slammed his head repeatedly into the ceiling until it lolled from side to side, unresponsive. The big warrior grinned widely and then tossed the unconscious heap onto his captain's equally unresponsive body. After a moment of stunned silence, cheers erupted around the tavern and a round of drinks were thrust into the victors' hands as the losing crew was dragged off to recover someplace else. *They're probably just going to toss them out in the alley.* He accepted the offered ale and the accolades for what apparently was a stunning display of hand to hand combat on that backwater world.

The next morning, while Omega Force was in the galley fighting valiantly against the collective hangover they were all suffering from, the proximity alarm sounded to warn them something was approaching the ship. Doc, who had already treated himself in his own infirmary, hopped out of his seat and went to the terminal in the galley to see what the alarm was about while the others relived, and mostly embellished, their exploits from the night before.

"Looks like it's Dowarty, Captain," Doc said loudly to cut over the chatter. Jason frowned, while he had wanted to stick around to see if they could pick up some more intel on the operation on Oorch he had expected to be called over the com. An in-person visit rarely bode well since it was unlikely the officious little administrator was visiting each ship on the pad.

"He's outside the ship?" Jason asked, wanting confirmation.

"His vehicle just pulled up and he's standing outside by the rear ramp," Doc confirmed.

"Shit," Jason muttered as he stood up and stumbled towards the armory. He was angry at himself for letting things get so out of hand the previous night, not so much the fight itself, but the fact that almost none of them were functional and a potential threat had just appeared at their back door.

He grabbed a high-powered plasma rifle from a rack out of the armory and made his way to the rear of the cargo bay to lower the ramp, he was not surprised to hear Lucky and Crusher coming after him. *Thank God Lucky doesn't drink. At least one of us will have some reflexes still.* He slapped the controls to open the ship up and waited as the ramp lowered, revealing Dowarty standing by himself in front of the same powerful ground car he had arrived in before.

"Oh dear," he said. "We're you expecting someone else, Captain?"

"Not expecting anybody, to be honest," Jason said, keeping his weapon casually over his shoulder and realizing he must look ridiculous with bloodshot eyes, no shirt, dirty fatigue pants, and the sandals he wore while shipboard. "Was there an issue with the merchandise?"

"Oh no, I can assure you, my employers were ecstatic by both your results and your methods," Dowarty assured him. "There was much laughter at imagining the mark's anguish when he realizes his prize has wondered off. I'm here for a different reason."

"Care to come aboard?" Jason asked cordially. "I can't imagine it's something you want to discuss on the tarmac and it's chilly out here."

"Don't mind if I do, Captain. Wisely discreet of you," the small man said as he walked up the ramp and followed Jason into the ship. As Crusher closed the rear pressure doors to the cargo bay, Jason couldn't help but notice two things: Dowarty had come alone, and he also had reverted back to the subservient persona he had displayed when they had first met him while he was in the presence of his bosses. What he couldn't figure out was why, on either count.

"Guys," Jason said as they walked into the galley, "you remember Dowarty, our gracious benefactor on the last job." Dowarty bowed with a flourish and smiled, playing along with Jason's joke. "So, what brings you out here again?"

"As you have no doubt noticed, this spaceport serves as a sort of staging area for my employers' various endeavors," Dowarty began. "A large part of what I do is organize our assorted… contractors… into small sub-fleets that can tackle larger projects together." Jason's heart began to pound and he struggled to look casually disinterested. This was what they had been waiting for; one of the facilitators that had been organizing raiding parties out of independent mercenary and pirate crews.

"We had a planned operation that would be launching tomorrow, but it seems one of my crews was brutally attacked last night at a most disreputable tavern. The captain and pilot were seriously injured and the others only slightly less so. This puts me a bit of a bind, but I'm hoping you can help me out of that."

"What sort of job is this?" Jason asked, playing the money-hungry mercenary. "Lots of ships means a big target, and big danger. I'm hoping there's big pay to go along with that."

"Payment will be quite ample, Captain," Dowarty smiled, feeling he had the upper hand in the negotiation. "The target is challenging, but important, so we don't take the chance of one or two ships; we send a dozen to make sure the operation goes as planned."

"I take it you need an answer immediately."

"That's why I came all the way out here personally. Are you in?"

"Hmm," Jason made some show of looking around at his crew before turning back to Dowarty. "I suppose we are. People in our position aren't ones to quibble over the details if the pay is good. When and where?"

"A ship will be landing within the next twelve hours," Dowarty said, smiling. "I'll ping you on this," he tossed Jason another hand held com unit, "and let you know when it's here and where it's parked. You, and you alone, come and get your instructions. Maybe get cleaned up a little beforehand as well."

Jason ignored the barb and led Dowarty back out of the ship and to his vehicle. "So your other crew got themselves jumped?" Jason asked casually.

"The accounts vary from each member of the crew. Their claims range from a dozen well-armed and trained fighters to a full regiment of Eshquarian Marines," Dowarty said blandly. Jason snorted out a short laugh.

"We were out and about last night and didn't see anything like that. What's their captain look like?"

"He's about your size, covered in fur from head to toe. Sound familiar?"

"Can't say it does," Jason said with a straight face. "But, their bad luck is our good fortune I suppose."

"I'd say it is, Captain," Dowarty said as he climbed into his vehicle. "Don't be late." Jason watched him drive off before heading back up the ramp and closing the rear doors.

"Well... we can thank Crusher for this lucky break," he said as he walked back into the galley where his crew was still lounging around.

"How's that?" Twingo asked, eyeing the big warrior skeptically.

"By beating the shit out of the crew last night that was supposed to be on this job he opened the slot for us." They all stared at Jason, and then at Crusher in pure disbelief.

"Of all the dumb luck..." Doc mumbled, shaking his head. Crusher was positively preening as he smiled at the rest of the crew.

"You all continually doubt me... but I always have a plan. *Always*," he said. This was met by catcalls from the rest of the crew and a thrown breakfast pastry by Jason. Crusher deftly caught the sugary projectile, took a savage bite out of it, and strutted outrageously from the galley back to his quarters.

"So, Jason, how did Omega Force crack the case? Well, Crisstof, we unleashed a terrible beast into their midst to eliminate the competition until we were the only ones left in the Cluster," Twingo conversed with himself in his best Jason Burke and Crisstof Dalton impressions. Jason realized that Twingo's impression of him was far too polished for that to have been the first time he'd done it. He gave the little blue-skinned alien a flat, unfriendly stare before going to his own quarters to clean himself up.

Chapter 10

Jason walked toward the large, gleaming ship that had touched down at the spaceport hours earlier. As he approached the lowered ramp on the port side, he could see two heavily armed guards at the base and two more just inside the entrance, but not the sloppy, amateurish thugs that his line of work seemed to attract. The four men guarding the ship were unmistakably professionals. He stopped a few feet in front of the ramp, identified himself, and raised his arms to allow the search he knew was coming. One of the guards nodded his appreciation at the gesture and patted him down. Jason had not taken the chance of trying to smuggle a weapon on board. If anything went down on someone else's ship, a single shooter with a hold-out weapon only made themselves a target.

"Captain, you're clean," the guard said crisply. "Go ahead and board and please follow the gentleman at the top of the ramp."

"Thanks," Jason said absently as he climbed up the ramp, taking note of how clean the ship and its crew were. One of the guards at the top nodded with his head, indicating that Jason should follow him, As they entered the ship's interior he could hear the second guard turn and follow him, ensuring he was covered from all sides. *These guys are taking no chances, must be a big fish on board.*

When they arrived in a well-appointed room, dominated by a circular table in the center, the guards gestured for Jason to enter and wait. There were two other scruffy looking individuals already there, presumably other captains to be involved in the raid. More out-of-place captains arrived one by one until there were eight total. Shortly after that, Dowarty walked in. "Thank you for being prompt, captains," he said as he walked to the front of the room and keyed the intercom panel. "We're all here, sir."

"Excellent," a disembodied voice said. A moment later the forward display flicked on showing a seated being behind a large desk and completely obscured in shadows so that no features were discernible. Jason resisted the urge to roll his eyes at the melodramatic show. *If he's going to hide his face why bother with the screen and the cheesy lighting effects?* "As you've probably guessed, you're here because you've shown yourselves to be capable and trustworthy. Well... as trustworthy as any pirate or mercenary can be." A polite chuckle rippled through the room.

"We have a window of opportunity to strike a fleet coming into the Cluster by way of Eshquaria. The same rules will apply as with the others, any debris or captured passengers are yours to keep, just make sure nobody gets their ship captured or disabled. If anybody can't make it out, the survivors are to destroy the disabled ship."

Over the next ninety minutes the Voice filled them in on the mission details with the help of Dowarty. Their target was a colonist fleet that was coming into the Cluster to settle an open continent on one of the sparsely populated worlds that dotted that region of space. There was no real reason given, and the other men in the room needed none, save for payment. Jason knew this was nothing more than a terrorist attack meant to garner sensational headlines and shock those in power on Eshquaria into a rash action. What he couldn't figure out was why... what could blowing up a load of poor colonists push the Eshquarian government into that would be of benefit to anyone? The more he tried to puzzle it out, the more confusing it all became, so he compartmentalized the problem and concentrated on his little corner of it: find those responsible for conducting these raids. It seemed like he was close.

He was tempted to call in the *Diligent* and tag the ship he was on so it could be tracked, but he knew that would be a premature action. Impressive as the vessel was, there was no way such a wide array of organized attacks were being launched from that ship alone. The logistics involved made Jason think they had a major base somewhere that had yet to be found. For the time being, he would continue to play his part and see where it led him. His most immediate concern, however, was how to play along while at the same time thwarting the attack on a fleet full of innocent civilians.

After they had been given their individual assignments and escorted back off of the ship, the gleaming vessel powered up its drives and lifted off almost immediately. Jason also wasted no time, breaking into a quick jog all the way back to the *Phoenix*. When he arrived Lucky and Crusher were standing watch over the open ramp, both armed and alert. "Expecting trouble?"

238

"Hopefully not, Captain," Crusher said. "But if you found some, we were ready."

"That's why I love you guys," he said as he hustled past them. "Button her back up and meet me in the galley. We've got some decisions that need to be made, and quickly. After that we'll be launching as soon as possible."

Two minutes later all the members of Omega Force were back in the galley and waiting for their captain to fill them in. "This is the group we've been looking for," Jason told them without preamble. "We've just been hired to hit a colonist fleet, and hard... we were told the more carnage the better." He paused to let that sink in. Flying all over the Cluster to help out a major power's government, the kind of government that had used up and spit out most of them, had not been sitting well to begin with. But now, they were the only thing standing between a huge group of innocents and a grisly death at the hands of a terrorist group and their hired guns. This was exactly the reason they were all out there. "While we still need to try and push in a little deeper and find their base of operations, there's no way in hell we're letting these colonists die."

"Damn right," Twingo said to the nods of agreement by the others.

"I think we're going to have to bring the *Diligent* in on this, Captain," Doc said. "We can't take on seven other ships without exposing ourselves, if we can even take them out at all."

"I agree," Jason said. "We're all supposed to be converging from different vectors to mask our slip-drive signatures as well as eliminate the possibility a ConFed or Eshquarian patrol ship getting lucky and taking us all out. So, how do we get a message to Captain Colleren and not blow our hard-earned cover?"

"One of the twins," Twingo volunteered. "We tell it to fly directly away from the spaceport and climb up and out to send the message: we'll pick it up on our way out of the system."

"The twins don't have slip-transmitters," Kage disagreed. "Can you fit one of them with one of our spare com packages?"

"Sure."

"You have forty-five minutes," Jason said forcefully. "We need to be lifting off in an hour. Who do you need?"

"Kage and Lucky," Twingo said.

"Go. Now. Doc, I want you to compose the message. It needs to be short and concise, the smaller the packet the better. Crusher, you're with me. We're going to go over the intel brief I got and start forming contingency plans if this one goes belly up on us." Jason ended the meeting by standing up and striding off towards the bridge with Crusher in tow.

The next thirty minutes of frenzied activity by the crew resulted in one of the twins being fitted with a slip-transmitter from their spare parts locker and an auxiliary power pack so it could actually use it. The message had been uploaded and the drone had instructions to fly out towards the open plains beyond the spaceport perimeter before making its ascent. It would then transmit its message four times, which was addressed specifically to the *Diligent*, and then shut the transmitter down and continue on course away from the planet. They would grab it on the way out once they launched. The risk was that by transmitting blind, without waiting for a confirmation from the *Diligent*, there was no guarantee the short message would be received or understood. It was a risk they had to take, though, as any lengthy contact with the other ship would greatly increase the chances of them being discovered.

"Talk to me," Jason said as he climbed up into his seat on the bridge.

"Primary flight systems are online. Our messenger has delivered his package and is flying away from the planet and everyone else is reporting that they're ready to go," Kage said.

"Very good. Go ahead and let ground control know we're leaving," Jason replied even as he fed power to the drives and lifted the *Phoenix* off the landing pad. He swung them around on a course that would take them directly away from the spaceport and throttled up into a lazy climb up out of the atmosphere. As the sky blackened around them, he saw that Kage had given him an indicator on his display to let him know where his wayward drone was. He steered towards it and continued accelerating, closing in fast on the small, underpowered craft. He continued to fly towards the indicator until the proximity alarm chimed and forced him to decelerate to match speed. Finally, he saw the drone with its little engines still lit up bright pushing hard away from the planet like it had been told to do. "Chirp the transponder once and tell it to come aboard," Jason told Kage. Once the drone knew they were there, it cut its engines off and let Jason maneuver up under it as they continued to drift away from Oorch Prime. Once they were underneath the drone it fired its exoatmospheric jets and grabbed onto the docking cradle, allowing itself to be pulled inside.

"Drone is aboard," Kage reported. "You're clear to maneuver and the slip vector is programmed. Ready when you are." Jason didn't waste any time flying further up the gravity well before meshing out of the system. Under the circumstances, the fuel savings seemed trivial.

They now had a nine hour flight to wait and hope the *Diligent* received their message and was in position to do something about it.

"We've got a pretty long flight, everyone," Jason said over the intercom. "Try to stay loose, get something to eat, and rest up. Once operations start, I don't know when we'll get any downtime again and I don't want anyone falling out on me." He stood up and stretched his lower back out. "That goes for you too," he said to Kage.

"Of course," was the insincere reply. Of everyone on the crew, even Twingo, Kage was the one who seemed utterly incapable of keeping calm before an operation. Jason had thought he would eventually acclimate, but every time the little Veran sat there buzzing, like he was hooked directly to the slip reactor. But, he had never once failed to perform during a mission so Jason let him be. Instead, he made his way down to the galley for a quick, light meal before doing his rounds to check on the rest of the crew individually.

He found Lucky in the armory cleaning weapons while Crusher laid across one of the benches snoring like thunderstorm. "Cleaning weapons you don't even use?" Jason asked with a laugh in his voice.

"I am just trying to make sure I pull my weight, as you like to say, Captain," Lucky replied quietly.

"You do that and then some, my friend." Jason watched him for a moment more. The polar opposite of Kage, Lucky was calm and serene just before a mission, even though he was often the pointy end of the spear on dangerous ground operations. He knew the synth had a full range of emotions he was beginning to explore, but he seemed to be able to keep his anxiety from ever showing. The only time Jason had seen him show any stress was when he was in a large crowd and people were staring at him. "So... any regrets about signing on with this outfit?" Lucky stopped cleaning the plasma rifle he had broken down and turned to his captain.

"No offense intended, but is this not an odd time for a discussion like this?

"Maybe. But we've got nothing to do for another seven hours at least, so I may just be trying to distract myself," Jason said as he fidgeted with tools on the bench.

"Distract yourself from what?" Lucky asked, now focusing all his attention on Jason.

"What could happen if we fail," he admitted. "Before, it was just an abstract fact that ships were getting attacked. Now, we're in the thick of it, and a misstep on my part means a lot of people will die for no other reason than some sick bastard wants to prove a point."

"But we cannot let the fear of failure stop us from trying. We have made our plans as best we could under the circumstances, and we will try our best when we arrive. Fear and guilt will not save a single life, Captain. Having the courage to try, and even fail, is what makes a difference," Lucky turned to look at Crusher's sleeping form before continuing. "Since I have been a member of Omega Force I have saved untold lives, helped those who had given up all hope, and made friends like I never dared to hope for in my previous life. So, yes, I am still happy I am here in the place you have made for us."

"I didn't make anything, Lucky," Jason told the synth. "We were all broken in some way or another when we were forced together." The pair fell silent as they each thought about what the other had said. "Well, that's enough introspection. I'm going to go fuck with Twingo."

"I hope that you are able to come to terms with the consequences of when we fail one day, Captain, as we inevitably must," Lucky said as Jason stood up. He paused, but didn't reply as he left the armory and headed for the engineering bay. Every time he engaged Lucky in any sort of meaningful conversation he was forced to again reevaluate how he viewed the synth. At each turn, the artificial man was forcing Jason to come to terms with what his humanity really meant to him out among the stars.

The last couple of hours before they hit their objective seemed to crawl by at an ever-slowing pace. Everyone was rested, prepped, and at their station as the *Phoenix* hurtled through the ether of slip-space towards the unsuspecting colonist fleet. They had brought all the weapons and defensive systems online already and were ready for anything when they meshed in. The plan had them breaking into real-space quite close to the target so as to not give them any time to escape. They were to catch them at their last rally point before they would make their final slip-space hop to their ultimate destination. Larger civil fleets tended to make long journeys in a series of jumps so they would know if a ship was having trouble keeping up and to not get too spread out. Jason just hoped their navigators were of the precise sort since they were planning on meshing in relatively close to their intended position.

"It's almost show time," Jason said over the open intra-ship com channel. "Everybody give me one more check-in and then get ready for anything." One by one his crew checked in with an affirmative status, so then it was down to a tense fifteen minute countdown until they arrived.

5... 4... 3... 2... 1...

"...*break off and retreat! I repeat, break off the attack, they were waiting for us!*" The voice that broke over the secure com channel sounded stressed, but not panicked. Jason watched as the sensors began populating his tactical display and noticed there were seven more ships than they were expecting, one of which was familiar: the *Diligent*. He knew his own ship would be recognized by Captain Colleren's crew, but the remaining six looked like Eshquarian light-cruisers who would have no idea the *Phoenix* was on their side. He also saw that two of the raider ships were drifting dead in space, their momentum taking them away from the battle as they tumbled powerlessly.

"It looks like everyone's making a break for it," Kage said as he watched the sensor feed. "Should we follow?" Jason didn't answer immediately as he watched the remaining raiders turn and accelerate away from the defending fleet, a few winking off the display as they meshed out of the system. Even though they had jumped in close, he had begun decelerating as soon as he heard the com traffic so they were just now coming into the outer effective range for the cruisers' weaponry, he was assuming Colleren wouldn't fire on him with her frigate's larger main guns.

"One raider is losing power," Doc said before Jason could respond to Kage. "They took a nasty shot from one of the cruisers and are no longer accelerating."

"I see them," Jason confirmed as the ship in question rotated around to bring its forward weapons and shields to bear as it shot away along its original heading. "It looks like they've lost their engines, but not main power."

"That's the ship the commands were being broadcast from," Kage said. "Uh, oh... looks like Captain Colleren is going hunting." On his display Jason could see the *Diligent* break formation and begin accelerating towards the stricken ship. It looked like they would close into weapons range within minutes. Playing a hunch, Jason swung onto a course that would bring him up behind the *Diligent* and accelerated away from the colonist fleet. He happily saw that the Eshquarian ships had no intention of pursuing him.

"Dial the forward plasma cannons back to ten percent power," he said.

"Ten percent?" Kage asked. "That will just make a big flash against their shields."

"Just do it. I don't have time to explain," Jason said while he lined them up directly behind the *Diligent* and accelerated hard. *I really hope she understands what I'm doing.* When he was within range, and the larger *Diligent* was directly between the *Phoenix* and the stricken raider, he opened fire with the forward plasma cannons. With the power being so low, the bolts hit the frigate's aft shields and flared in a spectacular coronal discharge, but caused no damage. He continued to accelerate past the *Diligent* at an incredible velocity and bore down on the still-drifting raider. It was a tense few seconds before he got confirmation that Captain Colleren had understood his ploy.

"The *Diligent* is breaking off," Kage reported. "She's decelerating and turning to rejoin the fleet."

"Good," Jason breathed out, relieved. "Lucky, Crusher, get to the cargo bay and get ready to bring that other crew aboard. This is a rescue, but don't trust them."

"Copy."

"Whoever the point man for this operation was is on that ship," he explained to his somewhat bewildered crew. "We're more likely to make a large gain by rescuing him than letting the *Diligent* capture him and turn him over to the Eshquarians." With the aid of the computer, Jason began the delicate dance of matching speed and orientation to the other ship and slowly closed the gap until Kage could extend the ventral gangway and link up to their airlock. "You know the drill," he said as he hopped out of his seat. "If that ship makes a suspicious move... blast it."

Jason jogged through the ship and arrived in the cargo bay just as the drop-hatch in the floor was irising open. Immediately the acrid smell of burning composites and wire assaulted them through the opening. Lucky reached into the opening and grabbed a coughing and injured man who looked like he had some serious burns on the right side of his body. When Lucky laid him on the cargo bay floor Jason could see who it was, and he was quite honestly shocked: Dowarty. *Why is this little weasel out here on an op?*

"Is there anybody else alive in there?" Jason asked him loudly. The small man only shook his head, his eyes squeezed shut against the pain. "You're sure?" Only a nod in response. "Kage, cut us loose and move us away…" Dowarty's left hand reached up and grabbed his wrist.

"Destroy my ship, Captain," he whispered before passing out.

"Better get up here, Captain. One of the Eshquarian cruisers has started to head this way."

"Get him to the infirmary," Jason told Lucky. "I'll send Doc down there in a minute." He ran back up to the bridge and saw that the cruiser wasn't accelerating too quickly, so they had some time before there was a risk. Once he confirmed they were floating free from the damaged ship, he moved them away to a safe distance and brought the nose back around.

"Target the aft drive section and the reactor core," Jason told Kage.

"Target locked."

Jason squeezed the trigger on the stick and let loose a salvo of high-energy plasma bolts into the unprotected vessel's main drive and reactor. A brief, explosive flash and all that was left was a cloud of high-density metal particles drifting outward. Satisfied, he turned them about and accelerated away from the closing cruiser while Kage entered a jump point into the nav system. Once they had meshed out of the system, Jason hopped up and went to check on Dowarty in the infirmary.

Chapter 11

"He looks bad," Jason observed.

"He isn't great," Doc confirmed. "He has significant burns over much of his body, but the immediate danger is the caustic fumes he was breathing in on his ship. I've stabilized him and the nanobots are beginning to map out the damage to his lungs, in the meantime I'll be oxygenating his blood artificially. It could have been worse though, his hearts are beating strong and his brain scans show normal activity."

This little wisp has more than one heart? They must be the size of walnuts.

"We're heading back to the Oorch system," Jason said as he looked down on the small facilitator. "We'll hang out just inside the heliopause until he regains consciousness and..." He broke off as he saw Dowarty's personal effects laid out on the far table, much like his own were when he was first brought into the infirmary by Deetz. Among the various decorative pieces of jewelry was an only slightly singed miniature tablet computer. "Kage! Get down here," he called over the intercom.

"What's up?" Kage asked as he rushed into the infirmary a moment later.

"Can you do anything with this?"

"Hmm," was all the Veran said as he grasped the computer in the smaller of his four hands. Silver threads of nanobots seemed to spin from his hands like a spider's web as they glided over the surface of the computer, searching for a way to make a hard circuit path that would enable Kage, with his highly specialized neural implants, to try and access the unit. His eyes glazed over for a moment and Jason realized how well secured the small device must have been; he'd seen Kage slice through supposedly locked-down systems within seconds.

"The encryption is top-notch," he finally said. "I can't break it without dismantling the unit, and even then there may be safeties in place to let him know I've been there."

"So it's useless to us?" Jason asked, trying to not let his disappointment show.

"Maybe not," Kage said, again seeming to drift off. After a much shorter pause he was back; "There is a flaw in the device's security."

"I was hoping you'd find at least one," Jason smiled.

"It's not a guarantee, but I can copy the entire contents off the storage medium. It's sort of like cloning a computer core; it will exist on a section of our computer and the software on the device will never know it was tampered with since no attempt at forcible entry was made. Then I can try and slice into the copy stored on our computer."

"That seems like a glaring security flaw," Doc said. "You sure it's not a trap?"

"It's designed to protect against direct slicing attempts," Kage explained. "There's no external connectors, so it's not likely someone could attempt this without permanently damaging the unit. The outer case cracked during the fight, however, and I can just fit four pairs of nanite tendrils into the gap."

"Go ahead and start," Jason decided. "You're routing the data stream through your implants and into the main computer?"

"Yes."

"Keep alert then, if anything suspicious happens break the connection."

"You got it, Captain," Kage was already getting comfortable in a chair. "With only four pairs the data stream is going to be a bit thin, this could take a few hours."

Jason simply nodded to Doc, who reached up without question and adjusted the stream of sedatives being pumped into Dowarty to ensure he didn't awake at an inopportune moment. With Doc and Kage busy, Jason felt he was just in the way, so he walked out of the infirmary and back towards the bridge.

*   *   *   *   *

He must have dozed off sitting in the pilot's seat because Jason nearly jumped out of his skin when Kage's voice came over the intercom; *"We're all set, Captain. The copy went off without any trouble. Doc says this guy is ready to wake up if you want to come down here."*

"On my way," he replied through a yawn. He hopped out of his seat and made his way back down to the infirmary. There was quite the crowd when he arrived, Doc and Kage were both still there, but sometime during the previous few hours Lucky decided an armed guard needed to be present. "Kage, why don't you head on back to the bridge? The less people it seems to have been rifling through his stuff, the better."

"Probably not a bad idea," Kage said wearily and walked off without any further argument. Jason watched him trudge off, practically dragging his feet. *The data transfer must have taken a lot out of him.*

"Ok, Doc," he said, "let's wake him up." Doc reached over and shut off sedative stream and injected Dowarty with a mild stimulant and stood back expectantly. Within minutes Dowarty's eyes began to flutter and the small alien looked around in alarm.

"Relax," Jason said firmly, stepping into his field of vision. "You're on my ship, we pulled you out of your own flaming wreckage. Remember?" He watched as Dowarty slowly relaxed and finally nodded his head, closing his eyes at the pain.

"I apologize for the discomfort," Doc said as he saw the grimace. "There were some questions about drug interaction and, of course, the substantial injuries you sustained. Now that you're awake I can go ahead and up the dosage and observe for any adverse reaction."

"Thank you, doctor," Dowarty said, finally gathering up the energy to speak. His voice came out in a raspy croak, but he seemed lucid enough. "It seems I owe you a great debt, Captain."

"Don't worry," Jason said offhandedly. "I'm sure you're good for it."

"A true mercenary, through and through," Dowarty said with a painful sounding chuckle. "Where are we currently?"

"We've retreated back to the outer edges of the Oorch System," Jason said. "With the ambush by the Eshquarian fleet we're not sure if Oorch Prime is still a safe harbor, so we're not chancing it just yet."

"Very prudent, Captain," Dowarty approved. "You're correct, the Oorch operation may well be compromised after the attack we just survived. If you'd be so kind as to give me a bit more time to recover, I'll be able to direct you to a safe place to regroup and avoid any other unpleasant engagements. I will, of course, make it worth your time."

"Sure, at this point I'd say our fortunes are linked together. At least for the time being," Jason shrugged. "You're superiors won't mind you making contracts on the fly like this?" Another rasping, coughing laugh.

"I can assure you, they will be fine with whatever decisions I make," he said, confirming some of Jason's suspicions about his actual place within whatever organization he represented. "You destroyed my ship as I asked?"

"Oh yeah," Jason laughed. "That thing is nothing but vapor."

"Another thanks for that, then," Dowarty said, his head sinking down into the pillow as the effort to talk sapped his strength. He opened his eyes one more time, "I had a small computer when you pulled me off my ship..." Wordlessly Doc handed the small tablet to him. Dowarty clutched at it with his bandaged hands and pulled it tightly to his chest. "It is most fortunate that it survived." A few minutes later and the steady rise and fall of his chest told the others he had fallen asleep.

"Lucky, would you mind keeping watch over our guest?" Jason asked the synth, who had been standing silently during the exchange.

"Of course not, Captain," he answered. "I had intended to do so anyway."

"Thanks. Doc, if there's no particular reason for you to stay, I could probably use you on the bridge," Jason said, giving Doc a meaningful look as he did.

"Of course," Doc said, understanding immediately. "He'll likely sleep for a while more and I have some things I should be doing up there anyway." The two turned and exited the infirmary, leaving Lucky to stand watch over the presumably sleeping Dowarty.

"So," Jason asked once everyone had made their way up to the bridge. "How does this change our plans? And Kage... could you unplug for a minute?" The Veran was sitting at one of the sensor stations and was hooked directly into the ship's computer, obviously working on cracking the download from Dowarty's computer.

"Sure, Captain, just give me..."

"Now," Jason said firmly. He wasn't being intentionally harsh, but Kage would become more and more enamored with the problem he was working on until he tuned them all out completely. With obvious reluctance, he paused the processes he had been running and pulled his hands away from the terminal, raising all four to prove he was completely disconnected. Jason just stared at him, not breaking eye contact as he accessed the ship's computer via his own terminal and shut down the wireless links on the bridge.

"Oh!" Kage exclaimed. "I must have forgot about that one."

"You really don't think I learn, do you?" Jason asked rhetorically. "Anyway... Lucky is currently guarding Dowarty down in our infirmary, who is sleeping a bit more to try and heal up some before we make our next move. I'm assuming he's going to negotiate for us to get him back to his own people. Thoughts?"

"It could work to our advantage," Doc said speculatively. "That's assuming he's not just going to arrange for another of his own ships to meet up with us to hand him off."

"That's doubtful," Crusher offered. "He's likely to assume that someone in his own organization tipped off the Eshquarians, he may have us fly him all the way to their main base of operations. At least that's what I'd do."

"Yeah, but we're not sure if he's going to suspect that we tipped off the military," Kage said, his hands fidgeting in his lap.

"We're probably in the clear there," Jason disagreed. "It'd be almost impossible to trace the Eshquarian fleet movement to us, not without someone on the *Diligent* being a traitor."

"So what do we offer him?" Crusher asked.

"We'll keep playing the money hungry pirates, for now. If he knows we can be trusted so long as the pay keeps coming in, I think we're in an advantageous position," Jason answered. "We really could be rolling up on the endgame soon; if he has us fly him to their main base then we simply make a discreet exit and call in the cavalry."

"You think an underling like that would risk exposing their operation?" Doc asked.

"I think Dowarty has been quite good at hiding who he really is," Jason argued. "His multiple personalities aside, too much evidence points to him being a *lot* higher up than a simple errand boy."

"So we're agreed?" Kage asked eagerly. "We keep playing along for now until we can call in the Eshquarian fleet if we find their main base. Simple and brilliant, Captain." Jason affixed him with a steady glare even as he reactivated the links for his neural implants. A broad smile came over the Veran's face as he turned to his terminal and dove back into his work.

"Remember, Kage," Jason warned. "I still need you to fly right-seat, so don't get too comfortable there." He looked around a moment before snapping irritably, "Where the fuck is Twingo?" He was more annoyed at himself that he hadn't noticed his engineer was missing during their strategy meeting.

"Sleeping," Kage answered absently. "Don't worry, I'll be ready to fly when you are." Jason took in a deep breath, held it, and let it out slowly.

"Nice of him to let me know he was going off shift," he said simply as he exited the bridge. Doc had already left, presumably to monitor his patient, so Jason did a quick flyby of the galley to grab a sandwich and a glass of water. The plan was thin, even by their standards, but like most aspects of this mission; it was all they had. It felt solid enough that he was fairly certain they would find the base that had so far eluded the authorities, but he also knew these people were smart enough not to just let them go off on their merry way with a cheerful wave. An organization like this survived by being smarter than the people hunting for them, and letting an unknown group of strangers find your main logistical hub, and then simply leave, wasn't all that smart. So, the trick will be to convince them to let them leave once they have the location. Not an easy trick by any means.

"Captain Burke, please come to the infirmary," Doc's voice came over the intercom. He winced as his real name was used in front of Dowarty. *I had thought we'd progressed past these rookie mistakes...*

When Jason entered the infirmary Dowarty was sitting up slightly and appeared to be quite a bit more alert than the last time he'd seen him. "Captain... Burke, was it?... Odd name. Anyway, I think I'm well enough that we can progress to our destination, but it will require that I be on the bridge with you."

"If you think you're up to it," Jason said, giving Doc a hard stare.

"I think I'm as ready as I will be for some time," Dowarty said, starting to swing his legs over the side. Jason slapped Lucky's arm;

"Help him up to the bridge. I'll meet you there."

"Yes, Captain."

Jason hustled out of the infirmary and towards the engineering bays to let Twingo know they would be getting under way shortly.

"Ok, Dowarty," Jason said from the pilot's seat. "Where the hell are we going?" Instead of answering, Dowarty activated his tablet computer and went through an insanely convoluted recognition ritual before he could access the information inside. He scrolled through various menus, entered some commands, but still provided no answer. Just when Jason started to become seriously irritated he rose from his seat in obvious pain and shuffled towards him. Jason pointed to Kage, causing the injured alien to turn and trudge around the command dais to show the Veran the display. Kage took a seemingly cursory glance at the display and began entering the information into the nav system without so much as a grunt. Jason cringed inside as Dowarty fixed a suspicious glare on their flighty code slicer before moving back around to his own seat. He started entering commands frantically into his computer the moment he had situated himself. *Probably trying to see if our slicer tried to break into it. I hope Kage was right about the security protocols.*

"We're only six hours away at maximum slip velocity," Kage said as he transferred control of the slip-drive to Jason.

264

"That close?" Jason asked, surprised. "Let's get on it then; I'm sure Dowarty is good for the fuel tab."

"You can be assured of that, Captain," Dowarty said in a labored breath. He had slipped his computer back into the pocket of the odd, tunic-like garment he wore, apparently satisfied no attempt had been made to crack it. *Either that or his poker face is as good as Lucky's.* Jason remembered when he had first met the man and he had appeared as a servile boot-licker, now he seemed very accustomed to being in charge. His duplicity at every turn meant no amount of body language would let them know what he did, or didn't know until it was too late.

"Meshing out now," Jason announced unnecessarily as he slapped the control to send the *Phoenix* streaking towards their destination; an open patch of space within a gaseous protuberance of the nebula that spawned the Cluster. It was probably a nightmare of gravitational anomalies and interstellar particles, but he assumed Dowarty had shown them a safe route given he was on the same ship they were.

They rode in silence for the most part, limiting their chatter to terse status updates with an interloper sitting amongst them. Kage had found a new way to communicate, however, and gave it a try as they all pretended to be fascinated by the displays in front of them:

"I THINK WE MAY HAVE A PROBLEM." The text appeared to float in Jason's field of vision and he realized that it was being projected by his ocular implants. He blinked and looked around, trying to decipher the source. *"THIS IS KAGE, BY THE WAY."* Jason rolled his eyes, he should have realized who would be able to hack into his neural implant. Since he had no idea how to reply he made a rolling gesture with his right hand to indicate to Kage that he should continue. *"I CAN'T BE CERTAIN, BUT I THINK DOWARTY IS TRYING TO ACCESS OUR COMPUTER THROUGH HIS HANDHELD."* Jason tried to think of a way to reply, but came up with a blank. Now it was Kage's turn to roll his eyes. *"THAT'S WHY I'M ACCSSING YOUR IMPLANT DIRECTLY, I DON'T WANT TO RISK HIM INTERCEPTING A MESSAGE TO YOUR CONSOLE. I'M GETTING SOME SUSPICIOUS ACTIVITY PIGGYBACKING ROUTINE DATA PACKETS. SHOULD I LOCK HIM OUT, OR BEGIN ISOLATING ALL OUR SENSITIVE DATA THAT'S IN THE COM CENTER?"*

Jason held up his right hand with his first two fingers raised, indicating he wanted the second option. He didn't want Dowarty knowing they were on to him, if he was indeed trying to break into his ship's main computer. Fortunately, due to the nature of the DL7's original purpose, the com center that was located in a small room on the command deck had isolated computers that stored sensitive com traffic and intel data. Those cores could be disconnected, and even remotely destroyed, in the event any attempt was made to break into the main computer. As a warship that was often tasked for reconnaissance, Jepsen Aero had had the forethought to make safeguarding their sensitive information as easy as sending a command with the proper coding.

After some more seemingly innocent plinking at his computer, Dowarty put it back into his pocket and leaned back in his chair, staring off into space for a moment before his eyes slowly closed. Since he couldn't do much more, Jason pulled up all information their computer had on the region of space they were flying towards and settled in for some dry, boring facts on astral navigation and interstellar phenomena. *As the captain of an interstellar space ship I should probably be more interested in this shit.*

The *Phoenix* dropped back into real-space right at the edge of the nebula, but with the distances and dimensions involved, there really wasn't much to see. There was also no ship or space station on the sensors. "You put in the coordinates correctly?" Jason asked Kage.

"I'm sure he did, Captain," Dowarty said before Kage could answer. He had gotten up again and walked over to Kage with his computer display active. "Please send out this repeating message on the indicated frequency from your slip-transceiver. We won't have long to wait after that." Kage looked to Jason, who nodded his ascent, and then began to program the sequence into their primary com node. It wasn't even encrypted, but it included their current position. Apparently whoever was to receive the message would be able to contact them for further directions. "Forgive the secrecy, but we can't be too careful," Dowarty said to Jason.

"No sweat off my brow," he shrugged with an exaggerated indifference. "I'm being paid to drop you off, however you want that accomplished is between you and your credit chit." Dowarty simply smiled indulgently and made his way back to the seat he had occupied during the flight out.

Another ninety minutes elapsed before they had any confirmation their message was received. A small, autonomous, slip-drive equipped drone flashed into real-space near their position, transmitted a coded burst, and then meshed back out just as quickly as it had appeared. Jason looked at Dowarty expectantly. Instead of answering, he again pulled out his abused tablet computer and accessed it.

"Could you scroll that message in a loop on one of these displays, please?" He asked.

"Sure," Kage answered and complied with the request. On the terminal in front of Dowarty a raw, encrypted data stream began to scrawl across. He simply held the tablet up so it could "see" the screen and waited for a moment before a double beep from his device told him the process was complete. When he turned it around it had a new set of coordinates clearly displayed. He smiled as he showed Kage the new destination as well as the new transponder code they would need to squawk when they arrived. "Simple, but elegant," Kage said admiringly at Dowarty's sign-countersign encryption scheme. His tablet had held the key and the slip-drone had given him the data to decode

268

to provide them with the exact location of the base. "We're ready, Captain. It's only another forty minutes away," Kage informed him.

"Here goes nothing," Jason said as he re-engaged the slip-drive. Once the canopy darkened and the engines were humming out their hypnotic song, he pondered the nature of their destination. It couldn't be a fixed base on a planet or moon, otherwise there wouldn't be the need for such an elaborate method of gaining access. It could be a station, but those weren't very mobile. Even the big commercial harvesters were broken down and flown separately to the work site. He also didn't think it was a ship, not to support the size and scope of an operation that was attacking shipping lanes up and down the entire Cluster. He resisted the urge to ask Dowarty directly as it would break character with the hired gun mentality he was trying to project. *I guess I'll just have to wait and see like everyone else.*

"Everyone look sharp, we're five minutes out," Jason announced to his crew as he prepared the ship to re-enter real-space. Kage started transmitting their passcode a few seconds before they meshed in, it wouldn't be received, but there wouldn't be a delay from their appearance to their code confirmation. Sometimes those precious few seconds were the difference between one arriving safely or being blasted to one's assorted molecules.

The gunship shuddered slightly as she flashed back into real-space. Immediately upon their arrival, their defensive systems began blaring alerts and putting a threat assessment on their displays. There were a *lot* of ships sitting in that region of space with their weapons charged. Jason didn't hesitate as he abruptly brought the *Phoenix* to a virtual standstill, the gravimetric drive killing their forward momentum so they didn't drift into weapons range before they could confirm that they belonged there. It was a tense few seconds before they had their answer.

"Unidentified vessel, we have confirmed your passcode. You're clear to approach The Complex."

"Don't worry, Captain," Dowarty said with a smile. "They wouldn't have opened fire until they verified friend or foe."

"You'll forgive me if I don't want to bet my ship, or my life, on that," Jason retorted as he throttled up the drive and steered on course for the largest sensor contact, assuming it to be The Complex. Whatever that was.

One of the things Jason had found difficult to adjust to was his instinct to look out the canopy to view objects that were "close." This may have been from watching too many science fiction movies, or just a lack of comprehension about the vast distances involved, but either way after a little over two years in space he still looked up expecting to see The Complex looming large in front of him. Instead, he saw a small speck of light moving slightly faster than the other specks of light against the backdrop of space. This region was a little more interesting thanks to the copious amounts of interstellar gas they were flying through, but that was mostly due to it reacting with their anti-collision shields.

At their rate of closure, Jason didn't have long to wait before he did get his first eyes-on view of The Complex, and what he saw concerned him tremendously. The Complex looked to be six large cargo haulers that had been highly modified so that they could be docked to each other and form a sort of space station. The advantages were immediately apparent: the station could be broken down into its base components (the ships themselves) and slip-spaced out of any location, and on different vectors, only to meet up again and reform the base later. He was sure each ship provided a unique function and that it was all very well engineered and constructed... and that's what concerned him the most. This type of thing was *not* employed by a gang of pirates and smugglers no matter how well organized they were. This type of operation positively reeked of military, and it gave Jason grave misgivings about who may be responsible for the attacks on civilians within the Concordian Cluster.

"Impressive, isn't it?" Dowarty's question broke him out of his musings.

"That's one word for it," Jason said. "I'll admit, I've seen a lot of crazy shit while in this line of work... but nothing like a bunch of pirates building a mobile space station."

"Oh, we're more than just pirates," Dowarty said drily. "We also smuggle, kill, overthrow governments... we're equal opportunity entrepreneurs."

"Whatever pays the bills," Jason replied just as deadpan. "You getting docking instructions?" His question was directed at Kage.

"Coming in now, I'll give you fly-to indicators in a moment and tell the computer which docking arm we're supposed to head for," Kage replied. Jason was silently elated they were heading to a docking berth instead of a hanger. Hangers were quite a bit more challenging to escape from when, invariably, the mission went belly up on them. A docking arm was usually a flimsy structure that wasn't even remotely capable of holding them in place if they really wanted to leave.

The closer they got, the more detail of the docking complex he could make out; a spider's web-like network of airlock gangways that had a smattering of ships linked to it, looking like so many flies in the aforementioned web. They were being directed to a tall spire that, when docked, would give them a decent view over the entire Complex. All things being equal, Jason couldn't complain about their position if they were forced to make a quick getaway. He relinquished his grip of the controls as the computer used the thrusters to gently nudge the gunship against the docking collar and allowed it to lock onto the hull.

"We're all locked up," Jason said. "Dowarty, I assume you'd like me to accompany you to arrange for our payment?"

"I could have your money brought up, or you could come with me. Whichever you prefer, Captain," Dowarty said with a humorless smile.

"I could stand to stretch my legs a bit," Jason replied blandly, making it clear that he didn't trust the smaller man to return with their payment.

"As you see best," Dowarty agreed, already making his way slowly off the bridge and towards the airlock.

"Crusher, you and Doc are with me," Jason said as he eyed the retreating back of their injured passenger. He held up a hand to stop Lucky's protest before it started; "I need you on the ship. We're in the belly of the beast right now and I can't leave the *Phoenix* unprotected by taking all our fighters with me."

"So what do you want us to do?" Twingo asked.

"Keep her ready to rock and roll, that includes keeping the weapons ready. I want the quick-start capacitors fully charges, but keep the emitters and projectors cold; I don't want a causal scan to reveal we're armed up for war while docked."

"You can count on us," Kage said absently as he turned back to his computer console, already focusing all his considerable mental power on his pet project of Dowarty's computer download.

Jason, Doc, and Crusher jogged to meet Dowarty at the airlock. Thanks to the other man's injuries, it wasn't too difficult.

"What's the procedure for coming aboard?" Jason asked.

"Just open the door, Captain," Dowarty smiled. "If you weren't authorized to be here this ship would have been destroyed well before docking." That was good enough for Jason, who shrugged and cycled the outer hatch. The gangway that led down and away from the ship was empty, Jason half expected some sort of armed escort or at least a guard. *There must really be honor among thieves here.*

They followed Dowarty at a snail's pace down the curving passageway until they came to a bank of lift doors within a larger room. The space also had a half-dozen other passageways branching out in all directions to other docking points. As they approached one of the lifts, the doors slid open and revealed what Jason had been expecting all along: armed guards. In addition to the guards, who looked to be pros, there was an alien of a species Jason couldn't place who looked like *she?* was probably a doctor and was pushing a type of wheelchair.

The guards nodded respectfully at Dowarty, but kept their eyes on Jason and his crewmates.

"Sir, we must get you to medical at once, there's no telling what some hack of a pirate medic has done to you," the doctor said in a distinctly feminine voice. As Dowarty sat in the chair Doc cleared his throat loudly.

"*I* stabilized his condition by injecting class two medical nanites into his bloodstream to begin repairing the damage to his lungs due to the inhalation of caustic fumes, applied synthetic skin layers to the more severely burned areas of his epidermis, and kept him relaxed and asleep with a mild universal sedative so his body could begin to recuperate naturally. I can transmit his treatment record from my ship if you'd like." Doc's speech had that insufferable tone of superiority to it that Jason thought had been burned out of him by now. The other doctor simply stared at Doc and harrumphed before wheeling Dowarty back into the lift.

"Please show our guests to the crew rest area while I'm being worked on," Dowarty ordered his armed escort as the doors slid shut to the lift. Jason looked to the hired goons expectantly.

"This way," one said simply as he led the way to the far set of lift doors. They all climbed in, Crusher ducking a bit as he did so, and rode the lift tube into the heart of the ship they were docked to. Jason quickly gave up trying to keep track of where they were in the ship, the twists and turns were simply too convoluted. There was evidence everywhere of the heavy, and hasty, modifications the ship had gone through to be part of the linked space station that it helped comprise. But even within the chaos of the construction Jason could see a definite purpose, this was no haphazard idea that evolved slowly over time. The nature of The Complex distressed him greatly, there was no way in hell this sprang up just as a convenient dock for pirates and smugglers.

"You'll be staying in this area until called for," the same guard spoke to Jason as they approached a large set of heavy doors that were flanked by another pair of guards. "Do not try to escape, do not try and tamper with the ship's functions, and try not to kill any of your fellow low-life friends."

"Escape?" Jason asked innocently. "That would imply we are prisoners. I'm just here for my just rewards for the safe return of your leader." The guard just stared at him with thinly veiled contempt and keyed the door open.

"Get in, or you can go back to your ship and leave when you're given clearance." Jason shrugged and led the way in. *He didn't flinch or try to correct me when I mentioned Dowarty was in charge around here.* As soon as the door slid shut a familiar, and wholly unwelcome, ambiance assaulted his senses. It was the same miasma that clung to the walls of every seedy tavern or gamers hall they'd been in during their time on the job. It was an obnoxious combination of poor hygiene that manifested itself differently across a dozen different species as well as the spilled drinks, spilled bodily fluids, and whatever disgusting off-world muck was treaded in on boots.

They were in a large common area that was dotted with tables and couches, off of that were alcoves and passageways that led away to other parts of that section of the station. After a moment Jason began to pick his way among the scattered beings lounging around. "Let's find a quiet corner to wait this out."

"I couldn't agree more," Crusher said with obvious disgust in his voice. As they made their way around the perimeter of the common area Jason could see one of the passageways seemed to lead to a bar of some sort. He was in no mood for a drink, but places like that seemed to be the best location to pick up intel on the locale.

As they made their way down the darkened corridor they became aware of the branching alcoves that jutted off of the main passage and were covered with thin, decorative curtains. The pitiful sounds coming from beyond that flimsy barrier left little to the imagination as to what was happening just out of view. Jason's jaw set in an angry line and, seemingly before he realized he was doing it, was making his way for the first alcove. Kidnapping females on raids was hardly rare, nor was holding them captive in such a depraved and vicious manner, but it was one of the few times Jason had been personally close enough to do something about it. Before he reached the curtain Doc grabbed his shoulder and spun him around.

"Are you insane!? We're trying to keep a low profile so we can get out of here," he hissed. Jason looked at him with open contempt.

"So you're perfectly content to allow that to continue?"

"Of course not, don't you dare insult me like that," Doc said vehemently, still keeping his voice down. "But we're trying to save the lives of hundreds, maybe even thousands. What do you think will happen? These animals will see the error of their ways? Or is it more likely we'll be swarmed and torn apart? Is the life of one person worth all that?"

"I don't know... maybe we could have asked your sister, had she survived such a place..." Doc struck so quick that Jason didn't have time to block or dodge at all, and the punch hit him square in the mouth, snapping his head back and drawing blood.

"You sanctimonious ass," Doc snarled, shaking. "You think a day goes by I don't think of her and what was done? Why do you think I'm here? I'm answering *your* call to action; to step in and end this type of thing..." He trailed off at Jason's enraged glare, realizing the fatal flaw in his own logic.

"We're starting to attract attention," Crusher murmured. "Let's take this someplace else."

"Good idea," Jason said, hitting Doc with his shoulder as he brushed by the pair and made his way towards their original destination.

The next twenty minutes sitting at a corner table were tense, to say the least. Doc and Jason refused to meet each other's gaze or otherwise acknowledge the other's presence. Crusher watched this as long as he could before rolling his eyes and standing up.

"I'm going to walk the perimeter of this place and get a feel for the layout," he said, glaring down at the pair. "When I get back, this bullshit better be done with. We have things to do that are too important to have them jeopardized with your infantile squabbling." Jason glared at the warrior's departing back; he didn't appreciate hearing that his righteous indignation in reality was making him look like a jackass with a maturity problem. Doc broke the thick silence first;

"I'm sorry I hit you... Captain."

"I guess I deserved it. I'm sorry I brought up your sister, Jorvren," Jason said, using Doc's real first name for the first time since he had given him his nickname. "I was out of line. I hope you can forgive me."

"I understand, Jason, I really do," Doc said, also dropping rank and monikers from their conversation. "I feel much like you do, but I'm used to *not* being able to directly do anything about it. I don't have the strength or training you and Crusher do, and I was serious about answering to a higher calling. While I would have never dreamed that I'd end up in a crew like Omega Force, I'm committed to the idea that the few of us really can make a real difference."

"Ok," Jason said brusquely, not entirely comfortable with all the soul-baring. "We're both sorry, so let's move on to something that's been bugging me. This space station was purpose-built, and by pros."

"Agreed," Doc said. "And they're also keeping us low-lives segregated from the operational centers and the regular crew. These are significant, but I'm not entirely sure why yet."

It was another fifteen minutes before Crusher ambled back over to their table, the other patrons giving him a wide berth as he didn't bother trying to dodge them. He sat down and leaned in conspiratorially, "This seems to be a holding pen for the pirates and other assorted scumbags being used to pull off these raids. Every once in a while the guards open up the main doors and send a runner in to bring out one person or another, but other than that nobody ventures out of this area."

"We were just discussing that," Jason said. "I'm starting to think the dimwits in here are simply a distraction, or camouflage. If one, or even a few, are caught it just looks like an uptick in crime. These aren't all local boys either; there isn't enough work to go around in the Cluster to support an underworld this extensive. I feel like we're missing some critical piece to all this."

"So where does that leave us?" Doc asked.

"Fuck if I know. But I doubt it's anyplace good. We're either going to be roped into participating in another raid or we're not going to be allowed to leave at all," Jason said glumly.

As it turned out, none of them were entirely correct. A pair of guards entered the small bar area and, after a brief look over the room, walked directly to the three. "We're to escort you outside," the one said simply.

"What for?" Crusher asked belligerently.

"To receive payment for the rescue and transport of Dowarty," the guard said, giving no indication that Crusher's demeanor was getting under his skin.

"Lead on," Jason said as he stood up from the table.

They followed the guards back through the stinking common area they had entered through and into the open space beyond, each taking a refreshing breath of shipboard air that had been scrubbed by the recyclers. Dowarty himself was waiting for them, now changed and apparently feeling much better after a trip through the Complex's medical facility.

"Gentlemen," he smiled broadly. "I believe we have an account to settle up. I don't wish to be rude, but the quicker you're paid, the quicker you can be on your way."

"Can't argue there," Jason said. "We're not making any money sitting around here, as nice as it is."

"Of course. I think you'll find that the amount is far more generous than what we originally agreed to," Dowarty said. "The extra amount is for your... discretion... about what you've seen here. If you agree I'll have it sent to your ship's treasury at once."

"Looks more than fair to me, our added discretion considered," Jason said, not being able to help his eyebrows shooting up at the amount Dowarty had shown him on data tablet.

"Excellent!" Dowarty clapped his hands once, enthusiastically. "Now then, we've got a bit of a situation developing here, so my men will escort you back to your ship where you can await clearance to depart. Know that you have my personal thanks, Captain. Had I or my ship fallen into the hands of the authorities, things could have been quite bad for me."

"Happy to help," Jason said with a forced grin, "and of course happy to lighten your account a tad." Dowarty laughed genuinely at that.

"Worth every credit, I assure you. Between the saving of my life, and creative acquisition of rare antiquities, I'm somewhat sorry to see you depart. I'm including a secured inbox address with your payment, if you ever are looking for work, or even a permanent arrangement, let me know." With that Dowarty turned and walked through a side hatchway before Jason could answer him. Without a word, one of the guards nodded to indicate they should follow him back the way they had originally come towards the lifts that would take them back to the docking arms.

They rode the lift in complete silence until they arrived at the junction that would let them enter the gangway that led back to the *Phoenix*. When they entered the junction, however, they were unprepared for the familiar sight, and sound, of someone they least suspected to see.

"...needs to understand that timing is everything, too much longer and our fleet will be in position to act. Colleston is losing control of the legislature, the time for half measures is over. Tell Dowarty that..."

The other set of lift doors closed, blocking off the remainder of the conversation. But the man had been unmistakable in his fine suit and slick talking manner. It had been Prime Minister Colleston's Chief of Staff: Mr. Kross. Jason and Doc exchanged a meaningful glance before turning back to their escort.

"I suppose this is where we part ways," Jason said. "Good luck with everything you guys are into. Tell control to let us know when we're cleared to depart." When the guard nodded disinterestedly he spun and walked as fast as he could manage up the gangway where his ship was waiting for him. *What the FUCK was Kross doing here? This can't mean anything good.*

"Lock her up and meet us on the bridge," Jason said to Lucky as he rushed through the hatch and ran from the airlock chamber up to the command deck with the others on his heels. When he ran onto the bridge, he was pleased to see Twingo and Kage were alert and looked appropriately worried. *Wait... they don't know what's going on yet. What are they worried about?*

"What?"

"Show him," Twingo said. Wordlessly Kage turned to his panel and projected a time-lapse sensor feed onto the forward canopy. Jason could see three large contacts mesh in, followed by a slew of smaller ships. The passive sensors showed massive energy signatures on the larger ships. That usually indicated one thing: warships.

"Whose are they?" Jason asked, slightly dry mouthed. Three destroyer-class ships was a lot of firepower in the hands of a bunch of "pirates."

"No idea," Kage said. "They came in dark, no transponder squawks. They look to be of the same origin as the ships that make up the station. Same goes for their smaller escort ships. They've parked seventy-thousand kilometers off our starboard side and are holding formation there. This doesn't seem good."

"It's worse than that," Jason said. "Doc?"

"While we were coming back we ran into one Mr. Kross making his way down into The Complex." Doc said.

"Kross? As in Eshquarian Executive Chief of Staff Kross?" Kage asked incredulously.

"One and the same," Jason confirmed. "This was just a few minutes ago. What ships have arrived on this docking junction recently?" Kage's four hands flew over the controls.

"Nothing Eshquarian. There is a private high-speed transport that docked twenty minutes ago and... now *this* is interesting... a ConFed VIP transport came in and docked an hour before that."

"What?!"

"No mistaking it, Captain. They're not transmitting ConFed codes, but the configuration is unmistakable," Kage said with raised hands.

"What in the fuck is going on here?!" Jason asked to nobody in particular. "Ok, we're way out of our league here... as soon as we get cleared to leave, we're jumping a short hop and calling Crisstof to turn this over to him. We're not equipped to handle whatever the hell this is."

"If Kross brought a private transport, we can assume he is not here at the behest of the Eshquarian government," Lucky said.

"That's a safe bet," Twingo said. "And I'm sure that ConFed ship is no coincidence either. So are they really just going to let us fly off, Captain?"

"It seems so," Jason said with a shrug. "Between the theft and the rescue, it seems Dowarty has taken a bit of a shine to us. He also seems to be a lot higher up than we originally thought, Kross mentioned him by name when we passed him."

"Ah, the intrigue of politics," Kage said, suddenly leaning forward in his seat. "Captain, quite a large sum of money has been transmitted to our onboard treasury. Should I accept it?"

"What the hell kind of question is that?!" Crusher exclaimed. "Yes accept it." Kage wisely took that as confirmation as he keyed in their access code to accept the payment from Dowarty.

After another two hours passed, the crew began to get anxious, wondering when their clearance would be granted so they could leave. Jason didn't think they were in any direct danger. Whoever was running the operations center seemed to have more pressing issues than a single, banged-up gunship and its six outlaw occupants. That and it made no sense to torture them with an extended wait just to forcibly board and kill them later when they already had half the crew in their hands.

"Ping their controller," Jason told Kage, who typed a message to transmit to the station's docking controller and leaned back to await the reply. When his console chimed he read it aloud;

"*Unidentified vessel, remain docked until clearance is granted to power your drives and detach. Fleet movements take precedence.*"

"What fleet movements?" Jason wondered. Within the next few minutes he had his answer.

"Captain, the docked raider ships are beginning to power their drives," Twingo said. "It looks like they're all getting ready to leave together."

"Shit. I feel like we're running up on the end of something big here and we're stuck to this dock." Jason worried at his scalp with his right hand and glared at the sensor display that showed ships detaching and drifting up into a loose formation above their relative position in space. The members of Omega Force sat on the bridge of the *Phoenix*, transfixed at the sensor feed of the "pirate fleet" assembling over their heads. For the next sixty minutes different ships within the formation jockeyed for position and the amassed fleet began to separate into three distinct groups and started moving away from the station and towards the edge of the gas pocket they were in.

"There they go," Kage said softly. Sure enough, the indicators on the sensor display started winking out as the raider ships meshed out of the system.

"Fuck!" Jason raged as he smashed his fist into his right-hand console, nearly startling Kage out of his seat. "Where the hell could that many ships be going at one time?"

"Captain, look," Doc said, his eyes also glued to his sensor display. Jason's head snapped around and he saw the recently-arrived fleet of warships also begin accelerating out of the area, obviously preparing to depart the system.

"Get someone on the com and get us out of here. Tell them to ask Dowarty directly if you have to," Jason said to Kage. The Veran began trying to raise anyone in the station's control center that could get them clearance to detach and leave. "Twingo, get us ready to move. I don't care if they know we're powering up the drives or not."

"On it, Captain," Twingo said, sliding into the engineering station on the bridge and sending the necessary commands to bring the *Phoenix's* powerplant and main drive up to flight-ready status.

"I'm getting stone-walled, Captain," Kage said in disgust. "They say we're not cleared to leave and that Dowarty isn't available." Jason fumed for a moment before coming to a realization.

"He isn't there," he said quietly. "He told them to hold us and then he left with one of those fleets, probably the newcomers in the shiny warships."

"While that's probably true," Doc said, "where does that leave us?"

"Can we raise the *Diligent*?"

"Nope," Twingo said before Kage could answer. "Slip-space radios won't operate worth a damn this far into the nebula. Too many funky gravitational anomalies."

"Bullshit," Jason insisted. "Slip-drive still works, it's the same principle."

"Captain," Twingo replied in a pained voice. "The energy required to transmit a signal in slip-space is miniscule compared to the massive amount of power the drives need to output in order to transition a whole ship. The signal would just gets lost in the background noise."

"No boosting the signal?" Jason asked, not willing to give up.

"Oh, of course... why didn't *I* think of that?" Twingo's acerbic tone convinced Jason to abandon the idea.

"A simple 'No' would have been fine." Jason said flatly. "Looks like we're back to doing things the way we usually do them," he said in a resigned tone. Crusher perked up at that.

"Hell yeah! Let's break some shit!" Jason couldn't help but smile at his enthusiasm.

"We can assume they're getting com traffic in and out of the nebula using the relay system we used on the way in," he said, thinking aloud. "Would that be a specialized type of com node that could reach just outside of this mess?"

291

"Possibly," Twingo said, looking up to the ceiling to ponder the issue.

"I can tell what you're thinking, Captain. It won't work," Kage spoke up. "If we destroy the com node they'll just send a ship from their hanger to make contact. If you really want to leave in secret we'd have to blow the whole station, and we're not carrying the firepower for that."

"When you're right, you're right," Jason conceded. "Ideas?"

"We sould just leave," Lucky said. "Nobody knows that we are reporting to the Eshquarians, or we would be dead already. It is imperative we leave to warn somebody about the fleets that have departed here. We should just blow the airlock seal and mesh out."

"Twingo," Jason said loudly, smiling at Lucky while he did. "Arm us up... tactical condition Alpha."

"Yes, sir!"

The ship's interior lighting dimmed and took on a red tinge. It was to reduce the degradation of their low-light vision, but Jason always felt like his ship was also tensing up for war, becoming angry when the switch was flipped. A steady, building, sonic thrum was felt on the bridge as the reactor poured power into the offensive and defensive systems while simultaneously bringing the drives online.

"*Unidentified ship, you WILL power down your drives and weapon systems and remain docked as instructed.*" The irate voice of one of the controllers broke in over the emergency broadcast channel, causing everyone to look to Jason.

"It's about to get real, boys," he said quietly. "Target the gangway with the port plasma cannon."

"Target acquired and locked. Let 'er rip, Captain," Kage said with a misplaced feral grin on his wide mouth. Jason mirrored the expression and squeezed the trigger on his stick. The massive plasma bolt blew the gangway in half and still had enough energy left to continue on and strike another docked ship on a different junction, destroying it.

"Oops," Jason said as he advanced the throttle and yanked back on the stick. The *Phoenix* turned her nose up and pulled away from the station on a wave of gravitational distortion before the

293

controllers could even think about raising an interdiction field to stop them. "Shields!"

"We're pulling part of the gangway with us, Captain," Twingo said. "Shields have a coverage gap on the forward, port quadrant."

"Blow it!" The outer airlock couplings were equipped with explosive squibs that could blow a coupled seal off the hull. He sheepishly realized that he should have ordered that course of action before firing one of his main guns through the gangway.

The squibs blew the remnants of the airlock coupling away from the hull, sending it drifting slowly away from them as it maintained its forward velocity relative to the ship. Once it cleared away enough, Jason steered towards open space and slammed down the throttle, sending the gunship streaking away before a response force from the station had a chance to launch.

"Clear to jump," Kage reported, having already programmed in a short escape hop.

"Jumping now," Jason said, pulling the throttle back to idle and smacking the oversized control on his right to mesh the *Phoenix* away from The Complex.

Chapter 12

"Still can't raise the *Diligent*?" Jason asked. They'd been in slip-space for twenty minutes and had been unable to reach Crisstof or Captain Colleren.

"No. I can't tell if they're not listening or if their node is offline," Kage said. A soft beep from his console distracted him and he promptly ignored his captain. Jason glared at him and climbed out of his seat to walk around the bridge and stretch his legs a bit. They were flying at maximum slip-velocity towards Oorch Prime to try and catch the trail of the raider fleet. They had no idea as to the origins, or the destination, of the other fleet of warships, so they had been trying to inform the *Diligent* as to the position of The Complex as well as keep a tail on the mass of pirate ships that had moved out. They had failed miserably on both counts. The tension on the bridge was palpable, they knew that something major was afoot, but they had no idea as to what that may be, much less how to stop it.

"Doc," Jason said, still glaring at the inattentive Kage, "put a message on a loop to the *Diligent*..."

"Captain!!" Kage's strident call was of utter distress. He looked up at Jason in abject horror, but didn't speak.

"What?" Jason asked, perplexed.

"I know where that fleet of warships is heading, and it isn't good."

"How not good?"

"Millions of lives are at risk. Right now," Kage said in a tone that made Jason's stomach drop. *Millions? What are you into, Kross?*

"Better start from the top, bud," Jason said gently as the other members of the crew moved to hear Kage better.

"I finally cracked the download from Dowarty's computer," Kage started. "The reason there were so many sophisticated safeguards in place is because it was loaded with operational data for all the shit that's been going on in the Cluster. We're even in there for the theft of those crystal birds and transporting Dowarty to the Solic System.

"The raider fleet is scattering into six attack groups as we speak, they'll do hit and runs up and down the outer edge of the colonies to try and coax the Eshquarian fleet out, nothing too major, but enough that it can't be ignored. They want the bulk of the fleet away from their home port."

"Are they actually going to attack Eshquaria Prime? With all its orbital defenses?" Crusher asked, dubious. Kage simply shook his head slowly.

"They're going after Shorret-3, one of the main raw material producers that feeds the Eshquarian industrial complex with refined metals," he said.

"I take it there is something about this attack that has you so... distressed?" Jason prompted.

"Shorret-3 is home to six million people planetside, all in one massive settlement... and another one-hundred thousand on the main orbital platform; an older tether-type installation that stages the refined ore for the big cargo haulers.

"Even though the platform is a bit outdated, it's simply enormous; nearly four kilometers across. It's mass requires an extra long tether that the cargo cars ride up and down. Since the mass of the platform can fluctuate wildly as ore is taken up, and then offloaded, the tether can be retracted or played out using the machinery that's in the ground planetside at the anchor site. Dowarty plans to hit the platform to disable its thrusters and repulsors and then retract the tether." Kage waited, letting the situation sink in.

"Oh shit," Twingo said softly. "If the platform can't correct its forward velocity, and they retract the tether quickly enough..."

"They've just created a four kilometer wide kinetic weapon that will wipe out Shorret-3's entire population," Jason finished in an emotionless voice. The platform relied on inertia to keep it aloft, its mass dictating the length of the tether while its relatively weak propulsion system made fine corrections. It was reliable, economical, and safe; if the tether failed and snapped during normal operations the platform would just float away until it was recovered.

If the tether were to be shortened dramatically, however, without the platform being able to compensate it's mass or velocity... it would simply fall to the planet.

"Defenses on the platform?" Jason asked hopefully.

"Minimal. They rely on the Eshquarian fleet, and the threat of that, to protect them," Kage said sadly. "They're profit driven, and they're in a safe zone, so defenses are an afterthought."

"This will be one of the worst terrorist attacks ever perpetrated in this region of space," Doc said, horrified. "In addition to the loss of life, it will completely destabilize the Eshquarian government."

"We still can't raise the *Diligent*?"

"No."

"There's no point contacting Eshquarian Fleet Command," Jason mused, pacing along the forward canopy. "They'd never believe us. ConFed Fleet is out... I have a feeling they're hip deep in this after that ship we saw at The Complex. Who does that leave?"

"Us," Crusher said simply, giving voice to what Jason wouldn't.

"You all saw that fleet," he began. "The *Phoenix* is no match for them head-to-head. We've done what we could, what we were asked... there's no dishonor if anyone would rather not do this... I can't ask this of you. You know we won't survive."

"Whether we survive or not isn't the point, Captain," Doc said. "We're the only ones who know this is coming, the only ones who stand between them and millions of innocent lives... do you really think there's a choice here?"

"No," Jason said finally, looking around him. Five grim, determined faces looked back. He couldn't have been more proud to stand with those individuals in that moment. "New course. Get us to Shorret-3 as fast as she'll take us."

"Course correction confirmed," Kage said. "We're on our way, twenty-six hours until we mesh in."

"Best guess on how far behind the attack fleet we are?" Jason asked.

"Oorch Prime was a bit out of the way, but we're a lot faster... maybe an hour," Twingo said as he consulted his own terminal.

"We'll hit their fleet hard and fast with all she's got, but we have got to get planetside quickly," Jason told them. "To retract the tether, they'll probably need to go to the anchor point. We'll make our stand there. Crusher, Lucky; we're on... I want full armor and break out the heavy weapons."

"We'll prep your gear, Captain," Crusher said crisply as he and Lucky left the bridge. The Galvetic warrior had a noticeable snap in his step as he walked, obviously relishing the thought of an epic battle in which he was all that stood between the innocent and their certain deaths at the hands of a superior force. The frustration of the past couple of months was gone, the slogging through shitty bars and hives of bottom-feeding scum that had been wearing on the crew, now all but forgotten as the very ideal of Omega Force was reaffirmed in that one, crystalline moment. As the *Phoenix* tore through slip-space toward Shorret-3, each member of the team busied themselves making sure they were ready.

"Doc, prep a message to the *Diligent* informing them what's happening. Tell them to inform the Eshquarians that Chief of Staff Kross is to be arrested on sight," Jason said to his friend. "Once you have it ready, put it on a continuous transmit loop to all known com nodes. There's no point in secrecy now.

"One other thing, all of you need to rotate down through the armory and gear up," he told the rest of the crew. "I know you're not usually 'tactical assets,' but I don't know what's going to happen when we mesh in, so I want everybody ready for the worst. Tell Crusher to outfit you with whatever we have that will fit as far as armor and weapons. In fact... Twingo, I want you to use the fabricators to make sure everyone has at least some level of body armor. Nothing too fancy, just enough to ward off a couple lucky shots."

"You can count on me, Captain," Twingo nodded solemnly, for once not having a sarcastic quip or insult as an answer.

Jason strode off the bridge and headed for his quarters for a little bit of privacy to try and prepare himself for what he knew was coming. The job had started out easy enough: gather intel on a group of overly ambitious pirates. After the boredom, the shenanigans of stealing some dolt's prized artifacts, and the juvenile fun of a few good ol' bar fights, he knew he was flying his crew to certain death. The fact they did so willingly did nothing to assuage his guilt and his guilt did nothing to deter him from the course of action he knew he had to take. *Millions* of innocent lives stood to be lost... they'd all try until they had nothing left to give to stop that.

The crew went about their tasks with an almost desperate efficiency, not wanting to dwell on what may happen when they emerged from slip-space. Getting the three members of the crew who were usually not involved in ground operations kitted out with weapons and armor would have been a humorous proposition any other time, but now Lucky and Crusher worked quickly to make sure each knew how to operate the gear they were given. After a short period of quiet contemplation, Jason was in the cramped com room pouring over the sensor data they had been able to collect on the fleet they were streaking towards. It was scant, at best; only the passive array and navigational sensors had been active so they weren't able to determine specific tactical capabilities. He had the computer scouring their records for the build and model of each ship to try and get a general idea of what they were up against, but he had little hope it would amount to much before they arrived in the Shorret System.

Once he had reached the limit of his patience, and the others had filtered through the armory, he went down to get his own gear prepared. When he entered the armory, he saw that Lucky and Crusher were nearly complete with their own equipment. Lucky, in a rare instance of opting for external weaponry, had two large, articulated plasma cannons mounted on his back, just inboard of his shoulders. These were specifically built for him and designed to run off his considerable internal power cells. He could also direct them independent from each other, this added some serious punch to his already formidable arsenal.

Crusher, also dressing for the occasion, had set aside his usual penchant for going sleeveless and sported a set of heavy body armor, complete with pauldrons, gauntlets, and protection for his arms. He was checking two heavy plasma rifles that would be almost impossible for someone Jason's size to wield. He also had a large sidearm and two wicked-looking molecular-blade weapons strapped to him in various places. The pair of warriors looked utterly terrifying.

Jason walked through with only a nod as he made his way to his own area. He opened one of the wall units and stared at the assortment of gear inside, all looking pitifully inadequate for the upcoming task. He moved to the next unit over and slid open the door, pressing a button just on the inside. A rack slid out silently on rails until it extended about a meter and a half away from the wall. Hanging from the rack was a specialized piece of gear; Jason's custom powered armor. He rarely had a need to use it, which unfortunately also meant he didn't have near the amount of training time in the machine that he'd like to. While it wasn't the most advanced unit one could buy, it was incredibly expensive (wastefully so, according to some of his crew) and gave him an advantage on the ground the other, lighter units he owned didn't

The term "powered" was a bit of a misnomer when comparing the armor to some of the more sophisticated models; it actually did nothing to enhance the user's strength. What it did have was a set of full motion actuators that were designed to eliminate the weight of the armor so the user could move as if they weren't wearing it at all. It also offered limited energy shielding over vital areas and a full sensor suite within the helmet. His own particular unit had also been programmed by Doc to render emergency first-aid when possible.

Jason stood in front of the apparatus for a moment, running his hand over the Greek letter "Omega" that was embossed on the upper part of the chest plate. He then touched a few controls on the rack's touch panel and watched as the suit hissed and opened up. "Everyone else all geared up?" He asked as he stripped off his shipboard fatigues and reached for the fitted undergarments that went with the armor.

"As best we could," Crusher said. "Twingo is a little scrapper, but the other two are next to useless if we get into any real fighting."

"We gave Doc a long-range kinetic kill weapon and Kage a small plasma carbine so he could act as spotter and protect him," Lucky said more helpfully. "Twingo insisted on the biggest energy weapon he could carry, so I am not certain where he plans to be when we land."

"Hopefully he hangs back and keeps any ground forces from closing in behind us," Jason said. "Give me a hand with this, Lucky." He turned and slipped his feet into the armor and grabbed Lucky's proffered forearm and pushed himself up and back into the unit. Once he had slid in his arms one at a time, he nodded to his synth friend. Lucky reached over and activated the armor via the external control panel, causing the suit to close slowly over Jason and seal.

There was the usual moment of claustrophobic panic Jason experienced each time the suit swallowed him up before the helmet linked to his neural implant and he could "see". A moment later and a gentle rush of air swirled through the helmet and indicators for individual subsytems began to wink green on his heads-up display. After it was fully activated the locks on the rack released and he was able to step off of the platform with a heavy *thud.*

"Are you sure you want to wear that contraption, Captain?" Crusher asked doubtfully. "Your training time in it is woefully inadequate."

"I'm in full agreement," Jason said through the helmets audio projectors. "But without it I won't last long if we're right about what we'll be facing." Crusher seemed to consider this before nodding in ascent.

"Thankfully, the one thing I did train for is flying the ship while wearing this thing," Jason quipped as he approached the weapons rack. "Otherwise, this would be the galaxy's shortest offensive on record." Even as he contemplated the array of man-portable weaponry hanging on the wall, he knew which he was going to carry; his second generation railgun. The first unit had been designed in a rush by Deetz and was based off his own AR-15 carbine he had boarded the gunship with when it had made an emergency landing on Earth. It had been incredibly powerful, but flawed in some significant ways. The newer version, designed by himself and Twingo, fired a slightly heavier tungsten-carbide projectile and sported a much-improved cooling system for the firing coils. It also had selectable fire; he could fire the rounds sub-hypersonic at a higher rate when in close quarters combat against a lightly armored enemy. If he needed maximum damage, however, the rifle would accelerate the round past Mach six as it left the barrel, slightly faster than its predecessor. The overpressure and muzzle blast from the weapon were considerable, so the low-speed fire mode was a necessity in confined spaces.

"Please tell me you're not bringing that damn thing," Crusher lamented, having been on the receiving end of the aforementioned muzzle blast before.

"Oh yeah I am," Jason smiled behind his helmet visor. He grabbed a load bearing harness that held several spare magazines, which were a combination magazine and powerpack for the weapon, and a heavy plasma sidearm that he affixed to his right thigh. Jason, like Crusher, also carried a molecular-blade weapon, but only one and significantly smaller at that. He wasn't nearly as well trained in the use of melee weapons like the big warrior was, so he kept his contingency weapons basic. The nanotech in the blades kept the molecules along the edges aligned like they'd just been hit with a sharpening steel, effectively allowing the weapon to re-dress the cutting edge after each use. There were more exotic, energy based edged weapons available, but Crusher was a traditionalist and Jason like his weapon-of-last-resort to be as simple as possible.

"Are we ready for this?" Jason asked his friends.

"Not even close," Crusher snorted, "but let's give it a shot anyway." The trio secured the rest of the items in the armory in preparation for heavy maneuvering and then left.

"Twingo," Jason shouted as they walked through the engineering bay, "I want you up on the bridge and strapped in before we mesh in." Twingo, half buried in an access panel, just waved at him in an ambiguous response that promised nothing. Jason gave the ship a cursory inspection as he made his way up to the bridge, ensuring everything was secured as it looked to be a bumpy ride. When he arrived on the bridge, he could see Doc and Kage sitting at their respective stations, each trying to remain busy as the minutes counted down until they'd blast into real-space and engage the fleet of warships they'd seen at The Complex.

He sat in his seat and waited while it began to adjust for the additional bulk and weight of his armor. "Sixty-two minutes out, Captain," Kage volunteered without having been asked. The Veran looked absurd in the body armor that Twingo had quickly had fabricated for his slight frame. Doc looked no less out of place, but at least more proportional.

"Thanks," Jason said. "Everybody make sure your weapons are secured on the bridge, we don't need them flying around or someone accidentally shooting something when we start maneuvering."

"Who would accidentally fire a weapon on the bridge?" Crusher asked, as if it were the most ridiculous thing he'd ever heard. Jason remained silent, remembering that the first time he had set foot on the bridge he had inadvertently squeezed off a single round that took out the navigation subprocessor with his AR-15.

"It doesn't matter," he said. "Just secure everything like I asked." When Crusher just shrugged he turned to Kage.

"When we're thirty minutes out, bring all the weapons systems online, including all the missiles in the launch bay, and start self-testing them. I want them primed and ready as soon as we're out. I also want the shields up the instant you see stars through the canopy."

"I'm on it," Kage said nervously. Jason looked over and saw that Doc was fidgeting at his seat as well. A moment later Twingo walked onto the bridge wearing an unusually subdued expression. Only Lucky looked calm out of them all as Crusher had a disturbingly eager expression on his face as he watched the timer that was projected on the canopy count down. *That's one sick bastard.* He keyed the control to pop and raise the forward part of his helmet so he could talk to his crew directly.

"Ok, boys," he began. "We've been through this before, so let's settle down and focus on the small things. Get the systems all checked and re-checked, make sure the safeties on our missiles are disengaged, and just concentrate on your small part in the big picture." He wouldn't dishonor them by suggesting they could still turn back, not after they'd made their decision.

"This is what we're here for, only this time we're saving the lives of millions of civilians... there will be statues of us and schools named after each of you," a few chuckles at that part, "We're going to hit them hard in orbit, but we're not going to burn-in trying to stand toe-to-toe with those bigger ships. Our main goal is to try and get planetside and stop their ground assault team from retracting the tether. It won't be easy, but we'll make a few passes with the *Phoenix* to try and soften them up first."

They each sat a little straighter and went back to their individual tasks as the importance of their mission was reinforced. Jason, with little to do until they meshed in, let his thoughts wander to the things he'd left unfinished in his life. In particular, the beautiful blond woman he had left on Earth to pursue his calling among the stars. She would never know that he had died out here in a blaze of glory, fighting to protect a planet of innocent lives, but he hoped she would have been proud of him if she had.

"We're five minutes out," Kage said crisply. Jason flipped his visor back closed and slaved his visual input to the ship's tactical sensors. They all sat in silence, anticipating what they would see within the next few moments.

"Meshing in-system in 5...4...3... 2... 1... NOW!"

As the slip energy dissipated and the sensors began populating the threat board they could see the orbital platform was already taking a beating.

"Shields up!" Kage announced over the alarms.

The *Phoenix* streaked into the system towards the fray, largely unnoticed. Jason could see on the display that the three larger warships were firing on the platform, but were staying out of range of its meager defensive measures. From what he could tell, they were content to hammer at its weapon emplacements until it could be jerked out of orbit by their ground team.

"There is zero com traffic coming from both the platform and the surface," Doc reported.

"That explains the leisurely attack we're seeing," Jason said. Even at their current range they could see the flashes of energy bolts splashing against the enormous orbital installation. "They took out communications and now they'll just toy with them until the tether is retracted. Arm up the big boys, I'm going to line up directly behind the closest ship and stuff them up his engines. We'll then get one clean pass on the second ship with the main guns before that third ship in higher orbit can get a bead on us. Hopefully."

The "big boys" were two missiles they had inherited when they took possession of the DL7 gunship; a pair of high-yield tactical nukes. They were as old as the ship, but if they flew up into a ship's engines, the results should be quite dramatic. Unfortunately, they only had the two... while the missiles were sure to help even the odds a bit, they were still hopelessly outgunned once the remaining ships turned their attention on them.

"We're locked," Kage reported. "We'll be in range in fifteen seconds."

"Hold back, I don't want to risk their point defense taking them out, surprise is out only advantage right now," Jason said as he pushed the throttle up and raced towards the exposed rear of the closest ship. The sensors told him they had their shields up, but the section of shielding that was covering the engine emitters would be significantly weakened due to the gravimetric distortion propagating outward. Typically, that outward distortion would offer a significant level of protection when the ship was under way, but not when it was sitting

311

in a station keeping mode. The relatively small missiles should be able to punch through and deliver their payload... in theory.

He watched the distance between them and their target dwindle rapidly until Jason thought he could just make out the tiny speck of the targeted ship against the backdrop of Shorret-3. "Open the weapons bay and prepare to deploy. Two shots, no interval."

"Weapons bay open, ready to deploy," Kage said, his hand over the fire control. These particular missiles required they both initiate the launch sequence, so Jason squeezed the trigger on the control stick and waited just a few more seconds before pulling their speed back.

"FIRE!"

Kage hit his own fire control and two thumps were felt through the ship as the missiles came off the rails and fired their engines. A split second later, two brilliant blue sparks raced away from the Phoenix at over two-hundred g's of acceleration until they were quickly out of visual range.

"Close us back up, we won't get a second shot with missiles," Jason ordered as he throttled the ship up to pursue their two nukes. He wanted to pass over the target just as they realized they were under attack and hit the second ship hard before they could get a bearing on

312

the small, speedy gunship. As the larger ship began to resolve itself in the optical sensors there was a sudden, brilliant burst of light that washed out the displays and automatically darkened the canopy for a moment. A split second later the canopy cleared and Jason could see the ship listing badly, now unable to keep its position over the planet.

Still aiming to pass over the ship and pop out around it to hit the second ship, Jason was unprepared with their first target exploded right in front of them, the chain reaction that had been started by their missiles hitting the engines sending the reactors into meltdown.

"SHIT!!"

It was too late, the *Phoenix* plunged into the quickly expanding debris cloud before Jason could even think about steering away or stopping. Chunks of ship ranging from large to very large pummeled the combat shields and shook the ship violently as it battered through the heavy metal storm. Alarms began blaring and a list of warnings began to scroll over the tactical display, alerting them that all was not well. *Fucking stupid bastard! You've killed us all before we've even started!* A series of loud pops that sounded throughout the ship were their first indicators something critical was about to fail.

"Power couplers are failing all over the ship!" Twingo shouted. "We're losing the shields! I'm trying to stabilize and re-route..."

"Second target coming up," Kage said, still on task. Since he could do nothing about the shields getting ready to give out, he slammed the throttle down and relied on the *Phoenix's* speed to get them through the mess he'd flown them into. He lined up along the lateral seam of the hull and squeezed the trigger. Brilliant red bolts of plasma shot out in rapid fire mode from both of the forward emitters, causing the enemy ship's shields to glow and waver as they fought to absorb the onslaught of energy.

The main guns began to overwhelm the enemy's shields as a handful of bolts passed through and caused massive damage along the ship's starboard side as the *Phoenix* shot past. Just as they cleared the aft most portion of the target's hull, they were rocked by a blast so violent Jason almost bit through his tongue. Two more hit them in rapid succession before they were out of range.

"That was bad," Twingo said unnecessarily. "Shields are gone. Slip-drive is gone. The port engine is out altogether and the starboard engine is highly degraded."

"We were hit by the third ship, the orbital platform, and the point defense of the ship we just strafed," Doc said. Jason cursed himself for flying too close to the orbital platform, whose crew could not realize they were trying to help. In such a defensive mode they were just firing at anything within range. He cranked the controls over in an attempt to come about and try to make landfall near the platform, but all that happened was the ship rotated attitude, but continued along the original trajectory.

"I've lost maneuvering," he reported.

"I'm not surprised," Twingo said. "One gimpy engine isn't enough to maneuver freely in space, especially so close to a planet. We're now at the mercy of standard physics... The grav drive is dead, Captain, better shut it down and bring the mains online. We'll have to do a complete orbit and try and enter on the other side."

Jason chaffed at the delay, but began to reconfigure the ship's propulsions systems anyway. As he was doing that, another detonation rocked the ship and yawed them violently towards the planet. "What the fuck?!"

"Kinetic weapon, Captain!" Doc reported. "It just took off a large portion of the starboard vertical stabilizer." A kinetic weapon was like a missile, but didn't have an explosive warhead, just a solid chuck of metal that would tear through the hull. They were notoriously hard to detect because they were so small and fast.

"It's better than that," Twingo groused. "The heat exchangers run through the stabilizers, we're already losing capacity on exchanger two." The two vertical stabilizers that protruded from the ship's back also housed critical parts of the cooling system that kept the engines and weapons from overheating. The reduced capacity meant picking one or the other: thrust or weapons. "I'll try to run it closed-loop, but I wouldn't expect too much."

"We've done all we can here," Jason said, somewhat surprised they were still alive. "Let's get on the ground and try to finish this." The main problem was that even if they stopped the initial ground assault team, he had no doubt there were reserves waiting on board the remaining ships in orbit. It would just be a matter of time before they were overwhelmed.

Using the momentum they were carrying from their initial attack run, Jason guided the *Phoenix* around the planet in a descending orbit as they prepared to make atmospheric entry. He was concerned about the missing stabilizer now that the gravimetric drive was completely shut down. The repulsors would have to fight to compensate, and that meant taxing their damaged cooling system. *This has turned into a serious cluster-fuck of the highest magnitude.*

They began to feel the buffeting of the mesosphere as the gunship began to plunge into the atmosphere well before they would have line-of-sight again of the battle presumably still taking place in higher orbit. Soon the canopy was engulfed in superheated gasses as the *Phoenix* roared into the atmosphere without the aid of her gravimetric drive to slow the descent. With the structural integrity of the starboard stabilizer compromised, the fiery entry into the atmosphere was causing further damage to the cooling system. Twingo watched the capacity of the system continue to drop and hoped it would last long enough to get them safely to the ground.

Once the plasma had cleared from the canopy and the ship was flying in clean air, Jason turned them on course for the tether anchor point. He fervently hoped the population on the ground had fled to the outskirts once the assault had begun, but he doubted that many people could get out of the city center in time. He began to throttle up with the intent of circling the area, but as soon as he advanced the power the temperature on his engine readouts spiked.

"We've got a problem, Twingo," he said. "I've got no thrust, I can't get past ten percent power before the temperature spikes."

"I'm on it," Twingo said. "I'll re-route all the cooling capacity from system one to the engines... that means no energy weapons."

"Whatever," Jason said, "just get me the engines back or we won't even make it to the tether." After a moment of frantic control inputs from the engineer, the engine temperatures began to drop slightly from critical to just dangerous. "Best I can do, Captain."

"Copy that," Jason replied as he pushed the throttle back up again. The power climbed to twenty-five percent with the temperatures staying shy of dangerous for a moment, causing Jason to relax his left hand slightly. They should just make it if the repair held...

Before he could react, the temperatures spiked again and a loud explosion jerked the ship to port and caused the displays to go wild with warnings.

"We've just shelled out engine one!" Twingo shouted. "I'm not sure how much longer the others will keep pushing." As if on cue, the displays began to flicker and the interior lighting died as they crossed the outer border of the city. A moment later half the displays on the bridge winked out. "Main bus A is out, B is failing! Switching to emergency power. Beginning emergency shutdown of the main reactor." Jason could feel his ship floundering, dying underneath him, she couldn't leave the planet and he had his doubts about a safe landing. So far the repulsors were holding on emergency power... but would they last long enough?

The *Phoenix* slogged through the sky above the only city on Shorret-3, still maintaining a barely controlled descent toward the anchor point, but fading fast. They had lost enough altitude that the building tops of the residential area were streaking by just below them. A few moments later and they were knocking over com antennas and the right wing obliterated a rooftop greenhouse that Jason hoped was unoccupied. Whenever he tried any control inputs the ship vibrated and shook as the repulsors were unable to comply. With no control left he tried to lower the landing gear and prepared to tell his crew the news.

No sooner had he hit the landing gear control than an explosion of sparks erupted from port bulkhead and all power failed throughout the ship, including the barely-functioning repulsor drive. "It's out of my hands! Brace for impact!" Jason's warning left his lips a microsecond before the ship fell sickeningly out of the air, her airspeed not even a fraction of what was needed for the wings to keep them aloft.

The *Phoenix* fell, twisting slightly to port, and crashed through the roof of an enormous processing facility that was six stories tall and covered at least five acres. The gunship went through the roof like it was made of paper and kept its forward momentum, gutting the building as it went along. Inside, the crew was now just along for the ride as horrendous impacts slammed them to and fro against their seat restraints. Some large piece of something slammed into the canopy and cracked the ultra-dense material into spider web mosaic before flipping up and over the ship. Although it happened in the blink of an eye, Jason felt they'd been coring out the building for an eternity.

On the eastern road that ran along the processing plant, the ground began to shake and the building vibrated violently as if in an earthquake just before the right wing of the DL7 exploded out of the side of the facility, followed by most of the rest of it. The forward section burst through the building and swung around before dropping the remaining twenty-five feet and slamming into the road below. The ship lay there, still half buried in the structure, hissing and smoking, but otherwise still.

Jason blinked several times to clear his head as he hung from the restraints, the bridge canted at a crazy angle. Through the battered canopy he could see they had emerged from the building and were nose-down on a street. *Please let there have been nobody in this building.* There was a hiss of air as the emergency lighting glowed red along the walls and the chemical oxygen generators activated, signs of the *Phoenix* in her death throes.

"Is everyone still alive?" Jason asked. He got a chorus of affirmative responses, some less enthusiastic than others.

"Well, you finally did crash her," Twingo said in an attempt at humor that fell flat.

"Everyone try to get out of your restraints and get your gear without hurting yourselves or anyone else," Jason said, ignoring his friend. "Let's get to the port airlock and get out of here, we still have a mission to complete."

Over the next ten minutes the crew struggled to extricate themselves from their seats and collect their weapons and gear before struggling further to get off the tilted command deck and drop down to where the port airlock chamber was. Once they were all there, Jason manually closed the inner hatch, lifted the bright red cover, and smashed the large button down three times, then two more, activating the explosive charges that would fling the port hatch away from the ship. They heard and felt the muffled *whump* as the charges detonated. He waited a few seconds before opening the inner hatch, hoping most of the smoke had cleared out.

They made their way out of the gaping hole in the side of the hull one at a time, Lucky helping the smaller members of Omega Force so they weren't injured trying to make the jump. Standing straight, Jason took in the surreal sight of his ship jutting out the side of an industrial building and smashed onto the street below. The nose cone, a composite piece that covered the sensitive forward sensor array, looked to have taken the brunt of the fall, crushed and deformed as the weight of the ship pressed down on it. He deliberately turned away, becoming aware of the sounds of battle coming from the anchor point, which was still two kilometers away. Small arms fire and larger explosions were clearly heard as the surrounding area was largely silent, the citizens either in hiding or having fled.

"Crusher, Lucky, we'll be hitting the far access gate like we originally planned," Jason said crisply, trying to get his crew back into focus. "You three," he said, pointing to Doc, Twingo, and Kage, "get someplace high where you can see the complex and try to feed us what intel you can. With the twins stuck in the ship, we have no idea of what's going on until we're almost on it." Jason knew well enough that they'd be of little use as far as spotters since the battle was likely already inside the anchor point facility, but it would keep the three out of harm's way while not insulting them directly to their faces. He looked at them speculatively, and then changed his mind.

"Check that; Kage, you're with us. We may need your talents. Twingo and Doc, same plan; get high and get me intel."

"We'll take care of it, Captain," Twingo said solemnly, grasping the shoulder of Jason's armor. He understood the likelihood of ever seeing his friend again was slim, at best. Doc came up and wordlessly shook his hand before turning and leading Twingo away, down the street and around the corner.

"Kage, stay behind us as much as possible," Jason said to his small friend, who was now wide-eyed as the reality of going into combat sunk in. "No heroics. Let the three of us clear things since we'll probably need you to either gain entry into the building or access the computers controlling the tether winch."

"No heroics. Got it," Kage agreed quickly.

"Let's move out," Jason said, turning and taking one last, bitter look at the *Phoenix*. "I'm sorry," he whispered before turning and breaking into a run to catch up to the rest of his team.

The two klick run wasn't enough to wind him, but it did bring all the minute fitting imperfections of his armor into stark relief as the joints rubbed his inner thighs raw and pinched the skin of his elbows. They reached the last building that would conceal them before they reached the small service entrance to the compound and stopped. The sounds of fighting were now muted, which wasn't necessarily a good thing; they had either breached the facility or had killed the security personnel already. The portal through the solid wall that ringed the compound looked formidable. "Any ideas?" He asked.

"I will breach the entry, Captain," Lucky said.

"We'll cover you," Jason agreed as he watched, amazed, as Lucky's eyes began to glow a malevolent red and his weapons began to hum with power. This was the first time he had ever seen the synth in full "combat mode." *This should be interesting.*

Lucky burst from cover and closed in on the armored door with incredible speed. When he closed to within twenty-five meters he fired two blasts from his shoulder mounted cannons that crushed in and scarred the door, but left it somewhat intact. To the astonishment of his crewmates, who were running behind him, Lucky fired the repulsors in his feet and launched himself into a forward, spinning somersault and hit the door like a cannonball. The door disappeared in a screech of tortured metal and snapping bolts. The others burst through the opening in the wall, weapons raised, as Lucky stood up as if it were nothing. Jason looked over at where the door lay and saw it was reinforced steel nearly an inch thick at the edges. *Damn!*

"Captain!" Crusher whispered urgently, pointing to the sky. One of the assault boats that had delivered the ground force from the fleet in orbit was coming around the anchor point and heading in their direction. Jason raised his railgun and let the optics feed him ranging data, adjusted his aim, and squeezed off two rounds with a roaring flash. The hypersonic projectiles decimated the spacecraft, tearing the aft drive section completely off and sending in careening into one of the support buildings where it exploded.

"If we survive this," Crusher said, awed, "you're building me one of those."

"I hope to be able to," Jason said. "Let's go, we need to get out of the open." They ran as quickly as they could across the open ground of the compound to the edge of the main building. The tether, a twenty meter wide, five centimeter thick ribbon of an ultra-strong carbon composite, rose from the center of the building until it disappeared into the sky. They made their way along the side until they reached one of the many maintenance entrances that had no external handle. It was fairly flimsy compared to the main security door Lucky had crashed through, so Crusher stepped up and slammed his boot against it near the catch and was rewarded with it bursting inward on its hinges and slamming against the interior wall.

Alarms were blaring inside the building, but there was nobody to greet them. This wasn't really a surprise and was the main reason they had chosen such an out-of-the way place to make their entrance. Taking point, Jason flipped his weapon to close-quarters mode and began a steady, careful pace into the bowels of the anchor point control center. Next came Crusher, then Kage, and lastly Lucky covered the rear of the column. With a layout of the building floating in the upper-right side of his field of view, Jason sped up their pace as they moved to their first objective; a small conference room two levels above the secondary control room.

The massive machinery that controlled the tether was buried deep under the surface of Shorret-3 and anchored into the continental plate itself. The main control center was in a large, glassed-in room located above the primary winch. There was a small, secondary room that also could control primary tether operations in the event of damage to the main center. The trio wanted to make entrance into that room and try to disable the winch mechanism remotely without having to directly engage the forces already in the building.

They would gain access to the unsecured upper levels, which were mostly used for administrative functions, and use explosives to blow their way down the two floors into the room. If they were successful, they would be able to permanently disable the winch before the assault teams rushed their position and took them out.

After having to tear down three more security doors, they found themselves in the conference room in under five minutes from having first entered the building. Jason and Crusher grabbed the heavy table and tossed it into the corner of the room so that it was propped up on its edge. As they began to break out the small breaching charges they would use to try and cut through the floor, a deep, loud grinding sound began to shake the room slightly. They all looked at each other a moment before the significance of that sank in.

"They've begun to reel in the platform," Jason said sickly. "We're out of time."

"Step back please, Captain," Lucky said, coming forward. "In fact, everyone leave the room." He held his right arm out, palm outward, and a small projector of some sort deployed out from his lower forearm. Not needing to be told twice, the other three hustled into the hallway and stood watching as a brilliant green beam shot out of the projector and began cutting through the floor in an explosion of sparks and smoke. A few seconds later the beam stopped and the section of floor sagged slightly, but was held in place due to the angle it had been cut at. Lucky walked over and jumped directly into the middle of the section, disappearing though the floor as the section broke through.

Crusher, without hesitation, jumped through the same section. Jason gestured for Kage to come over and then lowered the Veran through the hole before jumping down himself.

"I wish you'd have mentioned before that you could do that," Jason said.

"My apologies, Captain," Lucky said as he cleared the floor for the next cut that would take them into the control room. "But you and Crusher seem to have such an affinity for using explosives, I didn't want to deny you that." Despite the adrenaline coursing through his system from the imminent danger, Jason had to chuckle.

After the floor had been cut again, the team jumped down one more level and looked around, trying to get an idea as to where to start. On a large monitor that showed a video feed of the winch itself, they could see that the tether was indeed being retracted at a fast clip and was accelerating. Kage wasted no time in approaching one of the terminals and entering a flurry of commands to gain access to the system. *Glad I brought him along after all.*

While Kage worked, Jason and Crusher took position by the entry to the room while Lucky went back up one level to watch in case anybody stumbled upon their entry method. Since the security measures were designed more to just deny unauthorized access from workers within the facility and not keep out a determined intrusion, it didn't take long for Kage to cut through the layers of pass code protection and gain control of the system.

"I'm going to try to stop the winch and then lock out the main system," Kage reported. "I'm not entirely sure how successful I'll be at that second part if they're actually in the main control center."

"Just do your best," Jason said. There really wasn't a backup plan as their sparse numbers ruled out a direct assault to disable the winch's mechanics. A few minutes later the monotonous grind of the winch stopped as Kage was successful in halting the mechanism. Then he cursed and his four hands flew across the control panels in what Jason assumed was a desperate bid to stop the other side from restarting it.

"I think they know we're here," Kage said.

"How can you tell?" Crusher asked. Kage wordlessly pointed to a security camera in the corner that was aimed at them. Before they could respond Twingo broke in over the com channel;

"*Captain, you've got trouble. Two more boats just landed and troops are rushing into the building you're in; it also looks like they found the door you entered through.*"

327

"Fuck," Jason swore quietly. "Showtime boys. Lucky, they found our ingress point, expect some company." He pulled out his sidearm and blasted the camera off its mount. The next few minutes were tense as the silence became almost too much to bear, knowing that in any moment they would be in for the fight of their lives.

The team that followed their entry method made first contact, which was unfortunate for them. Lucky, having heard them on the floors above, had used his repulsors to meet their charge in the hallway outside of the conference room. Jason and Crusher could hear his plasma cannons barking as the surprised troops sporadically attempted to return fire.

A heavy thud against the security door to the control room they were occupying announced the arrival of the team that had come through the main entrance to their position. With the battle being met, all the tensions and nerves left Jason and he stood to one side of the door, waiting for it to inevitably fall.

"Kage!" He barked. "Leave it! Get behind Crusher before they blow the door." For once, the Veran didn't argue as he left the console and gripped his weapon tightly, tucking in behind the big warrior. The thuds continued as whoever was on the other side was trying brute force to batter the door down, but so far it was holding.

"Captain, Doc and I have moved closer. We're going to start engaging the troops on the grounds and provide a bit of a distraction."

"Damn it, Twingo! Hold your position, we don't need a distraction, they already know where we..."

The rest of Jason's sentence was cut off as the door blew inwards from a shaped charge being placed on the outside by the assault team. It flew out of the frame and smashed into the console Kage had just been standing at. As smoke billowed in from the outside Crusher casually tossed a grenade out through the now open doorway. When it exploded, screams and the sound of debris falling met their ears.

Jason and Crusher both crouched and slipped their weapons around the edge of the ragged doorway and opened fire. Crusher's heavy plasma weapon was sending troops sailing back the way they came, often with smoking craters center mass, others missing appendages altogether. Jason, firing in controlled bursts, was having varied success against the well armored soldiers, but he couldn't switch his weapon back to high-velocity without injuring Crusher, who was standing too close.

Once the soldiers in the narrow hallway got over the initial shock of the reception they had received, they regrouped and began to change strategies. They brought up heavy, crew-served weapons and began blasting into the room with such ferocity that they didn't dare look around the corner to return fire. While the heavy bolts were doing nothing but blowing out the back wall of the room, they were keeping Jason and Crusher out of the fight, and they both knew that while the big cannon was chattering in the hallway others were advancing towards them along the edges. When he looked back into the room,

Jason's heart sank; the video feed showed they had reactivated the winch, which was inexorably pulling the orbital platform towards the surface at a quickened pace.

The cannon fire from the hallway had began to lull as the weapon began to overheat, but just when Jason was going to risk edging around the corner, he saw the barrel of a weapon entering the room from the other way. Crusher saw it too, and with a snarl, grabbed it and yanked the surprised soldier into the room with them. Before he could even get his feet under him, Crusher caved in his helmet, with his head still in it, with a massive overhand blow. Jason quickly rounded the corner to cover his friend's now-exposed back, but he was running low on ammunition.

He tried to take out the crew operating the large plasma cannon, but they were quicker on the draw than he was. A brilliant bolt hit him directly in the hip as he completed his turn, sending him rolling over backwards and sprawling out onto the floor. From the smell of scorched metal and flesh, he knew it was bad.

"Twingo! No!! Get up! Get up! We've got to move now, they're coming back for..."

The call over the open channel made Jason momentarily forget about his own predicament as he heard Doc's frantic call that had been suddenly cut off. He knew his best friend was most likely dead, probably Doc as well, and he wouldn't be far behind them.

He rolled over and saw Crusher in a heap against the far wall, a huge rent from the plasma cannon had been torn into his armor. The big warrior was stirring, but was out of the fight. Jason tried to rise, but the damage to his right side was too severe and he collapsed again, falling into the doorway as he did. Another two bolts from smaller weapons took him in the left shoulder and chest, knocking him back to the floor. The armor kept him alive, but the pain was excruciating and he knew he didn't have long.

"Kage!" He called as he coughed wetly. "Get out of here! Find Lucky and get out!" Kage ignored him as he kept messing with a panel against the far wall. Jason stared a moment, transfixed as the Veran pulled his weapon and opened fire into the wall once, twice, and then a third time. He reached into the smoking hole and yanked a handle down and held on for dear life. Suddenly, red, strobing lights and loud klaxons erupted from everywhere at once and a horrific rumble shook the entire building. Jason picked his head up and peered down the hallway, seeing that the enemy was also momentarily stunned. With a snarl he grabbed his weapon and flipped it to full velocity and propped himself up as best he could. "Sorry buddy," he wheezed to Kage before squeezing the trigger.

If the soldiers assaulting the room were surprised at the alarms, the hypersonic rounds tearing through their ranks positively shocked them. Jason was dimly aware of Kage screaming in agony from the weapon's muzzle blast and the pressure wave it created, but he kept firing, utterly devastating everything and everyone in the hallway until the trigger clicked and nothing happened. Out of ammo.

Kage was huddled in the corner, blood running from his ears and nose, completely incapacitated from being in front of the railgun when Jason had opened fire. For his own part, Jason's adrenaline had worn off, as had the shock, and he was beginning to realize just how bad of shape he was in. The rumbling in the building had stopped, or at least he thought it had, but he knew there were more of the enemy in the building that would be coming to finish him off. So he wasn't surprised when one of them stood over him, seeming to relish his helplessness as he aimed his weapon right at Jason's head. He closed his eyes, letting his thoughts drift back to her one last time...

Or at least he assumed they would be his last thoughts as he heard a wet crunch and a startled grunt. He opened his eyes and saw the hilt of one of Crusher's bladed weapons sticking out of the chest piece of his would-be killer. Jason wished the asshole didn't have a helmet with a face shield so he could see the surprised look on his face. The soldier let his weapon fall from his hands and then fell over sideways. Jason tried to turn and look at Crusher, but the pain in his chest and the blood loss almost made him pass out from the effort. "Thanks," he forced out instead.

"Anytime... Captain," Crusher said weakly. The sounds of renewed combat in the hallway outside both confused and alarmed Jason, they were all nearly dead... who could they be fighting? Without getting an answer, he let his eyes close and lay back, waiting for the inevitable.

*   *   *   *   *

What the fuck... I die and these are the people I have to see first? Jason's head swam as his blurred vision focused on the concerned faces of Captain Kellea Colleren and Commander Bostco. Colleren was saying something and he realized they'd taken his helmet off.

"Are you still with us?" She was asking.

"My crew... Find my crew..." Jason could barely get the words out before coughing up more blood all over his charred chest plate.

"Rest easy, Captain. We'll get your crew," she said, almost gently. Then, not so gently; "Get that fucking medical team in here NOW!!"

Chapter 13

Jason made his way slowly along the garden path, enjoying the heat from the Eshquarian sun after being bedridden for nearly a month. He still had a long way to go, but at least he was ambulatory now as the doctors at the capital's sprawling medical campus had worked miracles on his near-dead body. Beside him walked Prime Minister Colleston, having taken a special interest in his recovery since he had been brought there. "So you had no idea what he had done?" The Prime Minister was asking.

"None," Jason answered. "I was already hit, Crusher was down, so I wasn't sure what the tricky little guy was up to until Captain Colleren told me when I woke up on the *Diligent*."

"I see. Well, Kage's quick thinking saved the lives of millions on Shorret-3, a debt I'm not sure we can ever repay."

"I'm sure I'll think of a way," Jason said with a laugh.

While he didn't know it at the time, during the battle Kage had realized there was an emergency release for the tether hard-wired into each control room, but was behind a locked access panel. He had blown his way into it and yanked the handle down, blowing charges all along the winch's ratchet mechanism. After that, there was nothing actually locking down the tether, so under the inertial force of the planet's rotation the platform simply floated away, pulling the entire length of the tether out of the ground with it.

After that, the *Diligent*, and much of the Eshquarian fleet, had arrived and took care of the rest. The repeated message Doc had set up had been received, but they had already suffered damage to their own com array before the reply had come back.

"So how is he doing?" Colleston's question snapped Jason back from his thoughts.

"Pretty well, considering. He's still pissed at me. The damage to his ears from being near the business end of the railgun was irreparable. He'll be here for a bit longer while they clone replacement parts and install them."

"Colorful imagery," Colleston laughed. "We've been able to fully treat Lucky's... injury... as well. Witnesses on the ground are saying he was a force of nature, engaging two full loads of Dowarty's mercenaries and still not going down. His damage was really more superficial than functional, luckily we have someone here who can actually work on his kind."

"That is fortunate," Jason agreed. He chaffed at the slow pace, but was happy to be walking, or breathing, at all. "So what was this all about? What would the death of an entire planet prove?"

"It wasn't about proving anything," Colleston said sadly. "It was about leverage. Certain factions within our government would like nothing more than to merge with the Confederation, but it's a losing proposition for us: lose out sovereignty, pay an enormous tax, and for what? The privilege of being governed from afar?"

"Then why would anybody advocate that?"

"Same reason most politicians do anything: personal gain. The ConFed promised lavish rewards to whoever could deliver Eshquaria into the fold. If you hadn't seen Kross on that station we'd have never known where to start in cleaning out our own house," the Prime Minister paused and looked over the well manicured lawn the path meandered through. "We've arrested seven legislators on charges of treason and three others have disappeared, that's on top of grabbing Kross and Dowarty. Apparently the attacks on our shipping lanes weren't getting the job of convincing our citizens we couldn't protect them done fast enough, so they authorized Dowarty to pull off an act of terrorism that could tip the scale of public opinion in their favor."

"Wow," Jason mused. "There are people who would kill millions to get some shiny trinket from their would-be masters? It's hard to wrap my head around."

"It's the rarified air of living in the capital. The lives of the ordinary citizens become less and less significant when compared to their own personal ambitions," Colleston answered. "That's why we're introducing legislation that will require representatives to live in their districts at least ninety percent of the time. Maybe being around their constituents so much will remind them why they're here."

"Good luck with that," Jason said as they approached another pair waiting by an open aircar that was parked on the lawn .

"...look into it. But you realize she'll be almost impossible to track down if she's gone underground," Crisstof Dalton was saying.

"I understand," Doc answered. "Anything you can do. Jason! It's good to see you up and about!"

"You as well," Jason said to his friend, pretending he hadn't overheard part of his conversation. "Apparently without all of your tweaks to my body, I'd have been dead and gone before the *Diligent* arrived." Doc's answer was cut off as an indignant shout interrupted them.

"I can walk myself! Let me out of this contraption at once!" They all turned to see Crusher being ferried in a hovering medical chair from the building nearest them, he appeared to be restrained. The Galvetic warrior had taken a full blast from the large plasma cannon in the back and then a glancing shot to the chest when he fell. Despite all that, he still had enough fight left in him to hurl a heavy blade clean through the soldier that was about to execute Jason. The medical technician pushed Crusher up to the small group.

"He's all yours," the man said, completely oblivious to his Prime Minister standing right there as he turned and fled before Crusher could be let up out of the chair. The big warrior turned a vicious glare on his friends;

"Do I even need to say it?"

"No, just take it easy and quit scaring everybody," Doc admonished him as he moved around to the back of the chair and popped the restraints off. Crusher slowly stood up out of the chair and stretched his back with a loud pop.

"How're you feeling?" Jason asked.

"Better, now. I should be one-hundred percent in a couple days or so," he answered. Jason knew better than to argue with him, so he smiled indulgently and gestured for them all to get into the aircar.

"So where did Dowarty come from? He was more than just some local organizer," Jason asked once the aircar was climbing up and away from the medical center.

"The best we can tell, he's a ConFed operative. Beyond that, we're hoping the investigation will turn up who was pulling his strings and paying for his operation," Crisstof answered. "I know he's been out here on the fringe for a while running his own little kingdom, so it's possible he went rogue." Jason highly doubted it, but said nothing as the Eshquarian capital city gave way to the outlying industrial areas.

The aircar descended to a soft landing in front of one of the non-descript, albeit quite large, buildings that seemed to dot the landscape. All the occupants climbed out, the members of Omega Force quite a bit slower than the others, and entered through a door that was guarded by two visibly armed Eshquarian Security troopers.

They followed another guard that had been waiting inside to a large lift and began the descent below ground level in silence. After a moment the Prime Minister spoke up, "Are you sure there isn't anything more we can do for you and your crew, Captain?" Before

Jason could answer the lift stopped and the doors slid open. His heart caught in his throat at the view; amongst all the scaffolding, and a veritable army of engineers and technicians, was the *Phoenix*, her burnished hull gleaming under the bright flood lights. Yelling orders and gesturing wildly on the floor was a hobbled, but still feisty Twingo, refusing to sit in a hospital while his ship was being brought back to life.

"No, Mr. Prime Minister," Jason said with a smile. "We have all we need."

From the ashes once again, eh girl?

Epilogue:

"Gunship-class vessel, Phoenix, you are clear to enter the range hot. Proceed when ready."

"Phoenix copies," Jason said, "We're in hot." Pushing his ship into a steep dive, he slammed the throttle down and smiled in satisfaction as she surged through the crisp, cool air towards their objective. They were doing their last few shakedown runs at an Eshquarian military testing range before they finally departed the area.

When Jason had come around in the medical facility, he had been told that when the Eshquarians went to retrieve the *Phoenix*, they found the damage wasn't near as bad as it seemed. Prime Minister Colleston grandly offered him a choice: a brand new, top of the line ship, or they could rebuild the DL7. It was a no-brainer for Jason, and he suspected that if Colleston had known he would opt for the massively expensive rebuild of a thirteen year-old gunship over simply taking a new ship out of their own shipyards, he would have ordered the older ship scrapped while he still slept.

But, true to their word, the Eshquarians poured money and manpower into brining the ship back from the dead. Not only that, they upgraded nearly every system in the ship to the point where she was better than what was currently flying off of their own assembly lines. New, more powerful drives were fitted. An Eshquarian weapons suite that wasn't even available for outside purchase. A new computer core and sensor package... In every significant way, the DL7 was not the same ship it had been, and yet it was. Despite the impressive new systems, the *Phoenix* was still the seventh member of Omega Force, was still their home.

After he had completed a series of gut-wrenching maneuvers to test low-altitude handling, the smiles on the faces of his crew confirmed the wisdom of his decision. He let out a short laugh of and yanked the stick back, sending the *Phoenix* thundering into the darkening sky on her new main engines.

"Have you thought about my proposal?" Crisstof Dalton was sitting in one of the seats to Jason's left and had taken all the violent maneuvering in stride. As he reconfigured the ship for a nice easy cruise out of the test range, Jason turned to the older man.

"Are you sure you want us working for you? Some of us aren't house broken."

"You wouldn't be 'working' for me," Crisstof corrected, puzzling through the meaning of being house broken. "I'd be sponsoring you. Your ideals, and even your methods are noble, Captain... but surely you've come to realize just how hard it is to operate a warship like this as a privateer. How long until you'd be forced to take a high-paying job that didn't necessarily align with your charter?

"Within my organization, so many small things fall through the cracks and we just can't justify the resources to help only a few people. I'd like you to be my solution to that problem. You'd still be completely independent, but I'd be able to suggest places where you might be helpful, and then provide the needed support."

"And if we want to walk away at some point?"

"You walk away," Crisstof confirmed. "No contracts, no agreements. Just a mutual trust that we're both wanting to accomplish the same thing." Jason gazed out through the new canopy as he contemplated the offer.

"What is Captain Colleren going to think about this?" Jason laughed aloud at the thought of the *Diligent's* uptight captain having to regard him as a colleague.

"It's something she'll have to become accustomed to," Crisstof said, trying to suppress his own laugh. "But know that your actions on Shorret-3 have earned you a great deal of respect from Captain Colleren. You may come to view her differently after a time."

Jason looked around at his crew, who were all looking back at him just as interestedly. He had already discussed this with them when Crisstof had first approached him and they had made it clear they would trust him to make the final decision. The fact that they still

343

looked at him as the "Captain" after he had nearly gotten them all killed on the last mission humbled and honored him.

"Why not? We can give it a try, and if it doesn't work... no hard feelings." Crisstof looked visibly relieved at his answer. "So... what's our first job?" Jason joked with a laugh.

"I'm glad you asked," Crisstof said, pulling out a data tablet. "What do you guys know about the Tellefor System?"

Thank you for reading *Omega Force: Soldiers of Fortune.*

If you enjoyed the story, Captain Burke and the guys will
be back in:

Omega Force: Savage Homecoming.

Follow me on Facebook and Twitter for the latest updates;

http://www.facebook.com/pages/Joshua-
Dalzelle/287769144678448

@JoshuaDalzelle